kincaid

kincaid

LAURELIN PAIGE

Hot Alphas. Smart Women. Sexy Stories

ALSO BY LAURELIN PAIGE

Visit my website for a more detailed reading order.

The Dirty Universe

Dirty Filthy Rich Boys - READ FREE

Dirty Duet (Donovan Kincaid)

Dirty Filthy Rich Men | Dirty Filthy Rich Love

Kincaid

Dirty Games Duet (Weston King)

Dirty Sexy Player| Dirty Sexy Games

Dirty Sweet Duet (Dylan Locke)

Sweet Liar | Sweet Fate

(Nate Sinclair) Dirty Filthy Fix (a spinoff novella)

Dirty Wild Trilogy (Cade Warren)

Wild Rebel | Wild War | Wild Heart

Man in Charge Duet

Man in Charge

Man in Love

Man for Me (a spinoff novella)

Dating Season

Spring Fling | Summer Rebound | Fall Hard

Winter Bloom | Spring Fever | Summer Lovin

Also written with Kayti McGee under the name Laurelin McGee

Miss Match | Love Struck | MisTaken | Holiday for Hire

Written with Sierra Simone

Porn Star | Hot Cop

Be sure to **sign up for my newsletter** where you'll receive **a FREE book every month** from bestselling authors, only available to my subscribers, as well as up-to-date information on my latest releases.

PRO TIP: Add laurelin@laurelinpaige.com to your contacts before signing up to be sure the list comes right to your inbox.

DID YOU KNOW...

This book is available in both paperback and audiobook editions at all major online retailers! Links are on my website.

If you'd like to order a signed paperback, my online store is open several times a year here.

A NOTE FROM THE AUTHOR

My dear reader,

Donovan Kincaid was first introduced into the world in February 2017. Since then, he has become a beloved character, featured in all of the Dirty Universe books. Readers tell me everyday they want more—more of his past, more of his future, and definitely more of his love story with Sabrina.

Honestly, when I wrote "The End" on Dirty Filthy Rich Love, I thought that would be it for these two. Donovan wasn't the easiest of heroes to write. He toyed with me and remained elusive. He didn't want to give me anymore of his story. I had no idea what I'd write for him.

Then when I was wrapping up Wild Heart, formerly the last book of the Dirty Universe, suddenly Donovan showed up, whispering in my head, "This isn't over." And he was right.

Donovan and Sabrina have more to tell, and **Kincaid** is the book where it will all unfold.

So while Dirty Filthy Rich Love has delivered an ending, it's not *the* ending. You'll find that here in **Kincaid**.

xo
Laurelin

PROLOGUE

TWELVE YEARS *ago*

SEVEN MINUTES before my first class of the semester started, and I was stuck on the phone with fucking Raymond Aaron Kincaid.

Okay, technically not *my* class. According to the course catalog, it was taught by Martin Velasquez, and to be fair, he did give the lectures. But everyone in the master's program knew he threw every bit of the homework for his 101 classes to his T.A.s. And even though I was on year two of my master's and not required to fill any more T.A. positions, that class was mine for the same reason that I was stuck on the phone—because no one said *no* to Raymond Kincaid. Especially not his son.

Right now, he was laying out what he expected of me this year. "Listen for any tips you think will pay out. It's not just the professors that have useful leads. These days it's the youth. That social media site was created by a Harvard dropout. We could have been in on that, if you'd kept the right company, and that's a piece of tech that looks like it could go far."

I didn't bother to remind him that I'd been the one who'd told him about Facebook. "I'll keep my ears open."

"I'm expecting that Weston will come out of this year a star. Need that be said?"

I resented the question, so I didn't respond. Even if he hadn't demanded that I live with his business partner's freshman son instead of getting my own apartment, I would have bent over backward to look out for Weston. He was the closest thing I had to a brother. Despite our age difference and total lack of shared interests, he was also the closest thing I had to a friend these days.

That was a purposeful choice, one that a more compassionate parent might find concerning.

If Raymond Kincaid was concerned, it wasn't about me. "Jamison Stewart and the Sheridan kid both need to be on your radar."

"On your radar" was code for "give them an A". I didn't consider asking what favor he'd exchanged to make sure his friends' offspring made it through Harvard with accolades, mainly because the answer was likely boring—a doubling of investments in King-Kincaid or a promise to lobby in favor of fewer regulations in the financial district—but also because I lived by the *less you know, the harder to be charged as complicit* philosophy where my father was concerned.

And no, I didn't miss the irony that the class I was supposed to be passing these assholes through was Business Ethics. But the definition of ethical was objective, and I'd been raised to live in the gray. Obviously.

Already knowing what I was looking for wasn't there, I scanned the rosters on my desk, both the one for the class about to begin as well as the one I taught the next day. "Theo Sheridan isn't in either of my sections."

"Jesus, fuck. Are you kidding me?" As though it were my fault that his illicit bartering had been thwarted.

I looked up to see the first three students walk in and take seats in the middle front. Early birds. These would be the over-achievers. The brownnosers. The ones who would make more work for me because of their zealous efforts. I was already mentally attaching minuses to their A's just because they were guaranteed to be annoying.

Yes, there was power in my position. I didn't pretend that it hadn't gone to my head. It didn't seem like that big of an issue compared to the God complex my father had.

"You'll have to get him transferred in."

No concern as to whether or not I had that ability, or even whether Theodore Sheridan wanted to transfer in. Was the guy even in the school of business?

Those wouldn't be acceptable excuses for Raymond. *Make it work* was his motto, and so I would. A part of my brain was already laying out the best strategies. If Theo was in Markham's section, I knew that professor could be bought with King-Kincaid shares. If he needed to be transferred, I'd have to do some magic. But I was pretty sure the secretary in admissions was sweet on me, and if that route didn't prove fruitful, there would be someone else in the department who would accept a bribe.

"I'll take care of it," I assured my father, hoping that would get him off the phone. I'd half checked out of the conversation as it was. More students were filing in, and I was making a mental portfolio for each of them as they did. The one in the Chucks would fall asleep in class. The one with the Bottega briefcase sold coke to the faculty. The one with the bubblegum had ADHD. The one in sunglasses was considering changing majors.

For the girls, an extra assessment was added. Weston would fuck the girl with the French tips. And the one with the gel pens set out on the front of her desk. And the one with the nose job. And the one on her cell phone, but not the one next to her who was already reading ahead in the textbook.

Speak of the devil, Weston walked in. The two girls flanking either side of him were most likely the sole reason he'd shown up on time. My desk was tucked away in the corner, and when he didn't acknowledge my presence, I wondered if he'd been so preoccupied that he'd failed to notice me.

That theory was shot when, just after he took his seat, and without looking in my direction, he subtly flipped me the bird.

I'd pay him back later and "accidentally" mention his chlamydia meds within earshot of his new "friends". It was the little things I lived for these days.

Meanwhile, my father droned on in my ear. When he took his next breath, I slipped in. "Anything else?"

"Don't dismiss me like your time is more important than mine, Donovan."

"There's only one minute until my class starts. Do you want me to keep my T.A. job or do you want me to stay on the phone while you wave your dick around some more?"

"Cute," he said, with the same patronizing tone he'd used the entire conversation. "No. I'm done. Oh, but keep an eye out for the MADAR scholarship girl. Don't go out of your way for her, but the better our awardees look, the better we look."

I'd already registered that she was in this next class. Sabrina Lind, a Colorado kid who graduated from high school early. Low-income family upbringing, could write a compelling essay, even if her viewpoint was on the idealistic side. She didn't need my watching. I wasn't concerned about her.

"Yep," I said, placating. "Will do." Then, "Gotta go." I clicked END without letting him have the last word. Tucking my phone into my jacket pocket, I became aware of myself like I was split in two, a common state of being. One part of me was very present in the moment, noticing every detail of the students in front of me, fattening up those imaginary profiles, making assumptions I had no right making—assumptions that would, more times than not, be accurate.

Underneath those were murkier thoughts, ones that slithered around my head on constant replay. Thoughts without distinct shape, taking forms that sometimes resembled a dog on a leash and sometimes a car driving head-on into traffic and sometimes a man lost in the fog and sometimes a boy drowning in a waterless sea.

And then *she* walked in.

With less than thirty seconds before class officially started, her demeanor flustered like she'd gotten lost along the way. Her bottom lip between her teeth made her appear demure, while the set of her jaw revealed her as stubborn. She was equally plain (invisible, almost) and stunning (breathtaking, once she caught your attention). Both out-of-place and right where she belonged, and she seemed as unsure as anyone whether she needed to be boss or be bossed or needed to be a carefully managed combination of the two. While her big brown doe eyes searched for a place to sit, she pulled the end of her messy ponytail, and when she chose the front row for her seat and tucked her no-name Doc Martin rip-offs underneath her, top down, as though self-conscious about their appearance, I knew for sure she was the scholarship girl.

And I knew she'd be a strong student.

And I knew Weston would sleep with her—if he noticed her.

And I knew that I'd go out of my way to be sure he didn't.

And I knew, with the kind of conviction talked about in biblical tales, that, if there was anyone who could, she'd be the one to save me.

ONE

PRESENT

I WAIT until Weston and I are in my office, the door shut behind us before I voice my suspicion. "She knows."

"Who knows?" He glances back at the closed door, as if the answer is waiting in the threshold. "Sabrina? Why *wouldn't* she know? She doesn't know?"

"Since I just said that I think she does know—"

He cuts me off with a wave of his hand, correcting himself. "I mean, why wouldn't you have already told her? Elizabeth knows."

I'm stunned until it occurs to me we might not be talking about the same thing. "I'm talking about the drive with—"

"Yeah, yeah. So am I. Otherwise you would have invited Nate to come up with us."

Actually, I had invited Nate, but he was afraid of leaving

Trish alone with the wolves known as our wives and had passed on the offer. Weston isn't always as clued into our business partners' lives as I am.

No one is, to be fair.

But since it is just the two of us, I took the opportunity to bring up my suspicions, and now that I know we're talking about the same thing, I'm stunned again. "Elizabeth knows?"

"We're married. We don't keep secrets from each other."

I don't like his implication. "I only keep secrets that Sabrina doesn't care I keep."

His laugh says he's dubious. "Like, she doesn't care because she doesn't know? 'Cause that's the definition of a secret. And if my wife found out I was hiding things from her purposefully—"

I'm not in the mood for his self-righteous bullshit, so I interrupt to clarify. "I mean I don't flood my wife with information that doesn't pertain to her everyday life and/or that she isn't interested in knowing. Not secrets, exactly."

"Well, if you haven't told her, and you're worried about her reaction, then it's a secret."

I don't know why I thought that I could talk about this with the Boy Scout King. His ideals tend to get in the way of reality. Sometimes there are reasons to keep things mum, especially if those things might be dangerous. The only reason I've included Weston on this at all is because of the nature of the information. It didn't seem fair not to.

I'm beginning to regret that decision.

Running a frustrated hand over my face, I consider dropping the subject. The cigar box offers a suitable distraction. "You pick," I say, opening it toward him.

He takes one without examining the options. I match my choice with his—a Prensado with peppery, coffee, and bittersweet chocolate notes—and we spend the next few minutes with the business of lighting up. This was the excuse I'd used to lure him upstairs, after all, while our wives ignored Nate and Trish and mapped out strategies for our companies like it was a Monday morning at the office instead of a Sunday night in the living room with friends.

That's what we get for marrying modern women. I dare say neither of us are complaining.

It's Weston who, after occupying my favorite armchair and kicking his feet up on the ottoman, returns to the previous topic. "What makes you think she knows, anyway?"

I sit in the leather chair behind the desk and think about my response. It's not like she's said anything. That's perhaps the problem—how little she's said the past few months, like she's working out a puzzle in her head. At first, I thought it was just jet lag. She's been back and forth to London a few times to help her sister with her newborns. The twins' odd schedules and trouble latching were enough to mess with Sabrina's circadian rhythm, add to it the flying and time distance, and what did I expect?

But when I really think about it, I realize she may have been distant before that too. We'd both been so slammed with work, trying to manage Dylan's load as well as our own so he could take time off for the births, that I may have missed her pulling away.

Or maybe it was even before that. Maybe it started all the way back at Christmas, when I asked her to have a baby, and she'd said *not now*, and I'd let that be the end of it.

Except, I hadn't really let that be the end of it because I've wondered over and over what it was that could make Sabrina—a woman who is normally quite content to let me dominate her life and decisions—decide to put her foot down. The simple answer is that she really isn't ready for a baby. Fair enough. We're only just now coming up on two years married. It's too soon.

But I'm not a man who can settle on simple answers until all other possibilities have been ruled out, and I'm niggled by the chance that her wariness might be because of what I have hidden in the safe behind me.

Explaining all of that to Weston would be an exercise in futility. "Just a feeling," I say, instead.

He stares at me, as if he stares hard enough he can peel back my layers with his eyes. Though he's my best friend, I don't usually tend to share anything deep with him. He doesn't usually seem to want to know, to be fair. But right now, he looks as though he truly cares, and for the span of a few seconds, I consider what I'd tell him. That I've never been happier? That I'm relieved that all my friends have found women to love them? That watching him and Cade and Dylan proceed to bring children into their families makes me jealous as fucking hell?

When I say nothing, he prods me with words. "Are you keeping it here?"

"In the wall safe."

"Sabrina doesn't have the combo?"

"Sure, she does. Even if she looked in there, she wouldn't know what she was looking at."

"And you know without a doubt that she hasn't looked in there." It's not a question, and there's a hint of disgust in his tone, because he knows without me saying that I've examined the digital logs that report every time the safe is opened and closed and even watched the home security cameras that are focused on this room. It's the kind of action expected from men who distrust their wives. In my case, that's just another Tuesday, and it's something Weston will never understand. "Maybe that feeling you're having is guilt."

I lift my cigar and then adjust my hand to give him the bird.

"Ooo, Sally Sensitive." His grin goes full wide before he drops it. "If she really knows about it, why wouldn't she just tell you? Sabrina's not really the docile, keep-the-peace kind of chick."

"I'm going to pretend you didn't just refer to a grown woman as a farm animal." The fact that the grown woman was *my* grown woman is making it hard not to thwack him across the head instead.

"I'm just saying I think she'd confront you about it, especially if she was bothered by it."

Normally, I consider myself an expert at knowing how Sabrina feels about things, even when she doesn't understand herself, so it's irksome to not have any idea how she'd react to this—okay, I'll say it—this particular *secret*.

Or maybe the problem is that I do know how she'd react.

Except he's right—she would have confronted me. Definitely.

Still, something's off with her. And if Weston told his wife, I have even more reason to suspect that Sabrina will know soon if she doesn't know already. Hell, she could be whispering it to her downstairs right this very minute. "You really told Elizabeth?"

"Nothing specific. Nothing she'd tell Sabrina. Don't worry. Just that you're still doing favors for your father."

"I'm not—" I realize how irritated I sound and start again. "I'm not doing favors for him."

"You tracked down a hard drive full of the only copy of

information that could potentially ruin his company and put him in jail. How is that not a favor?"

"He didn't ask me to do it." Admitting I took care of it on my own accord doesn't sound much better.

The look he gives confirms that's exactly what he's thinking.

I lean back in my chair and puff on my cigar. "I wasn't trying to look out for him, all right? I was digging into something for Cade a while back with some people I know who deal in sensitive information, and while we were negotiating, I was told that there was someone trying to sell some info on King-Kincaid, and I was...curious."

Weston rolls his cigar between his fingers, nodding. I'd told him what I'd had soon after I'd obtained it, but this is the first time I've given him the details. I can guess what is going through his head, imagining himself in the same position—would he have been curious?

I don't need to think about it like he does to come to the conclusion that he would have walked away. Weston has managed to keep himself untangled from our fathers' empire, physically if not emotionally, for quite some time now.

The opposite could be said for myself. I've been numb about pretty much everything where my father is concerned, but I have my hands in several of his pots. Not just because Weston and I still both own stock in the family business, but because I like knowing. All of it. The good, the bad, and especially the ugly.

This particular info fell into the latter. I hadn't known our fathers had falsified their books and used their company to launder dirty money for some shady oligarchs in Eastern Europe until I'd seen the data. There've been rumors for a while that King-Kincaid isn't all on the up and up—rumors I believed—but nothing has had the potential to bring them down like this. They must have known they were dangerously close to being caught because they apparently hired a tech guy to clean their computer system of any trace of the bad dealings. The guy had done a stellar job, it seems—the company's books looked perfect when I audited them in January—but he kept a copy of the backup, probably to use as extortion at some point.

When I discovered he was holding it, I offered to buy it off of him without a second thought. It hurts to think about how much I ended up paying for the drive. That fact alone would have Sabrina's panties twisted in a knot.

But I know she hasn't examined the savings accounts the same way I know everything about her—I make it my job to know.

When I've finished explaining, Weston asks the question I've asked myself over and over with no satisfactory answer. "So why didn't you just let them blackmail our dads? Like you said, Raymond didn't ask you for this."

I give him the best I've been able to come up with. "Because I knew how to handle it. So I did."

His laugh turns into a sigh. "There you go again, thinking you're the only one who can do anything." He sits forward and points a finger at me with the insistence of past experience. "You knew how to get yourself *involved*. If it was handled, you wouldn't be worrying about it anymore. You wouldn't still have it in your safe...what, two and a half years later? Are you just planning on keeping it in there forever? Why haven't you destroyed it?"

Another unanswerable question.

He shakes his head and leans back. "Tell Raymond you have

it. Let him decide what to do with it. Make him pay you back. He owes you that much."

I prop my elbow on the arm of my chair and rest my chin in my hand. "Is that what you want me to do?"

"No, no, no. I'm staying out of this." He twists his cigar so he can study the label. "This is new. I like it."

I ignore the attempt at a subject change. "So you're not over there thinking that I should hand this over to the authorities."

"If I am, I'm not telling you. I'm not letting you put that responsibility on me."

I know it's not fair before the words are out of my mouth, but that doesn't keep them from escaping. "No, you're leaving me to carry it all by myself. As always."

"Oh, don't do that. You took this on yourself. I am not feeling sorry for you about it."

"No, you're feeling smug about it."

He turns toward me, and when my expression dares him to deny it, he doesn't. "Well, yes. Yes, I am."

Once upon a time, he would have felt sorry for me. He would have bent over backward to help bear the shame inflicted by our fathers' illicit business dealings. Elizabeth has been good for him. He's grown. I'm generally glad about it.

Right now, I resent him. "You're such a fuckwaffle."

His chuckle at the old joke takes the holier-than-thou look off his face. "But really, D, if you're still holding on to this because of me, don't. I can handle the fall out. If you need to protect them, then do it. I'm not going to fault you for it. Raymond's your blood. I get it. It's complicated. I feel the same way about Nash.

"And if it's not about me or them, then you should figure out what it *is* about. And you should tell Sabrina. She's your wife.

She's supposed to help you with these things. Let her. I guarantee you that's what you're feeling all twisted about."

I trust my suspicions over Weston's guarantees any day, but I let myself mull it over while we puff silently on our cigars.

A few minutes have passed and my mind hasn't been changed when there's a knock on the door. "Yeah?"

It opens, and Nate's on the other side. "Am I interrupting anything?"

Weston answers before I can. "We're done. You're good."

I let Weston go ahead and believe this was a bonding moment for the two of us. Truth is, I'd be better off unloading on Nate. His morals are closer to mine—let's call them loose—and even if it was his own father involved, he'd manage to keep feelings out of it.

But I suspect it's about time we return to the party. "Have Sabrina and Elizabeth eaten Trish alive yet with their work talk?"

Nate crosses to me and swipes my cigar for a puff before giving an answer. "Yeah, well, they've moved on to domesticity."

For Trish, that subject has to be even worse.

Weston and I exchange a glance. "We'll go down," we say in unison.

Nate nods in agreement as he hands me back my cigar. "Too bad. These are good."

"Take one for the road. Take one for Trish too. She'll like it."

After the business of putting out cigars and collecting new ones for Nate's pockets, we head down to the living room where the rest of our party is gathered. It's a small affair. Weston and Elizabeth are in town for a few days with their son and six-month-old daughter for Weston's mother's birthday. Tonight the kids are with the grandparents, and Sabrina offered to entertain.

While she's not usually big on these kinds of things, she's quite good at them when they're small and personal. I hang back a moment when we arrive downstairs, partly because I like to read a room before entering, but mostly because I like watching her. Her cheeks are flushed and her skin's glowing. The untouched champagne in front of her tells me this is genuine enjoyment on her part. She's so engaged, I can almost overlook the faint circles under her eyes and convince myself that I'm seeing problems where there are none.

"It's the only way to have kids," Elizabeth is saying, most likely promoting the unique co-parenting arrangement she and Weston have with his baby mama and her partner. They all liked it so much that they did it again, using in vitro this time, to implant Elizabeth's egg and Weston's sperm into Callie's uterus.

I dare say there are better ways to conceive, but bravo for them.

Trish is equally unimpressed. "Sell that to Sabrina. I'm not buying."

Elizabeth turns to my wife, ready to convince her, and I'm actually glad I arrived in time to hear this.

But before Elizabeth can say anything, Sabrina puts her hand up in a halt. "I'll keep it in mind. If we ever have a baby." She's barely finished speaking when her eyes lift.

Her smile fades as soon as she sees me.

I wonder what my expression has told her, or if she even needed to see me at all. She knew before she spoke the words they were a betrayal. When I'd asked her for a kid, she'd said, *not now*, which is a far cry from *not ever*.

She stands quickly. "I have dessert! Now that everyone's back, I'll go make us plates. Anyone not want tiramisu?"

Impressive. She's managed to avoid any follow-up questions

about motherhood from Elizabeth who instead asks if Sabrina's made the dish herself.

My wife laughs, and it's almost as if she isn't trying to hide anything at all. "No. I can make one thing in the kitchen, and this is not it. But Jean Claude Martin, our head chef at Gaston's, made it for us personally earlier today, and even though he's known for his French food, his tiramisu is to die for."

But I know her.

And I know all her tells.

So after she leaves the room for the kitchen, I make my own excuse. "I'll find us a nice dessert wine to pair with it."

Then I follow after her because, fuck whether or not I should tell her my secret, right now, my only concern is hers.

TWO

THE KITCHEN DOOR is still swinging from Sabrina's entrance when I push through after her. She glances in my direction, not surprised to see me, because of course I'd follow after her. Of course she can't escape my suffocation. She knows.

She knows, and yet she insists on rattling off mundanities, as if this conversation will go another way. "I really didn't expect Jean Claude to clean up after himself," she says, as she closes the refrigerator door with her shoulder, the dessert dish in her hands. "I mean, I'm grateful—Myrna will appreciate it when she comes in to clean tomorrow—but I couldn't find the pepper grinder earlier for the life of me. In the end, I found it in the pantry." She sets the dish on the island, next to the small plates she put out beforehand and starts opening drawers. "Do you want to make bets on where I'll find the spatula? It should be— oh, it's here." She holds up the stainless-steel utensil and grins. "How big do you think I should make the servings?"

I'm sure many men would fall for this distraction, and

honestly, I can't blame them. She's beautiful like this—her hair falling over one brow, her lips slightly parted, her eyes pleading for me to take the bait. *Just fucking take the bait.*

I don't take it. "You really think I came in here to talk about the damn tiramisu?"

Her smile slips, but again, she's not surprised. She begins to cut into the dessert. "I'd hoped you'd come in to help."

"Sure. I can help while we argue." Probably wasn't best to assume this would be a fight. Already, I've made this a confrontation when it should be a discussion.

But it's already said, might as well double down. I step over to the coffeemaker, already prepped with water and fresh grounds, and hit the start button before opening my mouth to begin my interrogation.

She beats me to speaking first. "Donovan, please. This isn't the time."

I close my jaw and bite down. Hard.

She's fucking right, of course. It's not the time. It's not the place. I'm not in the right mindset, and probably neither is she. I can concede that this conversation needs to wait.

But I'm also pissed.

Not just because she's put me off, but because putting me off means that there's actually a conversation that needs to be had when it could have been, *Oh, Donovan, I was just trying to get them to stop hounding me.* Or *It just came out. Of course we'll have a baby eventually.*

So now I really don't want to drop the subject.

I force myself to keep my mouth shut while I pass behind her to the wine fridge. Without examining my options, I pick the first Riesling, and slam the fridge door, which is really ineffective and ungratifying because of the rubber seal around the edges.

I truly do intend to take the bottle and leave. But my frustration is too big to tuck away from our guests. It's bigger than this one moment. Bigger than tonight. I am a man who demands control of the circumstances around me, a man who—never mind the toxicity of my nature—demands control over his wife, and Sabrina, being who she is, has made me a god by granting me that control in most aspects of our marriage.

But in this aspect, she's taken it from me.

The need to regain that power is raw and fierce. Instead of passing by, I stop behind her and slam the bottle down on the kitchen island with a satisfying thud. She jumps, but I don't move. I'm a wall at her back, my heat mixing with hers. She's scared of me, as she should be, and because fear excites her, I can smell it on her. Over her shoulder, I can see how her nipples have spiked and her breaths have become shallow. I place my hands on either side of her, caging her in, and this time her breath hitches.

And I'm hard.

I push my erection into the cleft of her lower back as I reach around her to grab the dish towel that sits near the stacked plates. Taking an end in each hand, I slowly bring it up toward her left shoulder, then pull it slowly across the base of her neck.

"Donovan," she whispers, and this time she's lost all her conviction. "It's not the time for this either."

"Perhaps not. But this I don't have to ask for."

She shivers as I pull the towel tight across her throat. Not so tight that she can't speak her safe word, but tight enough to let her know who's in control. It's not fair—I admit it. The recent distance between us hasn't kept us from fucking, but it's kept me from "forcing" her, and now I realize how much she's missed it. She's missed it, and she's desperate. She wants it too much. The fact that our friends are mere yards away only makes her more turned on.

So even though this is terrible timing, she won't use her safe word.

But she will fight me.

Her first effort isn't very valiant. It's a whispered plea. "Don't do this."

"I really don't think you're in a position to tell me what to do." I use the towel to pull her toward me so her body is flesh against mine, then I move both ends to one hand so that when she reaches back to slap at me, I can grab her wrist with my free hand and wrench her arm between us.

"Please." Her fight strengthens, so I pull her arm harder, until she squeaks from the discomfort. The sound fuels my arousal, and I know from past self-examination that it's not because her pain turns me on, per se. In a roundabout way, it might contribute to my lust because I'm turned on by her pleasure, and I know this sort of struggle gets her off, but even beyond that, I enjoy this sound because it means that, at this moment, she's weak. At this moment, she's overwhelmed and has no choice but to surrender.

That's what I'm here for—her surrender. Her submission. Whether she hands it over or I have to fight for it, it's all the same to me. I only care that in the end she knows that she truly and fully belongs to me.

I'm committed to being inside her now. As soon as possible. With that thought at the forefront of my mind, I still manage to realize that getting her covered in cocoa powder and mascarpone would not be ideal. Roughly, I use the towel to pull her farther down the island, then release it so I can twist her arms together and pin them with one of my hands at her hip.

With my other hand, I forcefully pull at the chiffon covering her bosom until the wraparound tie of her dress loosens enough to free one breast. She's braless, so it's plump flesh that spills out. I flick her taut nipple before taking her in my hand. Her back is arched because of how I have her pinned, and the position pushes her chest out, making her bosom appear fuller, and God help me, I'm tempted to spin her around and have a full course feast on that single breast, company be damned.

It's as if she knows what I'm thinking. "I need to..." *Get back to the tiramisu*, she means. "You need to..." *Stop*.

The word doesn't come, not that it would stop this anyway. Her breast is not my end game, though, so while I don't stop, I twist her nipple, eliciting a yelp that sends more blood to my cock, and then abandon her breast to gather her skirt at her waist.

Her fight renews, and she jerks, trying to throw me off of her.

"Just let it happen," I say, knowing the patronizing calm of my voice probably pisses her off. Gets her heart pumping. Makes her clit throb.

"Fuck you."

"If that's what you want..." I kick her legs apart, wrapping my arm around her completely when she struggles. Getting her panties off isn't easy with one hand, especially when she keeps trying to stomp on my foot. When she lowers her head, I'm too distracted to realize she's going for a bite on my hand. "Goddammit, Sabrina."

In surprise, I loosen my hold, and she escapes and turns to face me. There's anger in her expression. Arousal, too. Her stare is hard and hot, and for the first time in a long time, I feel a real challenge to our balance of power.

I could stop.

I should stop.

But I see the kitchen shears in the knife block, and before I'm aware of my decision, they're in my hands, and I'm pressed against her, the blades at her throat.

She swallows, and I worry that I've gone too far. Theo Sheridan held a knife to her neck, cut her clothes away, threatened her life. In a flash, I drop my hand and cup her face with my free palm.

Then I kiss her. And I tell her I love her. Not with words, but with my lips.

The kiss turns possessive. And violent. And by the time she's pounding at my shoulders with her fists, I've already managed to get the blade of the scissors around the band of her panties. A few cuts, and I'm able to rip the rest away.

"I'm getting in that cunt. Don't fucking fight me." I let the scissors fall to the floor and flip her around so I can wrap her loose hair around my fist and push her torso down to the island. She whimpers from the pressure I use, and I'm so intent on my goal, I wonder if I could stop now if she used her safe word.

For good or bad, she doesn't.

And after a bit of a battle with my zipper, I have my cock out and positioned. I know she's wet—I can see she is; I smell her arousal—but I thrust in like she's dry. Like I expect friction, and force is necessary to get as deep inside her as I want to be. As I need to be.

And I fuck her like this.

Angrily. My palm on her face to hold her down, even as she scratches at the back of my hand. My thighs slapping against hers. My cock driving like I'm racing the goddamned Indy 500. The control is mine, and I'm so sick with the power of it, that I'm barely able to hold on to it.

It's when Sabrina starts to tighten around me that I come to myself.

Somewhat.

Enough to slow down, take a breath, wonder what the fuck I'm doing.

I blink out of my haze and take stock of her. My cock is drenched with her juice, and she was close. My sudden decrease in tempo scared that climax away.

So I have work to do.

I wrap my arm around her and find her clit. "Show me you want it," I demand, careful to keep the nonconsensual scenario real for her while rubbing her nub with my thumb. "Show me how good my cock feels, and I'll stop."

"I hate you," she spits. "You're a monster." But she's tightening again, and my cock feels warm with a flood of moisture.

I tug on her hair until her neck is arching off the island. "Show me."

Show me you wanted this.

Show me I'm not really a monster.

Show me this sick relationship of ours still works.

When the sound of a glass shattering comes from the next room, she's close. "Don't lose it," I warn. "Stay with it. I won't stop until you come."

She lifts her head and angles it toward the door, straining to hear, but she stays tight. I increase the pressure of my thumb on her clit. I speed up my thrusts. We listen to our friends' voices rise as they scurry to clean up a mess. Nate mentions napkins.

Elizabeth calls Sabrina's name. Someone will come looking for us soon.

"I'll still be fucking you when they walk in," I promise. "I'm not stopping until you come on my goddamn cock."

That does it for her.

She erupts with a quiet cry. Her body is still shaking when I pull out and put my cock away. I grab the dish towel off the floor where it's fallen and swipe the bottle of Riesling, and when Trish pushes through the door, I'm already walking toward it.

"We're so sorry, but we had a party foul and—"

I cut her off. "On it," I say, ushering her back out, leaving my wife to pull herself together in privacy. "The broom's in the closet out here."

Surprisingly, I feel better, despite the hard-on that I manage to keep hidden with the business of cleaning up. While I gather broken shards of glass, I remind myself I don't really believe in God while simultaneously praying that Sabrina realizes our conversation is far from finished.

THREE

"I KNOW it's none of my business..." Elizabeth trails off, but I don't need to hear more to know that she's talking about my father and the contents of that disk drive in my safe.

I glare at Weston. It's just the three of us at the door to my apartment since Nate and Trish left earlier, and Sabrina made her goodbyes in the living room so she could get a head start on cleanup.

Though Weston doesn't usually excel at social cues, he seems to understand that my glare means *Thank you for running to your wife with the details of our private conversation; why am I surprised?* "I told you—we don't keep secrets," he says, with absolutely no apology in his tone.

"How the fuck did you even have time?"

"You and Sabrina were alone in the kitchen for forever," he says defensively.

Before I can attack—because believe me, I'm about to—Elizabeth intervenes. "When you were gone so long, I wondered aloud if you guys might need help, and Weston filled me in."

"I thought you might be filling Sabrina in," he explains.

A tasteless joke along the lines of *yes, I was filling Sabrina in* flits through my mind, but I quickly let it pass because I'm not twelve.

But Weston can detect an immature thought from a mile away. "Ah, I see from your expression that whole scene went down another way. Should we fist bump?"

"I could bump my fist in your face," I say without any hint of humor.

Weston's smile fades, and Elizabeth steps between us, as though I would actually throw a punch. "Obviously this is a personal matter between you and Sabrina."

"Thank you, Elizabeth," but I've spoken too soon.

"...But you really should lay everything out on the table," she continues, and now I want to punch *her* in the face. "Even if it's not a secret that matters, per se, if you're worried that it's causing tension, then it is."

Surprisingly, she's right. Though probably not how she intends to be. The reason my father's bullshit is an issue in my marriage is because I'm worried that it might be. Sabrina most likely doesn't know anything. I just need to stop worrying about it, and the issue goes away.

Good. Because I need the bandwidth to deal with the other issue that poked its head out tonight. Which first requires getting rid of our guests. "Thank you, again, Elizabeth. Your insight is nonpareil."

She scowls. "I'm pretty sure you're being facetious, but I'm going to pretend you mean it. In case I don't see you again before we leave town..." She leans in to give me a kiss on each cheek, in the European fashion that she's adopted in her time overseas. When she's finished, she puts a hand on my arm and nods toward the apartment behind me. "Take care of her."

Does she not know me? "Sure. Will do."

When she moves out of the way, Weston takes a step toward me, but I put a hand up. "I'm seeing you tomorrow in the office. Goodbyes can wait until then." Hopefully, he won't feel the need to copy the cheek kiss when his wife isn't around. I don't need another reason to want to hit him.

With the last of our guests on their way, I shut the door, lock it, and pause to take a breath. Switch gears. Prepare myself for the conversation that is about to be had. I don't want to fight with Sabrina, but I have a distinct feeling that it might be inevitable. It's part of the reason I haven't broached the baby topic again these last six months. I wanted to give her space, sure —space in my own way, anyway—but also it's the one thing in a very long time that I've wanted for myself.

And Sabrina's thirty now. This isn't something that can be put off forever.

I give myself a quick pep talk. *Be calm. Be patient. Be understanding.* Then I turn off the foyer light and head to the living room...

...where I find Sabrina asleep on the sofa.

Initially, I decide she's faking. But her breaths are regular and deep, and then I wonder if she's fallen asleep on purpose so that she can avoid this talk.

Then I decide I'm being a paranoid asshole. It was a long night, and she'd played hostess—a role she isn't naturally suited for. And then I fucked her pretty roughly. Of course she's worn out.

I walk around the sofa and scoop her up in my arms.

"Hey," she says, blinking up at me. "What are you doing?"

"Carrying you to bed."

"No, I can walk." But she wraps her arm around my neck and lays her head on my shoulder.

I chuckle. "Sure you can." The conversation will have to wait. Again.

And I'm not mad. Or disappointed, even, because I'm holding my beloved next to my heart, and for a long time, I'd thought that being in her life at all was an impossibility. I have her forever now, and this can wait a little longer.

I don't set her down until we've reached the foot of our bed. In the darkness, I undress her and tuck her in. She's barely awake, but when I start to leave, her dress in my hand, she calls out to me. "Where are you going?"

"To finish cleaning up."

"Leave it." She pulls the covers back in invitation. To sleep, not fuck. She's tired, and she wants to be held. I know her cues better than anyone.

For whatever reason, I study her, naked in our bed, before responding. The moonlight and the shadows sharpen her features. Her nose looks more prominent. Her breasts look more full. She's a goddess, and she's mine, and my dick throbs like a caveman beating his chest. It's hard not to want to ravage her, but I've learned how to tuck my wants away. They're always present—I never figured out the trick to suppress them entirely —just, I don't allow them to dominate me.

What dominates me is her—her wants, her needs, her love. She lets me master her because she trusts that I'll put her first. And I do. Every time.

So I leave the mess, and I ignore my cock. I throw her dress on the armchair and add my own clothes to the pile, and I shrug off the impulse to at least take care of our laundry before getting in bed next to her.

She turns so we can spoon, and I pull her into me, her flesh against my flesh. I kiss her bare shoulder and her neck, then lay my head down on the pillow.

"I love you," she whispers.

She's asleep by the time I make the decision not to respond. She doesn't need to hear I love her anyway. She already knows.

"IT SHOULD DEFINITELY BE A WOMAN," Sabrina says, and not for the first time in the million discussions we've had about expanding Reach. "This place is already overflowing with testosterone. If we're bringing in new blood, it should be female."

Although this is a stance she's taken repeatedly, today the statement feels directed toward me. We'd gone to sleep in each other's arms, and this morning we'd been cordial, but there was an unmistakable hint of animosity between us. It's a funny thing I've learned having been married to her for almost two years now—it's possible to be both madly in love and just plain mad at the same time.

I know why *I'm* irritated. I figure her irritation means she knows why I am too, and that she thinks it's invalid. She might be a little pissed that I'd pushed her for the fuck in the kitchen. She loved it, but that doesn't mean she doesn't resent it too. Considering how I'd used sex as a weapon, I can't really blame her if she does.

Whatever the exact causes are for her disposition, it's possible the tension won't get sorted between us until we talk, but I'm leaning into the notion that a talk about building a family might be better suited for when we're both in better moods.

In the meantime, we have our biweekly owners' meeting to focus on.

Across the conference room table, Nate nods. "I like women."

I hide my smile before Sabrina turns her glare from him to me.

"That's exactly what I'm talking about," she huffs.

"Personally, I like the Wilde guy," Weston says. "And not just because he has a cool name."

"Just because he has a cool name," I say at the same time. Despite his refute, I'm not sure I believe him. "Even if we can get him to come on board here for a while, he's made it clear he wants to end up back in Los Angeles."

"Which could work out great for us," Nate says.

Sabrina looks torn. She wants an L.A. office almost as much as she wants us to hire a woman, not that the two are mutually exclusive. "If we hire the Wilde guy, I don't know why we wouldn't just keep him where he is and open an office there now. Damn, I wish Maria was interested in moving to California."

"We can't put someone brand new—whether it's Cole Wilde or Maria Salvatore—in charge of opening a new office. They'd need to get some time under their belts, preferably in the New York office since it's our busiest." It's past time for the business to expand, but I want a second office on the East Coast, myself. We already have enough accounts here in New York to divide up, and selfishly, I'd like to see a satellite upstate or in Connecticut. Someplace that would be ideal for raising kids.

I recognize that this bias is a terrible reason for dismissing Cole Wilde as a candidate. The guy has a good resume, and both rounds of interviews were impressive.

But so were Maria's.

"One of us could go out to L.A. temporarily and set the place up with him." This comes from Cade via Skype. He's on the last leg of his one year travel-the-world with his family tour, and though he's still technically on a leave-of-absence, he's been participating in our owners' meetings more and more lately.

This time he's actually in a Reach office, having joined Dylan for this call in the London office.

"But you're not volunteering for that, I'm guessing, seeing how you just bought a house in Sherborn." I'm probably not supposed to say anything since Cade doesn't even know I know.

"Outside of Boston?" Nate asks. "That's a nice area."

"Guess the cat's out of the bag. Thanks, D." Cade only sounds slightly miffed, but he still takes a stab at payback. "Actually, I was thinking you and Sabrina."

Besides Nate, who could never leave the New York office since he's the glue that holds this place together, I know the others think Sabrina and I are the best option for relocating since we don't have kids to uproot.

Sabrina doesn't need another excuse to put off a family so I don't want the idea even on the table.

I attempt a redirect. "Boston would make a great location for an office."

"I was going to make the same suggestion." Dylan has been relatively quiet until now. The circles under his eyes suggest he stayed up late, drinking with Cade, or he still isn't getting much sleep with the twins.

I'm a little jealous of both possibilities.

Thinking about babies, I glance toward my wife. She's pinching her bottom lip with her fingers, and the look in her eyes is one I recognize. She has an idea of some sort. For once, I'm not sure I want to hear it, but I ask anyway. "What are you thinking, Sabrina?"

She puts her hand down from her mouth. "We could hire both Cole and Maria. Cade and Maria can open an office in Boston now. Meanwhile, Cole could work with us here in the New York office for a year or two, and then we could go help him open an office in L.A."

"We don't need an office in L.A.," I say.

She holds her ground. "In two years, we will."

"Not if we expand here now."

"The rate our numbers are growing says that we'll need both."

"If that's true, we can send Cole out on his own then." I don't mean what I'm saying. Reach is my baby. Two years would not be enough time for me to entrust a new office to be set up without my oversight.

Sabrina calls me on it. "You'd never send someone out on their own."

"We're not moving to L.A," I say definitively. *Subject closed.*

Sabrina's eyes narrow in rage, but she keeps her mouth shut, which means this will likely be an argument she'll save for later, when we're alone.

Goody me.

I'm surprised she's letting it wait, to be honest, especially since this tension is about much more than who we hire or where we expand the office. This decision has a far greater impact on our lives. She must realize this too, otherwise she'd keep pushing, audience be damned.

Speaking of our audience...

A glance around the table says that the tension between us has not gone unnoticed. Before I can smooth things over—because holding us together seems to be my job—my secretary sticks her head into the conference room. The interruption alone is unusual since Simone knows when I say *Do Not Disturb* that I mean *Do Not Fucking Disturb*. Even more unusual is that she's interrupted to tell me I have a phone call.

It takes effort to keep my voice down. "I thought it was obvious that—"

"I know, but he's insisting and—"

"Since when has—?"

Simone continues over me, "I didn't know if I should say no to Holt Sebastian."

The tension from earlier relaxes as curiosity takes its place. Even I'm intrigued, though I'm not the first to voice it.

"Holt Sebastian?" Weston and Sabrina say the name in unison though with very different tones—the former full of awe, the latter with something akin to disgust.

"That's what he said. The caller ID confirms the call is coming from the Sebastian Center." Simone is usually a tough, unflappable, no-nonsense kind of employee. That's why I took her with me when I moved from Tokyo to New York. I've never seen her get flustered, but right now she's dangerously close.

"Is he one of the main Sebastians?" Dylan asks. "I can't keep all the names straight."

It's a fair question. The Sebastians are modern-day Rocke-fellers who dominate in both industry and media.

"He's the newly appointed CEO of Sebastian News Media. Transferred over from the Industrial side. He's Samuel's son. Definitely one of the main ones, and definitely one with a lot of power. He's got a reputation for being kind of brutal about business. Very intimidating. Not that I, uh, have experience with that or anything. Real asshole." Weston sounds more impressed than put off, and I'm not the only one who notices.

"You finally find someone to knock Donovan off the pedestal you have him on?" Cade is also an asshole. Not that I'm complaining.

"Hey, I'm not the one with his name tattooed on me."

"His initial, and it's not his initial anymore, it's—"

Simone cuts off Cade's rant. See what I mean about being no-nonsense? "Mr. Sebastian is still waiting for you to pick up, Mr. Kincaid."

"What does he want?" Sabrina's terse tone proves she's just as no-nonsense as my secretary. I have a type, it seems. Unfortunately, that type doesn't seem to like competition in their playground so my wife and my secretary are prone to pissing contests—or whatever the female equivalent is.

"If he'd told me, I would have passed that information on to Mr. Kincaid already, Ms. Lind."

"*Mrs. Kincaid.*" I don't usually insert myself in their banter, but robbing my wife of her married name is not a petty behavior I'll tolerate.

"Excuse me, *Mrs. Kincaid.* It's an honest mistake. I really didn't expect the name to be relevant for this long."

Sabrina glowers, but the catfight takes a backseat when Nate shifts to look directly at me. "Do you know why he'd be calling you, Donovan?"

I shrug. "No idea."

"Does it matter?" Sabrina asks. "You're not really going to talk to him, are you?"

"It's the middle of the business day," Dylan muses over her.

"It's likely not a social invitation. Not if he's calling personally and demanding to speak to you at once. He'd ask for a call back."

Weston shakes his head. "I'm telling you, guys. He's a dick. You can't guess anything based on his behavior."

Nate ignores Weston's assessment. "What business would the Sebastians have with Reach? They have their own advertising division."

"Maybe he wants to pick D's brain about something," Cade offers.

"Or it's something to do with Raymond." At least Weston has the decency to look sorry about bringing up my father.

"Mr. Kincaid?" Simone prompts impatiently.

Even with the last suggestion being the most probable—so many of my relationships have started with my father—my interest is piqued.

That doesn't mean I'm going to come running just because some rich prick said so. "Tell him I truly couldn't be interrupted and get a better time for me to call him back."

"You're seriously going to talk to him?" There's the Sabrina that isn't afraid to bicker with me in public.

Simone ignores my wife's outburst. "Will do, Mr. Kincaid."

"Thank you, Simone," but she's already out the door.

"Oh my God. Really?" Sabrina huffs. "You're really going to take a meeting with Holt Sebastian?"

I open my palms up in a sort of shrug. "I don't see why I wouldn't."

"Because he's a Sebastian! They're the last people we want to be doing business with."

"We can't assume he wants to do business," I say coolly. "And if he does...might as well hear him out. There might be an opportunity there."

Now I'm not sure what her deal is with the Sebastians or if this is still all about last night, but I do know that she hates it when she gets worked up and I stay calm as a cucumber. This discussion would probably fare better for me if I injected a little passion myself.

But I am who I am, and I'm not interested in playing theatrics when they aren't warranted.

Needless to say, that only pisses her off more. "An opportunity? With a Sebastian? I can't believe what I'm hearing right now."

Next to me, Nate leans toward Weston and says, loud enough that I can hear, "Do you get the feeling this isn't just about Holt Sebastian?"

"D really doesn't want to move to Los Angeles," Weston says.

It's an opportunity to lighten the mood. I could crack a joke. Divert the conversation. Say I hear her, and I understand, and then meet with Holt behind her back to satisfy my curiosity.

But I'm overly aware of the fact that certain people in the room think I'm withholding too much from her already, and the undercurrent of tension from last night has me in tow. The circumstances are primed for me to behave badly.

And so I do.

I poke at her. I push her buttons. "I didn't realize the Sebastians were our mortal enemies."

"Considering who they are and what they stand for? You're being purposefully obtuse."

"Pretend it's not purposeful. Spell it out." My jaw is set, and under the table my knee is starting to twitch. This can't be going where I think it's going.

Except, I know her.

And that means I know exactly where it's going, and why I'm not surprised when she confirms it. "They're entitled rich boys, all of them, with no morals and questionable ethics in both business and their personal life. It was bad enough when it was just the five brothers doing dirty deeds at the behest of Irving Sebastian, but now they've all multiplied and Daddy Sebastian has an army of terrible people to do his bidding at his fingertips. It's disgusting, and Reach should want no part of them, financially or otherwise. As part owner, I'd like it on the record right now that I do not support engagement with any of the Sebastians."

It's prejudiced and overly simplified to lump all of the Sebastians into one box of good or bad. Irving alone has made several choices that fit squarely in the gray. Perhaps some of his practices have been morally questionable, but they've been legal, and he's made his business into an empire because of it. He made his company money. That was his job.

It was a debate I had with Sabrina back at Harvard, when she was a doe-eyed student in my ethics class, and I tried to teach her what it takes to belong in the world she longed to be part of.

It's absurd that her viewpoint is still so naïve. But her innocence turns me on, so I can live with it.

What I'm finding harder to live with is what she hasn't said, what's beneath her words. The description she's given for Irving Sebastian could very well be a description applied to Raymond Kincaid.

And if this is how she really feels, what the fuck is she doing with me?

The room is quiet. All eyes are on me, waiting to see how this quarrel will play out. As I've said, we've fought before in front of the team. Sabrina's stormed out of many a meeting. Generally all that means is that I'll have to grovel later, usually with my tongue, and my face between her thighs. It makes for a good marriage, as far as I'm concerned.

Today is the first time that I'm the one to leave.

"I think this is as productive as we're going to get today," I say when I reach the door. "We can pick up the discussion about our applicants at our next meeting."

I don't bother telling Sabrina not to follow me. She knows by now when it's best to leave me alone.

FOUR

I WATCHED as the two men uncrated the painting, careful to keep my expression even when the work of art was revealed. It was a fine enough piece with lots of detail and color, definitely a masterpiece. I'd maybe even love it if I were into dogs and horses and old British landscapes.

It wasn't for me, though, so my opinion didn't really matter.

"My girl needs some time to examine it for authenticity," I said, nodding to the expert my father had sent with me. Claudette was her name. A twiggy brunette thing with nice tits. I'd considered fucking her on the flight to Tokyo—my father's jet had a bed, and she'd definitely been putting out the fuck-me vibes—but I wasn't entirely sure my father hadn't already been there, done that, and the thought of sharing with Raymond had me shuddering.

Too bad. I had a thing for tits.

Or rather I had a thing for women who reminded me of the woman I always wished I was with. Four years since I'd last spoken to her, and Sabrina Lind was still my kink.

Yeah, I was definitely screwed in the head.

"Certainly," the dealer said. He was American. He hadn't said as much but I detected a hint of California in his dialect. He ordered his men to place the painting on the table. "Do you need gloves?"

Claudette was already pulling her pair out of her bag. "I have my own. I'll need some time with the piece."

"Take what you need." He gestured, and his men stepped back a foot, giving Claudette room to work while also making sure we both knew she was being carefully watched.

"Thank you, gentlemen," she said, moving to examine the painting, clearly unfazed by the military-looking guards and the guns openly displayed on their hips. Working with priceless art, she probably was used to the drill.

Or maybe she was just used to working with my father.

Still, I was glad I'd brought a bodyguard of my own. I liked having the numbers balanced. Two henchmen for the dealer, Claudette and a henchman for me. And my guy had the height and bulk of both his guys combined, though the tatted guy who'd called himself Cade—another American; East Coast, if I had to guess—had an intimidating handshake. It was clear he was a man who knew how to handle himself.

Despite all the armed men, the tenor of the meeting felt relaxed, which meant I didn't have to keep a close eye while Claudette did her inspection.

Stepping away, I pulled my phone out of my pocket and opened up my email and scrolled past the first three, all from my father. I already knew the gist of them—follow-ups on jobs I was doing for him and the like. I'd graduated almost three years before and though I'd told him over and over I wasn't coming to work for King-Kincaid, he'd managed to drag me in as a consultant on more projects than I liked to admit. It wasn't that I couldn't say no to him. It was more that it just felt easier to say yes. Part of the problem was that I needed more to occupy my time. I'd invested in a restaurant with my dead girlfriend's stepfather—yeah, I generally stayed away from describing Dylan as such—but that had been about it, much to Raymond Kincaid's chagrin. Gaston's was a contentious spot between us all on its own, not that my father disapproved of investing. He just sensed that I looked at Dylan as sort of a father figure.

I didn't. I liked Dylan too much to relate him to a father.

Point was, I either needed to bite the bullet and go all in with Dad, or I needed to start something on my own. Weston was graduating soon. He'd join me. Dylan would too, if I twisted his arm.

It was always in the back of my mind, but I didn't want to think about any of that right now. Instead, I scrolled to the already opened report from my PI so I could read it for the umpteenth time since I'd received it the night before. I'd print it when I got home so I could hold it in my hands. I liked tangibility where Sabrina was concerned. It made her more real when so often it felt like she was just a memory I'd invented. It was important to remember she was a living person. A living person that could easily be destroyed, if I wasn't careful.

This particular report included a recommendation from one of Sabrina's professors for her graduate school application, filled with enough high praise to make me both proud and irritated. Even if she was performing at her best—which she always was—

growth didn't happen under soft educators. She needed to be challenged. Harvard had challenged her. *I* had challenged her.

No. I wasn't doing that whole regret-what-I'd-done-to-her thing right now. It was in the past, and she was better off out of my life, despite the downgrade in her education.

Regrets aside, I was jealous. The professor's comments felt intimate. *With a curiosity and passion unmatched in her peers, Lind's strengths would be well suited to marketing or advertising. Her ability to think outside the box and her tireless drive make her a candidate that highly reputable programs will fight over.*

Did she fuck him? God, if she fucked him...

I shoved my phone in my jacket pocket and rolled my neck in an attempt to release the tension. She could fuck who she wanted. I didn't have a right to that any more than I had a right to any part of her life. Obviously, what I had a right to was never a deterrent, but I had vowed to myself to only intervene when I could give her something better. When I could lead her somewhere better. I would never be the definition of "better" so she could fuck who she wanted.

Besides, Sabrina wouldn't fool around with a professor. What had happened with me and her was on me. Take me out of the equation, and she was a good girl.

Or she thought she was anyway.

Her refusal to let herself be who she truly was frustrated me. It also let me be smug. Whoever she slept with, she wasn't going to get what she needed, not until she let that guard down. Hopefully, by the time she did, I'd figure out how to not let it destroy me.

"While you're waiting," the dealer said to me, "can I offer you a drink?"

Nathan Sinclair was the name he'd given me. Bold because, as far as I could tell in my research, that was his name legally, and I was pretty positive a lot of his dealings were not.

This one, for example. My father tended to give his orders with as few details as possible, but the discreet izakaya in Shibuya where Nathan had set our meet-up was shady as fuck. It was a complete dive bar with a nearly empty front room and lots of closed doors in the hallway back to the lounge.

Plus, the deal had been made in cash. As the son of a financial emperor, I'd learned that dealing in cash generally meant outside the law.

"I'm good." Actually, I could have gone for a drink, but I was also cautious.

"Something else, then? I just got in a box of Habanos straight from Cuba."

I hesitated. It was hard to turn down a good cigar.

"You're a cigar man," Nathan said, reading me better than I'd wanted to be read. "They're Maduros. Real quality. You can take your pick from the box."

What the hell. "Sure."

Claudette perked up. "You're going to smoke in here?"

"Of course not. We wouldn't dream of damaging the art. We can light up in the next room," Nathan offered, and when I seemed to balk he pointed to a mirror on the back wall. "There's a window. You can watch."

I'd suspected the mirror was a two-way.

"I'm good with that," Claudette assured me.

I exchanged a glance with my bodyguard, who gave a discreet nod of agreement, then consented. "Okay, but just a reminder no one here has any money. I have to text my guy in the limo to bring in the case after the piece is authenticated."

"Yeah, got it. We're cool. I'll take one of my men off her if that will help you relax." He turned to the tatted man. "Cade, join us?"

He grunted an affirmation.

I wasn't sure how bringing a man with a gun with us was supposed to make me relax, but I had a gun of my own in my pocket that I hadn't bothered keeping secret.

Which was probably the real reason why the Sinclair guy was taking a man off Claudette. He wanted his heavy with us. Fair enough.

On alert, I followed him into the next room, his man trailing behind us, and was a bit surprised to find that it was small and empty. Empty of people, anyway. There was a bar along one wall with dark leather stools and an armchair, sofa, and table on the opposite side, but no one in the room but us. I'd expected that our whole transaction was being watched. Apparently not. I doubted this dealer was working on his own, but it seemed at least that his boss trusted him.

And I trusted him. Possibly to my demise, but truly, my spidey senses weren't picking up anything that I thought I needed to be concerned about.

So not only did I accept the Cuban, I also accepted the Hibiki when offered it. "Smooth," I said, after my first swallow.

"Ah, you're a whisky man as well. This is a limited edition Suntori."

"Good stuff." Scotch was my go-to, but I could get used to this. Truth was, I hadn't had much of a chance to acquaint myself with Japanese liquor in the past. I was twenty-five, and had been to Japan a few times in my life—always with my father—but never for long enough to really explore. Most of the time, it had been a pit stop on the way to China, where

Raymond was always wooing government officials in an attempt to get US banking into the Chinese market. He had yet to succeed.

This time, I was here on my own.

Or, here with Claudette, I supposed.

I peeked through the window. She was still making her analysis.

"It's going to be a while," Cade said, plopping himself down in a leather chair in the corner of the room and lit up a cigarette. "Might as well get comfortable."

I didn't want to get *too* comfortable. So I took a seat on a barstool and angled myself so I could face the window, wanting to keep an eye on Claudette in case she needed anything.

Nathan, who'd been behind the counter, came around and sat on a stool a few spots to my left, giving me some space, which I appreciated. We puffed for a few minutes in silence.

"Not sure why someone would choose what you're smoking over this," I said, nodding toward Cade. "If you weren't smoking with me, Nathan, I'd wonder if these were laced."

Nathan chuckled. "Cade just has poor taste."

"Fuck you," Cade said, not seeming to be really bothered.

"I think it's really a sentimental thing with him. A girl got him hooked or something."

Well, I couldn't say I didn't know where he was coming from.

Cade put his feet up on the table in front of him. "She did not, and fuck you again."

"And it's Nate. I'm only Nathan on paper."

It took me a second to realize he was being genuine. Most people I dealt with for my father played the part of congenial. No one ever meant it.

It was an interesting change. "Donovan Kincaid," I said, because up until then I'd been communicating with him as D.K.

Nate extended his hand. I studied him for a minute before accepting it. He had to have a decade on me in years, maybe more. He had a scar near his ear and wrinkles near his eyes that aged him but also said he was quick with a smile.

Yeah, this guy was real.

I took his hand. He had a good handshake.

"First time in Tokyo?" he asked.

I shook my head. "I've passed through."

"Ah, that's no good. Tokyo is a destination. Spend some time."

"Definitely." It was a lie. My father's plane was scheduled to return to New York in the morning. He didn't need to know that.

"I'm happy to show you around the town. Not in a tour guide sense, but if you're looking for entertainment."

I couldn't help myself. "Entertainment?"

"Food, wine, women. Men, if you prefer."

"*Woman.* Singular." Not that I was celibate, but he had asked what I preferred.

"Me too. Sometimes. Doesn't mean you can't watch."

"I'll keep it in mind." As far as I was concerned, that ended the conversation. I'd moved on and was once again thinking about Sabrina. About her professor's report. Advertising, he'd said. Yeah, I could see her in advertising. I could see her in a New York high-rise with a view overlooking the Hudson, working in a firm that handled the nation's biggest accounts.

The only fucking problem with the fantasy was that I kept putting myself in an office down the hall.

It could never happen. And it wouldn't if I went to work for my father officially.

But now my head was beginning to spin with other ideas.

"Fan?"

"Hm?" I wasn't sure if I'd only caught the last word of whatever Nate was saying or if I'd missed the context.

He nodded toward the window. "Of Heywood Hardy."

"Oh, right." The artist of the painting I was about to hand over three hundred k for. I thought about my answer longer than I probably needed to. Did he think I was buying it for myself? Easiest to pretend that I was, but all of a sudden I wanted myself distanced from it. From my father, his money, all of it.

I took a swallow of the whisky, then answered honestly. "Nah. I actually have a thing for Japanese art."

"Like Hokusai? Or Hasui? Something older... Tōhaku?"

I tried not to look like a deer caught in headlights.

After a beat, I gave up. "You caught me. It's a new thing. As in, I really like the painting in my hotel room. A replica of something famous, I think. Autumn leaves, blurred and softened. Clouds. Unique style." Too abstract for my father's collection.

"Ah, Yokoyama Taikan. That's a nice piece. The original is in the Adachi, I believe."

"Be careful or Nate will offer to get it for you," Cade said from behind me. He was about my age, I realized now. I'd first pegged him for older, but now that he'd relaxed, I could see the boy beneath the man.

"That true?" I asked the dealer.

Nate chuckled. "Well. If you're looking to buy..."

"I'll stick with just the Hardy." The guy was a real salesman. Give him another minute on the topic and someone other than me as his audience, and he'd have the piece sold. A piece he didn't even own.

"But it's not for you."

It wasn't a question. So I didn't respond.

"A gift." When I again didn't respond, he clarified. "I'm just making conversation, not trying to nose my way into your business."

That's exactly what someone nosing their way in would say.

But he wasn't going to shut up, it seemed, so might as well do my own nosing. "More like a favor. And as long as we're 'making conversation', let me ask, how did you happen to procure this particular piece?"

"Oh, Mr. Kincaid, I do believe it was stated that would not be disclosed when the deal was originally made."

It had been my father who had made the original deal. Or someone else doing his bidding. I'd only been brought in to do the fetching.

I had a feeling Nate already knew that. "That sure does make it seem like the deal might not be on the level."

"Does it matter?"

I wouldn't want to own it if I couldn't display it, myself. But the painting wasn't for me. "As long as my girl says it's legit, it doesn't matter in the least."

"She will." He didn't even flinch. It was the real deal, I was certain, even without Claudette's say-so.

And this salesman...he was something special too.

"Donovan," I said. "Mr. Kincaid is my father."

"Donovan," he repeated with a smile. It wasn't the kind of smile that had women dropping panties the way Weston's did, but I would bet that Nate Sinclair's charm could give Weston a run for his money.

"And I wasn't trying to nose my way into your business." I waited for his laugh. "Just—"

"—making conversation," he finished for me.

"I was going to say 'curious'."

"Tell you what." He leaned an elbow on the bar. "If my boss came to me and said, 'I have a client who will pay for a certain artist'—a pretentious equestrian and landscape artist, for example—then I'd track down all the pieces by that artist in private collections, make some offers. See if anyone would bite."

"And if they wouldn't?"

"Then I'd start scoping out the private galleries. And say I found one in a summer home on an island in the Maldives—first of all, I'd be very interested in knowing whether the art was kept in a humid controlled environment, because someone who is leaving a piece like that to the natural elements doesn't deserve to own it. Am I right?"

I bit back my smile. "I see the logic there."

"And when I discovered that the piece was still miraculously in good condition, and that the owner's personal assistant seemed to have an attraction for me...well, then I'd hire someone to make a replica of the work—not as easy as it sounds, but not impossible—then get cozy with the assistant, which might only take one blowjob."

"Only one?"

"I give surprisingly good head."

I raised an eyebrow, but I wasn't actually surprised, even with the revelation that Nate had been the one on his knees. "So you get yourself an invitation to the house when the owner's out of town."

"Good thinking. That's exactly what I'd do."

"Slip away while he's sleeping and replace the original with the fake."

He shook his head. "I'd leave a door unlocked and the alarms off and then spend the night distracting the assistant while one of my partners replaced the original with the fake."

"Of course. Less risky."

His eyes twinkled. "More fun."

This time he did surprise me. I laughed. Then after a beat, I laughed again. "It sounds like you love your work."

He considered. "For now."

"It has its ups and downs," Cade offered, as though this was a topic they'd discussed before. I'd almost forgotten he was there. The man knew how to be a silent observer. Something about him made me suspect there was more to him than just brawn.

Nate gave a nod. "Would be nice not to have a boss."

I didn't think of my father as my boss, but that was essentially what he'd be if I worked for him. Was that what I wanted?

Not really.

But it wasn't like I could exactly cut the leash to Raymond Kincaid. I owned stock in his company. I was his heir. I shared his blood.

And if I didn't have him, what else would I have besides a dead girlfriend and a fat file on a woman that would never be mine?

As if he knew I was thinking about him, my phone buzzed with a text from my father. *Picked it up yet?*

Still authenticating.

"She looks like she's almost done," Nate said, drawing my head up from my phone toward the window. Claudette smiled and gave a thumbs-up.

I texted my father again to tell him we were good before texting the man outside with the suitcase of cash. By the time I finished with the latter, my father had responded.

I'll see you and the art tomorrow when you land.

I stared at the screen, rereading his message. Wondering how my blood could get so hot from one short sentence. No thank you, no praise. Just a summons.

"Everything all right?" Nate asked, apparently watching me.

"Fine," I said. "Money's on its way." I set down my phone. Took another puff. Considered what my father would say if I marched in the other room and put a cigar-shaped burn into his precious art piece.

"You're already out of here," Nate said. "Already on that flight back to the States." He wasn't just a salesman—he could read people well. With his knowledge of art, he'd be good at other creative work. Production, maybe. Design. Ad sales. "You really should stay awhile."

I didn't want to get on that flight.

I wanted something of my own.

I picked my phone up again and sent another text to my dad. ***The art will be there. I will not.***

I shut my phone off before putting it in my pocket.

Then I turned my full attention to my new friend. "Ever consider trying another line of work?"

FIVE

"SHOULD I get Mr. Sebastian on the line?" Simone asks when I get back to my office.

Part of me wants to take the call now more than ever, because fuck anyone's opinion, even my wife's.

But that's not really true. Fuck anyone's opinion *except* my wife's, and that's the problem, isn't it? That I care what she thinks. Isn't that why I'm still holding on to that disk drive? Otherwise I would have disposed of it immediately, without a second thought, protecting my father's corrupt business no matter the cost. Protecting the money. That's a stockholder's job.

Sabrina wouldn't agree, and if I'd thought she might before, I'm all but certain now that she won't.

"Not today," I tell Simone. She doesn't seem to like my decision—she's always been a bit starstruck by the rich and the richer—but like I said before, fuck her opinion.

It doesn't mean I won't talk to Holt Sebastian eventually, and even if it pisses him off to be put on hold, I'm not about to be someone's beck-and-call boy.

Isn't that how I got in this mess in the first place?

So if I call him, it won't be today, and for that matter, I'm not fit company at the moment at all. "Cancel my afternoon. I don't want to be disturbed by anyone."

"What about the partners?"

"Definitely not the partners." The last thing I need is Weston's puppy dog eyes and sappy advice.

"Even Mrs. *Kincaid*?" She emphasizes her use of the correct name, though it's dripping with condescension.

I scold her with my stare and hesitate only briefly before answering. "I'll see Sabrina." It's pathetic, but I hope she comes. It's our thing—I fuck up and withdraw, she comes running after me. She'll push me to make it better, and I will.

Only this time, she doesn't come.

All afternoon, I struggle to focus on my work. With the windows shaded and my door closed, I have to strain to hear footsteps outside in the hall, and that leaves little bandwidth for operational duties. Each time the phone rings, every time a snippet of muffled conversation reaches my ear, my fingers pause on the keyboard, my pulse quickens. When the sounds aren't followed by an intercom announcement that she's arrived or her bursting through the door, I become more and more agitated.

At four o'clock, I can't stand it anymore. I give up and go looking for her instead.

"She left for the day," Roxie informs me, without looking up from her work.

I don't even try not to snap. "What do you mean she's left for the day?"

Roxie doesn't put up with my bullshit anymore now that she's Sabrina's assistant than she did when she was Weston's. "I mean she left for the day."

I know I'd acted badly, but so badly that it had sent Sabrina home early? Fuck, was I the one who was supposed to come running to her this time?

When I'm still standing in front of Roxie trying to sort through what's what a whole minute later, she takes pity on me. "She had an appointment and said she'd go home straight from there."

"An appointment? An appointment where?"

"Didn't say." She goes back to her typing as though I wasn't still hovering.

Now, it's not unheard of for Sabrina to have appointments that I don't know about, though it is unusual. I can access her scheduler from my phone, and I do on occasion. Just not as frequently as I did before we were married. She's fully aware. She knows I like to keep tabs on her. She's the one who gave me access, which is so much easier than relying on my PI from the past.

Point being, if I don't know where she's at, it's because I didn't bother to look.

Today, though, I looked.

More than once, even though I'd memorized her agenda, because that's who I am. She'd had a meeting earlier in the afternoon that was supposed to be over by two. Nothing scheduled after.

That doesn't mean something didn't come up last minute,

but Roxie meticulously adds everything to the schedule, even if it's passed, just to have a record of what happened when. A girl after my own heart, in many ways.

All this to say that Roxie not knowing where Sabrina went is very unusual.

Immediately on high alert, I place my palms on Roxie's desk and lean in so she can't avoid me. "What do you mean she didn't say?"

"I mean, she didn't say."

"Not helpful, Roxie."

She shrugs. "It must have been personal."

"Personal like...what? She's buying you a birthday present? She's getting a mammogram? She's having an affair?"

She gives me a look like I'm being ridiculous because I'm totally being ridiculous. "There is no way on God's green earth that you believe your wife is cheating on you."

This is true.

But where is she?

"Have you tried calling her?" Roxie asks like I'm an idiot.

No, I haven't tried calling her. I was sort of not speaking to her all day because I wanted her to come speak to me. I'd planned on storming into her office and asking her just why she hadn't. Calling her would take away all the power in that move.

But now that she's not here, I have to pivot. "Good. Suggestion," I say tightly, pulling out my cell from my pocket.

Her phone rings twice before it goes to voicemail. Fuck, did she just avoid my call? I redial and this time it goes to voicemail immediately. I check the app that tracks her phone—an app she knows about but never touches—and she's turned it off. She's never turned it off.

My jaw ticks. I turn to walk away, then turn back toward

Roxie. "She had to tell you something."

Roxie sighs but looks up from her computer. "She told me many things. Earlier this week she asked me to keep this afternoon free. Then today, she walked out here at two forty-five and said she had an appointment at three thirty."

"And you didn't ask her for more details?"

"If Mrs. Kincaid doesn't tell me, she doesn't want me to know. I don't pry." There's nothing subtle about the accusation in her statement. I'm supposed to feel chided.

I don't.

I look for another angle. "What did you tell the driver when you called for him?"

"I didn't." For a beat, it doesn't seem like she'll say more, but she must suddenly remember who signs the paychecks because she goes on. "She said she'd take care of her own transportation."

"She called the driver herself or she took a cab?" Sabrina hasn't driven since she moved to New York, but it's not out of the question that she drove one of the cars we keep in the building parking garage.

"When she said she'd take care of her own transportation, that means without me. That means I don't know who she called or whether or not she hailed a cab or if she went where she was going on foot."

I'm too focused to bother saying thank you. Instead, I step away from Roxie's desk to dial my driver. "Danny," I say when he answers. "Did Sabrina use you for anything today?"

"No, I've been busy with Mr. King all day."

I swear under my breath. I mean, come on. When I'd offered him my driver while they were in town, I hadn't expected he'd actually take me up on it. He can afford to hire a service while he's in town, and even while I'm thinking it, I know that I don't mean it. That I'm only irritated because I can't find my wife. "She didn't reach out to you at all?"

"No, sir."

Then she took a cab. "Are you in the Jag?" I ask, to be sure.

"The Tesla," he says.

"Okay, thank you. I'm taking off early. Don't worry about coming back for me. I'll take the Jag." I'm sure it's still in the garage since Sabrina doesn't know how to drive a manual.

I hang up without saying goodbye. Blood is rushing in my ears. I'm very aware of my pulse. Symptoms of preoccupation, merely, but I'm not worried. Not really.

Okay, I'm worried.

I know there's no *reason* to be worried. She didn't disappear off the planet. She left work early is all. It's a couple hours— three tops—that she'll likely be off my radar. She's a grown woman. Not a child. It's not a big deal.

And yet I feel completely untethered.

I put my phone back in my pocket and stride back to Roxie. "Did she tell you not to tell me where she was going?"

"Look, Mr. Kincaid." She clasps her hands together, as if she's trying to keep herself from wringing my neck. "I wish I could be more helpful. No, that's not true. I don't want to intrude on my boss's personal life, and I definitely don't want to be involved in whatever spat the two of you are having, but if you want my advice, you should go home and wait for her there."

I'm not keen on unsolicited advice. Especially advice about my wife. I consider telling that to my employee, but realize I don't have the patience to explain.

Once again, I turn to walk away. This time when I turn back, I reach over Roxie's desk to pick up her phone. She lets out a disgusted breath as I dial Sabrina's number. Once again, it goes directly to voicemail.

I put the phone back on the receiver with more force than necessary, prompting Roxie to jump.

"Donovan," she says, which gets my attention, not because of her sharp tone, but because she rarely uses my first name. "Go home. Sabrina is the only one who can give you the answers you're looking for."

I don't tell Simone I'm leaving. I don't even go back by my office on my way out the door. I have my phone and keys. That's all I need. Anything in my briefcase can wait until tomorrow.

And I recognize the inanity of my behavior. I'm well aware I've put all reason aside, rushing home as though there's an emergency. I've felt this lunacy many times in the past, with Sabrina mostly. With Amanda before her. It's like claws inside my chest, scratching against my sternum, like my soul trying to get through a fortified wall. Trying to reach out. Trying to connect. Trying to clutch on.

It's a sort of mania, this obsession. This desperate feeling that if I don't find her, if I don't know, that I'll lose her entirely.

It's a hell of a way to love someone. I know she accepts me as I am, but it's also a hell of a way to be loved.

It takes almost forty-five minutes to get home. Rush hour and New York traffic in general—it would have almost been faster walking.

But it gives me time to think, and by the time I get to our apartment building, I'm more in control than I was when I'd left Reach. I don't know if it's the advantage of age or having the ring on my finger or of knowing Sabrina like I do now—in the flesh instead of from afar—but I find it's easier than it used to be to pull myself out from these spirals. There's plenty of reasonable explanations for Sabrina's unscheduled departure from the office and plenty of reasons why she hadn't told me. If I hadn't canceled everything, I would have been out of the office this afternoon at a meeting with Pierce Industries that I'd had scheduled for weeks. We would have come home separately. Thinking I was gone, she probably decided to meet up with Elizabeth for a drink. Probably even to complain about me. Turned off her phone because who wants to be interrupted during cocktail hour when you're bitching about your spouse?

And that's the real source of my anxiety—me. This frenetic desperation is about this wall between us, this wall that I've put up by not talking to her about things that I know I really should. Not to give Weston any credit, but...well. No, I'm not even going to say he was right. But he might not have been all wrong.

So as soon as I walk in the door, I immediately head to my office. I get what I need, and go back downstairs to the living room to make myself comfortable.

Then I wait.

It's only ten after five when Sabrina walks in. I hear her kick her shoes off by the door, then listen to her pad into the living room. She's got the mail in her hand, and doesn't notice me at first. When she does, she startles, which gives my dick a jolt. I'm not necessarily turned on by her fear, but she is, and that's all I need to get me going.

"I didn't think you'd already be home," she says, her voice breathy, and seriously I have to remind myself we need to talk, not fuck.

"Canceled my afternoon." I don't want to start this with an accusation so I don't ask where she's been. Not yet.

"Oh. And you're just sitting here...?"

"Waiting for you," I say. "Sit down. It's time we talk."

SIX

"I SEE IT," Sabrina says, when she finally sets the laptop down on the couch beside her.

It's been two hours since I handed over the disk drive I've been keeping in the safe. Two hours of me pacing and hovering and wondering if she'd realize the damning information without me having to point it out. I haven't been so stressed over a file since I sat across from her in the Reach conference room to go over every scrap I'd collected on her over the years.

In some ways, this is worse. Then, the fear was that she wouldn't let me in. Now, the fear is that she'll kick me out, and having truly been with her for the last few years, I know there's no life without her. Not for me.

"You see it," I confirm. Of course she sees it. She's smart as a whip—too smart for her own good sometimes—and her moral leanings drive her to naturally spot these sorts of business illegalities.

Now I'm also sure that this is new info to her. She hadn't known before. But now that she does, how will she react?

"Yeah. It's, uh. It's bad." She breathes in. She breathes out. "You said you've had this for two years?"

"Two and a half." I walk over to the armchair and force myself to sit. "Go ahead. Lay it on me. What are you thinking?"

"This information will lose people jobs."

"I know."

"It could put people in jail."

"Yes."

"Your father."

"Eh..." I've thought about this a lot, and the truth is that, while King-Kincaid would definitely be in hot water, it would never reach boiling point. Not for the CEOs anyway.

"Are you kidding me?" She doesn't wait for an answer. "Fucking capitalist society," she mutters under her breath. "I guess the money guys always get off, don't they? Can't have the faith in the American financial system destroyed, so we'll just ignore corruption."

I want to remind her that the American financial system is what keeps her in a job and pays for our nice home and lets her fly on a private jet anytime she wants to London to visit her sister, but it's probably not the best time. "I'm just being realistic."

"They'd get fined though. And a scandal like this could introduce legislation. It could protect innocent people from these kinds of scams in the future."

Ever the idealist. God love her for it. I hate being the one who has to remove those rose-colored glasses so I only say, "Maybe."

She stares at me, her eyes pleading. "It would hurt them

somehow, wouldn't it? They wouldn't have covered it up if they hadn't believed it would hurt them."

I've already been over the likely scenarios a million times in my head, so I don't have to take time to consider, but I do anyway. "They'd take a hit financially. Maybe they'd only do fifty billion in revenue instead of a hundred. My father could potentially be asked to step down as CEO, but he'd still own stock and he'd be sent home with a multimillion severance package."

She looks like she might be sick.

"He'd be embarrassed though. Which matters to him. King-Kincaid would lose big clients. It might never recover fully. It could take years, at the very least, and that would matter to him a whole lot."

She sighs. "It might have had more impact if the public had found out about this sooner to when it happened."

"Yes. It would have." It had already been a year in the past when I'd obtained the drive, but that was practically the present in financial terms. I'd let time go by. That was on me, and I was ready for the accusations to fly.

"But you've just held on to it."

I nod, guiltily.

"Where have you kept it?"

"My office safe."

Her turn to nod. "And no one outside King-Kincaid knows?"

"That I have it? No one inside King-Kincaid knows. Not even Raymond."

"I meant, no one knows about this scandal? It's not on anyone's radar? No accusations about dirty business? Nothing?"

I've believed all my life that this was the responsibility of a stockholder—work for the benefit of the company. Increase gains. Weigh the benefits of unethical decisions against the risk of getting caught, and if the potential is low, choose on the side of profits. That's why I bought the information. Because I knew it could hurt the bottom line if it got out.

But I held on to it because of this moment. Because I feared that if Sabrina ever knew, and if she looked me in the eye, that all I would see is judgment.

Now that this moment is here, I realize that judgment isn't worth any amount of money.

But when she lifts her eyes toward me, the look she delivers feels...sympathetic. "I'm sorry."

"...excuse me?" The only reason I can think that she'd be apologizing is if she's about to tell me something I don't want to hear. Like how terrible a person she thinks I am. Or that she can't be married to someone like me.

"You've been carrying this alone," she says instead.

I wasn't expecting that, and it takes me a beat to react. "Well. Weston knows."

"He helped you get the drive?"

"No, I did that on my own. I told him soon after. I thought he should be aware of what our fathers were doing. I thought he might have input."

She rolls her eyes as though she (accurately) wouldn't expect Weston to be much of a support, but behind that I see hurt. "Why didn't you tell *me*, Donovan?"

I have to clear my throat. "I couldn't."

"Why couldn't you? Because you don't trust me?"

"No. No, definitely not that. I trust you more than anyone."

"Then why?"

I don't say anything because every reason I can think of

sounds pathetic in my head. I'm sure they won't sound any better out loud.

She blinks a few times, but no tears fall. "What are you going to do with it?"

"I don't...I thought you might have an idea which way I should go."

She leans back against the couch, and I can tell that although she's hurt by my lack of disclosure, she likes that I've asked her advice. "What are the options you're considering?"

"I could destroy it." The disgust on her face tells me what she thinks of that option. "I could release the info myself."

"That turns you into a villain. In the financial world, in the media."

What she doesn't say is that she'd be dragged into it too, but I know it has to be on her mind. *Great fucking situation to want to bring a child into, Donovan.* "I could do nothing."

"And then nothing changes."

"Not exactly sure anything changes if it's released," I remind her.

"There's no *opportunity* for change if you hold on to it." An idea occurs to her. "Could we get in trouble for having this?"

I hate that she's including herself in that *we*. "If anyone were to find it, then yes. We could face charges."

"We have to get rid of it, Donovan. And you can't destroy it."

"Then what do you suggest?" I sound frustrated because I am. "I could give it to my father. Let him deal with it. Doesn't need to be our problem."

She shakes her head. "Giving it to your father is the same decision as destroying it. It's a cop-out."

"So I'll ask again, what do you suggest I do?" What have I

even gained by letting her in on this? She hasn't thrown the book at me, but only because she's dealing with the practicals first. Even if her wrath never comes, her pain is worse. "Besides to not have gotten involved in the first place, because I know that's what you're thinking."

She turns a hard stare on me. "Really? That's what you really think I'm thinking?"

Well, now I'm not so sure.

She looks down at her lap and shakes her head again. Then she lets out a laugh. "I don't know who to be more mad at right now—you or me."

"Why on earth would you be mad at yourself, Sabrina? This is all on me."

She turns herself so her whole body is angled toward me. "Because I obviously haven't made it clear where you stand with me. You still don't think I'm on your side in everything, Donovan. *Everything*."

I'm having trouble letting her words really sink in. "But this..."

"Even this, you asshole."

I deserve the asshole remark. What I don't deserve is how levelheaded she's being. I'd probably be more affected by her devotion if I wasn't so distracted by the details of the situation. It's throwing me off. "Am I missing something? Why aren't you mad right now?"

"I am mad! You should have told me. I'm more hurt, actually, but—"

I cut her off. "Right, right, I should have told you, but why aren't you mad that I got the drive in the first place? You think businesses that do this shit are bad guys. You know I didn't step in with plans to be a whistleblower, right?"

"Not a hero, I know. You've made it clear." She doesn't sound all that convinced, but she's already moving on. "How could you not have gotten involved? He's your father, and you saw this information, and you have this...this...insane drive to take care of the people around you—and believe me, it's why I love you. Mostly. Ish—but I have to imagine it's a weight sometimes. A lot of the time. And I would never expect you to put it down, but I really wish you'd let me carry it with you. Isn't that what a marriage is supposed to be about? Partnership?"

"Sabrina...I..." I don't know what to say. I don't deserve her. I could never deserve her, and I could never give her up. What am I supposed to do with that?

Then suddenly, she clasps her hand over her mouth. "Oh my God, Donovan...you thought..."

Her tone is urgent, and I drop the thread of thought I'd been holding, thinking she's realized something even worse. Something I'd somehow missed. "What? What did I think?"

But she's quicker than me. Within seconds, she's on her knees in front of me, her hands laced together on my lower thigh. "When I said that earlier today...about the Sebastians being an army for their despicable father...I didn't mean you."

My chest feels like it's caving in, and I have to swallow before I speak. "Didn't you?"

"No," she insists.

"Only because you didn't know about this."

"No, no. This is different." She reconsiders. "Okay, yes, I concede that there's a possibility that the Sebastians have the same complicated relationships with their father, and I shouldn't judge their actions, but you are not like them. You have separated yourself from King-Kincaid. You have made a name for yourself on your own. You are your own man—a man with a heart big enough to want to help your dad out of hot water, even when you know he doesn't deserve it—but that's you. Not him."

My throat feels thick. "I have been like them."

"I only care about now."

"Maybe I'm like them now too."

She doesn't hesitate. "I don't believe that." Before I can argue, she goes on. "Are you listening to anything I'm telling you? On your side, Donovan, means on your side. Stop fighting it."

I'm stubborn, and part of my brain is searching for evidence to the contrary. I'm manipulative too, and I could twist reality to fit my truth. If she's on my side, why did she push back so hard against me at today's meeting? Why has she felt so far away? Why won't she agree to having my kid?

The thing is, I believe her. Because I want to maybe, but also because I feel it in my bones. It's a certainty that doesn't need to be rationalized. It just is.

Fuck, I love her.

There aren't words to express how much, so I rely on action. Abruptly, I pull her from the floor and kiss her. Kiss her roughly. Like I'm trying to steal her air. Exactly like she likes it.

When she starts to pull away to catch her breath, I put a hand at the back of her neck to hold her in place. And then she knows what kind of kiss this is meant to be, but just in case she has any question, I slip my free hand down the front of her shirt, find her breast and squeeze.

She moans, and I devour the sound, but I don't let up on the kiss. There's been too much tension pent up between us with no release. We *need* this kiss. We need it to be more, and I know she knows it too when her fingers come to my chest, and she claws at me with desperation. Then she sets her ass on my thigh and grinds her hips like she's looking for relief. I can feel the heat of her cunt through our clothes. I can smell her desire. It intoxicates me.

We need the *more* to happen *now*.

Without giving her any warning, I stand, taking her with me. My hand stays firm at her neck, my mouth locked on hers until I'm sure she's steady on her feet. Once she's standing, I bend over and sweep the coffee table clean, sending three decorative bronze vases flying to the floor with a clang. With practiced skill—rough but not too rough—I throw Sabrina down onto the cleared space. It's as wide as her shoulders, but not long enough for her entire body, so she spreads her legs to hug the table. Her hands flat on the surface beside her, she looks up at me.

And she waits.

That's all it takes for me to get hard to the point of pain. Her —no matter that she's fully clothed—spread out for me, offering up what I had already planned to take. I take a beat to study her, and the only reason I take my time is because it's hard to know what I want to do with her first.

I decide to start by removing her shoes for no other reason than the pants aren't coming off with them still on. When her feet are bare, I move to the side of the table where I can reach the belt tied into a big bow at the waist of her trousers. It's frilly and I generally hate that, but right now I'm rather fond of the detail. It makes it feel like she's a present to be unwrapped.

A present that I unwrap slowly.

Tugging gently on one tail of the bow, I pull until the knot comes loose, then I keep pulling until it clears all the belt loops, and I'm left with a long string of fabric in my hands. Of course, I get ideas.

Maybe her patience is waning, or maybe she has ideas too, because the next thing I know, her hand grips my erection through my pants, and I let out an involuntary hiss. I'm too turned on for her to touch me right now. Too focused on her to be able to control what's happening with my cock. She's fully aware, and I half expect she's toying with me because she wants me to tie her up.

Which I'm game for.

But I don't like to be topped from the bottom. If I'm going to tie her, it will be on my terms. I toss the fabric to the couch behind me. Something else will have to be done about her roaming hands. "Grip the table above your head," I order.

She frowns, but after a reluctant beat, she does as I've asked.

"Good girl." Slowly, I prowl around the table and stop when I've made it back to her feet. This time when I bend over, I curl my fingers around her waistband. "Up," I say, and she lifts her ass so I can pull her pants down past her hips, then she straightens her legs so I can take them off the rest of the way.

I throw them to the floor then take a moment to arrange her legs like she'd had them before. When I spread her knees, I tuck her left foot behind the left leg of the coffee table and her right around the right leg, and since she rarely wears panties under her pants to avoid lines, her cunt is now completely exposed, shaved bare and glistening with her arousal. If I thought I couldn't be more hard, I was so very wrong.

I rub my hand over the bulge in my crotch, which only makes the situation worse. "Fuck, Sabrina."

"Sounds like a good idea to me."

"Are you trying to dictate how this happens?"

"No. But if you're going to take your time..." She brings one hand to her mouth, sucks on her index finger like a wanton little hussy, then lowers it down to stroke her pussy.

As if I wasn't suffering enough.

In two strides, I walk around to her head, grabbing the belt I'd tossed aside on the way. "I told you to keep a grip on the table. You seem to need some help. Give me your hands." She does, and I stretch her arms over her head before looping the belt around her wrists until tying it off in a knot.

Unfortunately, it's more for show than for impact since her hands are only tied together, not to anything to keep them in place. I'll have to figure out what I'm doing about that. It's a little hard to think with all the blood in my brain having gone south.

Right now, all I can think about is getting my cock out and getting some relief. I undo my belt, and pull my pants down just far enough to let my erection free. Then I fist myself and pump. Once, twice, three times. A small bead of pre-cum shows up on my crown.

"I could help you with that," Sabrina says. She reaches her bound hands toward me.

Time to decide what to do about those hands. Still not sure what, I grab the end of the belt and step to the side of the table. Since the ends of the knot are short, it's not just her arms that come with me, but her whole torso.

And now I've accidentally come across a good idea.

Using the belt, I tug her up and toward me, which brings her mouth level with my cock. Bingo. "Want to help? Open up."

As soon as she parts her lips, I shove in. All the way. Until my tip touches the back of her throat. And, fuck, it feels good. So fucking good. Pleasure runs down my spine and my body feels warm from head to toe, and I already feel like I'll explode.

Then she starts to suck. Her tongue runs along the base of my length, and she hollows her cheeks so that when I tilt my hips back and push back in, my cock feels sensation on every square inch, and fuck, fuck, fuck, I'm seeing stars.

"Sabrina," I growl. Because I feel fantastic, and that makes me mad. Fucked up, I know, but that's the reality of me and her. She wanted into my life, and the only way I could let her and live with myself was by making her my priority. Her happiness. Her pleasure. Everything about the way I love her is *for* her. I'm not saying I'm a martyr. It's symbiotic, actually, because there's nothing I want more in this world than to do for her.

And that's why I'm currently mad. Because this pleasure is selfish. The electricity spreading through my limbs, the fire at the base of my spine, the throbbing of my crown—it's all about me. I'm greedy, and I should despise myself for it. I don't, and that pisses me off.

Luckily, she loves my rage, and so I use it to refocus myself on her. I bend to stroke my thumb across her fat clit, with pressure, but not too much. She jumps, letting out a soft hum that makes my cock vibrate.

I curse under my breath, at war with myself now—torn between her needs and my own.

My own win out momentarily, and I pull at her shirt, suddenly desperate to see her breasts. The buttons are delicate and it only takes one tug before her bra is exposed. Sitting up and twisted the way she is, her tits look even more full. My eyes dart from them to my cock disappearing between her lips. I can't decide where to look. Everywhere I turn, the view is good.

Another burst of rage, and this time her cunt gets spanked.

Moisture pools between her legs, and I gather it to swipe across her most sensitive spot, then trail it down her pussy lips, smearing it like finger paint. Then lower, to that hole I haven't yet breached with anything thicker than my finger, which I insert inside her now, wanting to turn my anger into punishment, wanting to remind her that every part of her is mine. Even this.

That thought—or perhaps it's the roll of her tongue across my crown—brings me awfully close to orgasm.

And while I know she loves the degradation of my cum on her face, I'm feeling too into her at the moment. I need to be buried in her pussy for that.

I step back far enough that my cock falls out of her mouth, then use the knot at her wrists to pull her with me toward the armchair. I sit first, then turn her so her back is to my chest when I tug her down on my lap, onto my waiting cock.

I slide in easily, all the way to the base.

We sigh in unison. All the irritation disappears as my pleasure becomes hers, as we move together toward the same goal. We're so eager, our rhythm is sloppy at first. I place my hands on her waist to steady us out.

Then I give her the stage. "Bounce on my cock, baby."

Without hesitation, she brings her feet to the cushion on either side of my knees to brace herself, and I snake an arm around to play with her clit. Then she rides me with admirable gusto. The strength in those gorgeous thighs. The enthusiasm in her vigor. Like a goddamn porn queen. Like a dirty, little slut.

My thoughts aren't only depraved. She's equally a goddess. A woman worth worship. *My* woman. The only woman I want to live with and love and fuck, and yes, impregnate.

I end up there so often when I'm inside her—whether that's

a primitive yearning or a result of a higher love, I'm not sure—but soon it takes me over, the impetus behind my drive. I grip her hips and hold her in place so I can thrust up, up, up, needing to give her my seed. Needing to plant myself inside her. Needing to establish my claim on her in human form, birth control be damned.

She comes just before I do, her cunt clenching around me as though asking for my cum. And so I give it to her. My strokes become uneven, and I pump into her through the explosion, making sure to deliver every last drop.

When I'm spent, I sink into the chair. Sabrina collapses with me. I love her weight on me. This might even be my favorite part of sex—holding her, stroking her sweat-soaked skin, calming my breath by matching hers. It's when I'm most at peace. When my brain is quiet. When I don't feel like I have to try to do...anything.

When I feel like I actually have her.

I pull the remnant of her shirt down and kiss along her shoulder. Trail my mouth up her neck, across her jaw.

"Your father..." she says, breaking through my sanctuary.

With a groan, I rest my forehead on her shoulder. "I don't know how I feel about the mention of my father when my cum is still dripping from your cunt."

She laughs. "I'm not sure anything is dripping out yet. I still feel pretty plugged up."

It's true—I'm still rooted inside her, still half hard.

She's going to continue this conversation, despite our circumstances. Because she's Sabrina, and she's a dog with a bone when she wants to be. Reluctantly, I maneuver us so that we're no longer quite so attached.

She waits until then to go on. "I'm sure you've thought

about this inside and out, but I think there has to be another option you haven't explored."

"What option?" Another kiss on her shoulder. Another stroke of my thumb along her firm midriff.

"I don't know." She turns her head so she can place a kiss on the side of my mouth. "And I know that's not helpful, but I feel it in my gut that there's something you aren't thinking about. Another way to feel good about what happens with this information without...I don't know. Destroying who you are, I guess."

Our eyes meet, and I contemplate her suggestion. I have looked at this from every side. I've had two and a half years to imagine scenario after scenario. But now that I have her blessing, it suddenly feels like there might be some ideas I'd stayed away from considering.

"Like I said, not helpful," she says, trying to read me.

"No, quite the opposite. This is very helpful."

"Really?" She's practically giddy.

"Really."

"See? If you'd just—"

"I know, I know, if I'd just come to you earlier." I capture her mouth with mine, not wanting this to turn into a conversation. It's unnecessary. Have I learned a lesson? Yes. My wife can be surprisingly supportive when given the chance. Will I still keep things from her in the future? Probably so.

What can I say? I am who I am. She knows it.

We linger in the kiss, long enough that I start to get hard again. I'm already thinking about how I want to fuck her next when we're interrupted by a loud gurgling.

"Is that your stomach?" I glance at the clock. It's after eight. Shit, my woman needs to be fed.

"I guess I'm hungry," she says, standing up. She turns to face me, her arms outstretched so I can untie her wrists. "Should we order?"

"I can. You go clean up. Bento boxes sound good?"

She nods, then changes her mind. "Actually, I'm feeling more like teriyaki chicken."

"As you wish." I pull my phone from my pocket as she heads off, but before she reaches the stairs, I stop her. "Sabrina?"

"Yeah?"

"Where were you today?" I'm not looking at her when I ask, which is purposeful, to make the question seem innocuous.

But I regret the choice when she hesitates before answering, wishing I'd been able to study her thought process through her features. "You mean this afternoon?"

I turn my head in her direction. "Yes. You left early."

"Eye doctor," she says without missing a beat. "My vision's been fuzzy lately."

"Ah. Did they find anything?"

"Dry eyes. Too much screen time. She recommended Refresh Tears."

"Glad it was nothing serious."

She stares at me, her eyes narrowing. "It wasn't on my calendar."

"No, it wasn't."

"It must have driven you out of your mind," she teases. "Two hours of your life that you couldn't track me down. How ever did you survive?"

"You want me to order dinner or do you want me to chase you up those stairs and fuck you again in the shower?"

"Both?"

"Get out of here. I'll join you in a few."

She's smiling when she turns to leave.

I open the app and make our order quickly, switching out her usual for the chicken she's asked for. Then I toss my phone on the coffee table, and I let myself breathe.

Let myself evaluate.

She didn't know about the flash drive. Honestly, there wasn't any reason she should have. I know that now.

And I know that we're strong, that I still have her love. That she's still mine.

And I know that discussing a family is going to have to wait. Because despite all of that, I'm more sure than ever that my devoted wife is hiding something.

SEVEN

IT'S Friday before I have time to work a meeting with my private investigator into my schedule. While he's taken on new projects over the phone in the past, he's become more wary of recording software and now prefers meeting in person. It was harder to get him to consent to coming into my office instead of a neutral space, but I managed it. Not only did I have to promise to turn off all my surveillance, I had to promise he could scan the place for hidden mics.

He's high maintenance, but that's why he's good.

Despite understanding his modus operandi, the delay has me itching. When I get a bug in my head, I hyperfocus. I have to remind myself I'm a long game kind of a player, and that four days is nothing compared to lengths I've waited in the past.

"Mr. Fish here to see you," Simone announces at eleven on the dot, and I'm instantly at ease.

I count to ten before responding, though, just to prove I'm in control. Who I'm trying to prove it to—me or him—is up for debate. "Send him in," I say, simultaneously hitting the button to turn my glass walls opaque. Then I walk to my office door to greet him.

"Kincaid," he says, already eyeing the cameras in my office. He's the one who set them up so he knows exactly where they are. He nods when he sees that none of the red lights are blinking to indicate they're on.

"Mr. Fish," I say, shutting the door behind him. That's not his real name, of course. His name probably isn't even Ferris Clarke, but that's the one I use.

He puts a finger up to his mouth to silence me and pulls his bug detector from inside his jacket pocket. After a quick walk around the office, he seems satisfied, and slumps down in the armchair in the conversation area. "So, who am I looking into now?"

Nevermind that it's *my* armchair. Typically, I offer guests the couch.

I let it slide since I'm eager to get this going. "No one new. Just need to broaden the scope of one of your current targets."

Okay, it's probably not normal in my field of business to have a dedicated PI. And it's probably even less normal to have ongoing surveillance on any one person, let alone several. I long ago accepted that my interests are not normal. To be fair, it's only a handful of people—my father, Theodore Sheridan (who is easy to watch since he's in jail for assault and attempted rape), Nash King (Weston's father), a couple of suspicious people who escaped the arrests when Cade brought his former headmaster down for sex trafficking, and Sabrina.

Yes, I have a detective watching my wife. Like I said, my interests are not normal.

Ferris doesn't tail her like he once did. He doesn't need to do anything that in-depth because she's in my life now. I don't need reports about who she's seeing, what she's up to, how she's doing because I'm very often with her.

When I'm not with her, I still like to know. Not because I'm anxious or don't trust her—at least not generally—but because I like knowing everything about her. Everything. Even if she tells me herself, it's not enough. I want to know *everything*. That want consumes me. She consumes me. I wouldn't have it any other way.

I believe she feels the same. She knows that I keep tabs on her. Not the details, but she knows, and she accepts it. So I occasionally access the cameras in our house and office and Ferris checks up on her now and again—mostly just paper trails these days. It's for me, but I'm comforted knowing my preoccupation keeps her safe and secure.

I haven't explained any of that to Ferris. He doesn't tend to ask questions. He probably thinks I'm a controlling rich asshole or maybe he thinks this is all some kinky game we play. Neither is far from the truth.

Today's the first time since she's been my wife that Ferris's routine check-ups aren't going to cut it. "I need you to look into Sabrina," I tell him.

He squints up at me—rather than relegate myself to the couch, I'm still standing—and I already know what he's going to ask next so I beat him to it. "She went somewhere Monday afternoon. Didn't take the car. Didn't use a credit card. Didn't go to the bank. I need you to find out where she went."

"Okay," he says slowly. "Is there a particular reason why you didn't just ask her?"

I sit on the arm of the sofa, a concession of sorts. "She claims she was at the eye doctor."

"And is there a particular reason you don't believe her?"

Ferris scoffs at gut feelings, though my gut is rarely wrong. Fortunately, I have something more concrete to give him. "We have vision insurance. I checked the portal. A visit wasn't authorized. And like I said, nothing was charged to the card, and she's not the type to carry cash."

"Hmm." In general, Ferris is good at keeping his opinions to himself. He takes my money and doesn't cringe at the ethics, which is why I like him.

The glare he gives me now, however, feels awfully full of judgment.

I nudge him when his glare comes with silence. "Go ahead, say what's on your mind."

Despite my permission, he pauses a beat, his features giving nothing away. He's never been an expressive person, another one of his attributes that makes him so good for his line of work. He's plain. Not attractive, not ugly. Just a regular, middle-aged white guy who blends in with everyone else. Even his stoicism is unremarkable. No one looks at him and wonders what he's thinking. Most people don't even realize he's there.

"Look, I'm never going to turn down your money," he says finally.

"But...?"

"But I've been watching Sabrina for...what? Twelve years now?"

"Thirteen." Thirteen and a half, but who's counting?

He nods. "Thirteen years. I feel like I know her as well as you do."

"You don't," I say defensively. Maybe he came close during those ten years when Sabrina and I were apart, when the only connection I had with her was through Ferris's reports, but even then, I'd had experiences with her that he hadn't. I'd taught her class and graded her papers. I'd watched her ogle Weston at the weekly parties our college house had thrown. I'd fought with her —verbally and physically—and I'd fucked her. I'd tasted her on my lips, and like hell Ferris was going to compare his knowledge of her with mine.

But I know what he's alluding to. "She's not the type to keep secrets, I know. But there's definitely something she's not telling me."

"Since she's not the type to keep secrets, perhaps that means she has a good reason." He seems to know he's crossed a line because he puts a hand up before I have a chance to speak. "She's not cheating on you, Kincaid. I know that woman well enough to know that much. For some fucking reason, she thinks you're her lord and master. Even seems to like it. She's not stepping out on you."

"I never said I thought she was cheating."

"Good. You've always been intense, but good to see you're still sane."

"I prefer the term committed."

He grants me half a grin. "She's probably planning a surprise of some sort—a surprise that you're going to ruin because you can't exercise a little bit of patience."

What's trying my patience is this conversation. "I wish I appreciated your concern, Ferris, but—"

"No, you don't. You wish I'd keep my fat mouth shut."

I chuckle. "Now that, I appreciate." My smile fades quickly. "Maybe it is a surprise. I doubt it, because she knows I hate surprises, but I'll concede it's a possibility. And no, I don't think she's cheating. More likely, she's dealing with something that she worries I won't approve of. Something she doesn't know how to tell me about yet. She'll probably even tell me eventually." I consider that assumption. "I'm sure she'll tell me eventually."

"So then why not wait until she works it out?"

"Because I'd rather be prepared." And because, whatever she's struggling with, it's become a roadblock. I want us to get started on our future, but I can't approach that until this secret of hers is out of the way. "If it's going to be a problem..."

Ferris gives it a second. "No problem. I'll look into it. Just wanted to be sure you knew what you were doing. That this wasn't an impulsive decision."

"I'm not impulsive." I'm quick to action, but not impulsive.

"No, I suppose you're not." He takes out a notebook from his breast pocket. The man is textbook television detective. "I'm guessing you have no idea where this eye doctor she saw is located."

"Something close enough to the office that she was able to leave here in the early afternoon and arrive home by five."

"Her eyes dilated when she got there?"

"No, but she could have asked them to skip that." I always did. "I couldn't find any receipts or appointment cards in her purse or pockets either."

He rubs his hand over his forehead. "You know, I've done plenty of surveillance of one spouse on the behest of the other. None of this shit is new. But it's a little weird knowing you're going through your wife's things when we both know that woman is yours."

"She is mine," I agree. "Which means she completely expects me to keep tabs on her. You sure this isn't a problem?"

He stands up. "Just because she expects it doesn't mean she likes it."

I'm good with the power dynamics between me and my

wife. I wasn't once upon a time, and it was why I pushed her away, but she proved to me that she was all in, despite who I am. I know that, and still I'm bothered by Ferris's remark. Bothered enough to want to dress him down for crossing the line.

He holds out his hand, though, both a silent acceptance of the work and a request for payment, and I'm eager enough for him to get working that I decide to let the comment go. I stand, pull out my wallet, then hand over a few hundreds. "It's not going to be just the mysterious eye appointment," I tell him. "Whatever she's hiding, it's bigger than that. This is just a place to start."

"And you know this because...?"

"I just do." My tone is firm and final.

Ferris is smart enough to get the hint. "Got it, boss. I'll get back to you soon."

When he opens the door, Simone's voice floats in. "...and now he's not busy. I told you it wouldn't be long. Was it really so hard just to wait?"

I'm still standing by the couch, so I don't see who Simone is talking to, but it doesn't take a genius to guess. She can be snide with quite a few people, but that particular patronizing inflection is usually reserved for just one.

My suspicions are confirmed immediately with a voice I know like my own. "It's impossible for you not to be catty, isn't it?" Sabrina asks. There's barely a breath before she's changed to a much friendlier tone. "Oh, excuse me, hi." She must have noticed Ferris.

I wander over to the door in time to see him give a friendly nod in her direction on his way toward the elevator. It's obvious she has no clue who he is, but she must recognize something about him since her gaze follows after him as if trying to place him.

I'm not going to feel guilty. Like I said, she accepts me.

Instead, I direct my attention to my secretary. "How much do you like your job, Simone?"

"You'd have to pay me some serious hush money if you decide to let me go, Mr. Kincaid." She doesn't even look up from her computer.

"I won't fire you. But I will make your job a living hell if you don't start showing my wife—and your superior—some respect."

She smirks, unfazed. "But if I do that, you won't have any excuse not to give me a raise."

I open my mouth, but before I can say anything, Sabrina has strode over to me and placed a palm on my chest. "Don't bother. She's not worth the energy."

I feel the heat of that touch through two layers of clothing, and suddenly I'm annoyed that—I check my watch—I only have five minutes before I need to leave if I'm going to make my lunch meeting in time.

I put my hand over Sabrina's. "But you are. Unfortunately, I'm due somewhere else soon or I'd find some creative ways to spend that energy on you."

Sabrina grins, knowing the comment was meant for Simone, who makes a noise that sounds an awful lot like she's trying not to gag.

"Thank you," she says when I shut the door and pull her into my arms. I still have five minutes. I can't think of a better way to spend it.

"You really have somewhere to go?" she asks, her hands clasped around my neck.

"I do."

"Where? Is it important?"

"Not as important as you, but still important." Look at me gliding over a truth that I know she won't want to hear. Maybe I should feel bad about it, but I pride myself on being capable of shielding her from the bad, even when the bad involves me. "Is there something you need or can it wait?" I leave open-mouthed kisses on her jaw while I wait for her response.

"I was just going to see if you had time for lunch."

"Is that a euphemism for sex?" I slide a hand down to cup her breast, knowing I'm starting something that can't be finished.

Her breath hitches as I rub my thumb across her nipple, feeling it pebble through her bra and dress. "Does it change your answer if it is?"

I could change my plans. I could stay here and fuck her across my desk, and maybe then I could believe that everything is fine between us, that there isn't a widening rift. Maybe it would even actually be true.

Except it's not.

And my attendance at this meeting isn't our problem because she doesn't even know about it.

"No, unfortunately." I drop my hands to her hips and subtly push her away before my cock starts giving a show that will be hard to hide walking across the office. "Rain check?"

She cocks her head, and damn does she look cute when she's trying to read my mind. "Are you sure you don't want to cancel?"

"I *want* to cancel," I say, scanning my eyes down her curves to assure her I'm still into her. Her dress today makes her look particularly filled out in all the right places, and for a half a second, I consider whether or not I can fit in a quick fuck and still make my meeting. "But I really can't."

"Boo." She pouts. "Oh, well. Weston had said he was free today—I guess Elizabeth is tied up with work. I'll just give him a call and see if he'll have me for a meal. I mean, have a meal with me."

She knows exactly what will make me jealous, that little minx.

"Nice try. But he's getting ready to fly back to France this afternoon." I head toward my desk to grab my phone and a pen and shut down my computer.

She feigns innocence. "Whoops. I guess I lied. Might need a spanking for that."

"Don't tempt me," I say automatically, but then I stop to give her my full attention. She's not usually so playful at work, and maybe I'm making too much of it, but the fact that she's here right after Ferris, right before my upcoming meeting—is it possibly not a coincidence?

What is she up to? What does she want to know? What *does* she know?

As if she can read my thoughts, she changes gears. "That guy who just left? Who is he? Where do I know him from?"

"Ferris Clarke." I watch her carefully, even more on guard now. "You hired him once. Over the phone."

"I did? For what?"

"To investigate me." Or I'd hired him for her. It had been what I'd offered her when she was worried that my surveillance over her had given me an advantage in our relationship.

"Oh." Then, probably realizing that the reason he looked familiar was from all the times he'd tailed her, she says it again.

"Oh." She leans back against the closed door, her arms folded over her chest. "Should I be worried you have another girl?"

"What?" It takes me a second before I understand that she's insinuating I could be obsessed with another woman the way I'm obsessed with her. And then another second to see that she's teasing and not serious. "Ah, still just the one."

"Aw, shucks, I'm flattered."

See? She knows who I am. She knows what I'm like. She accepts that this is what I do, and even if she thinks I'm just teasing along with her right now, it's an opportunity to voice her complaints, and she hasn't.

But Ferris's comment needles me. *Just because she expects it doesn't mean she likes it.* "Are you? Flattered? Or are you bothered?"

"By what? The way you love me?"

I raise an eyebrow, waiting for her answer.

"Of course not."

I don't push her further. Because I believe her.

Or because I'm running late, but even if I wasn't, I'd let it go. Like I said, I like to be prepared, and I'm not ready to dig into what it means for us if she's lying.

TWO MINUTES LATER, I leave Sabrina outside my office with a kiss, but I'm stopped by Nate with a question before I can make it to the elevator, and by the time I get in my car downstairs, I'm running seven minutes behind.

"Gun it," I tell Danny, wishing I'd decided to drive myself since I'm the faster driver of the two of us. More willing to take risks. But then I'd have to deal with parking and that would lose me any time I gained.

It's for the best, I suppose. Now I have time to focus. I don't want to be scattered when I meet Holt Sebastian for the first time. He already has the upper hand since we're meeting on his turf, but after discovering Sabrina's vehemence toward him, there was no way I was inviting him to Reach.

I'm pretty damn sure he wouldn't have agreed anyway. After I'd ignored his call, he played hard to get, even though I got back to him first thing the next day. He'd only finally called me back this morning, and then it had been his assistant with a simple message: *Meet at Panache, Sebastian Center, today at noon.*

I thought about ditching him. After untangling myself from my father's affairs, I decided I'd never be another billionaire's bitch. I also considered siccing Ferris on Holt. Have him figure out what he wanted from me, without a face-to-face.

But in the end, I don't want to take Ferris from the Sabrina project, and the easiest way to have my curiosity fed is to just take the goddamn meeting.

As for telling my wife...well, obviously I haven't yet. Potentially, I will, depending on how the conversation goes. Right now it isn't anything that needs to bother her. I'm not getting in bed with Holt. I'm not agreeing to do business. I'm having a conversation. No harm in that, and better to know what he wants than let it sneak up on me.

Thanks to unusually light traffic and good luck with the elevators, it's only three minutes past noon when I walk into Panache. The skyscraper views over Midtown made the restaurant a posh dinner spot, but during the day, the locale made it a favorite for corporate types, particularly those doing business with one of the many branches of the Sebastian Corp.

I'd managed to avoid the Sebastian family for much of my career, partly because Reach did ad campaigns for Pierce Industries, owned by Hudson Pierce, a well-known rival of the Sebastians, and partly because our paths had just never crossed.

That doesn't mean I don't recognize Holt waiting for me at the hostess desk. There are plenty of Sebastians, many I would have a harder time pointing out, but Holt is too famous to not know him by his face. Thankfully, his notoriety made my internet search provide a wealth of information. At thirty-seven, he's recently become the youngest CEO of Sebastian News Media. The company has its own advertising division. He isn't connected with any specific charitable organizations. He is ambitious and works hard, but he also plays hard. Like most rich men, his hobbies are expensive—race cars, wine, women. I prefer bourbon, chess, and stalking my wife.

So what the fuck does he want from me?

"Donovan Kincaid," he says, his hand outstretched, brushing off the hostess who has stepped up to help us with his next breath. "I have it, Nora. He's with me." He keeps his eyes on me the whole time, a man aware of what's happening around him without being obvious. "We finally meet."

I take his hand, making sure my grip is extra firm. Holt isn't a man to be weak in front of. I know that much already. "Holt Sebastian."

"Just Holt. I can call you Donovan?" He doesn't wait for my response. "I have a private room this way." He starts walking through the restaurant.

What else can I do but follow?

"Look," he says, over his shoulder. "I wanted to meet you

out front for a reason. I don't mind that we have company, but I'm afraid you might have the wrong idea about why I've reached out. This isn't a business affair. It's personal. I want to make sure you know that before I say anything that you might prefer remain just between the two of us."

I'm grateful he is a step in front of me because I have no idea what he's talking about, and I don't like to look confused in front of men who wield so much power.

"So let me know right now if there are any topics that are off-limits."

"Off-limits to...whom?" But we reach the door to the private dining room just as I ask, and I see who the who is before he answers because she's sitting at the table waiting, a glass of iced tea already in her hand.

"Sabrina," I say in unison with Holt.

This meeting just got a thousand times more interesting.

EIGHT

SABRINA SEES US, and straightens. Kudos to her for not shying away when I arrived. In other circumstances, I'd be proud.

Fuck it, I'm proud now too. How she discovered this meeting was happening is beyond me. Clever to have figured it out. She's surprised me, and I'm not easily surprised. Her odd behavior in my office earlier suddenly makes sense. I knew she was up to something, and it's validating to have that confirmed.

But I have to make a decision on the spot. If I let on to Holt that I didn't know Sabrina was going to be at this meeting, then I look like a man who isn't in control of his domain. Traditionalist, patriarchal, and primitively alpha—yes, I know. I don't make the rules. I just know how to play the game.

Obviously, that option is out of the question.

I can pretend that I thought this meeting was solely about business (honestly, I had no presuppositions at all), thank him for the heads-up, and ask him to dance around his agenda until I A) reschedule for another time or B) convince Sabrina to leave. Lots of downsides there. I'm doubtful Holt is willing to give me another morsel of his time, and convincing Sabrina of anything lately is...

Well, she's here. That says it all.

I have one option, and it's potentially a landmine. "Sabrina," I say again, this time with more surety in my tone. "I didn't realize she'd already arrived. I hope it's not a problem."

Holt gives a challenging smirk. "Not unless you have a problem speaking frankly in front of her."

Summoning the confidence of Weston King, I smile. "I appreciate your concern, but I don't keep secrets from my wife."

I might have just dug my grave with that lie. Just to satisfy my curiosity. I hope to hell it's worth it.

"How very noble," Holt says. It's snide, but I detect a hint of envy too. Is the billionaire bachelor tired of his playboy ways? It's something to put in my pocket anyway. "Then, shall we?"

He leads the way to the table. I lock my eyes with Sabrina and don't let them go until I'm standing next to her. She stands when we get there—assertive; I'm impressed.

"You beat me here," I say, as though I'm surprised about her timing instead of her presence. Then I lean in so only she can hear. "I'm currently fantasizing that I have my hands around your throat. You've never been so hot."

When I back away, her cheeks are flushed, but otherwise she's unruffled. "I didn't get stopped on my way out like you did."

So she sent Nate to intercept me. How cunning.

And now for the first time since seeing her, it occurs to me that I might be in as much trouble with her as she is with me. To be fair, I never said I wouldn't meet with Holt. She did make her wishes clear, but I didn't intend my storming out to indicate that she'd won.

All that can be sorted later on.

I wait for Sabrina to sit before unbuttoning my jacket and taking the seat perpendicular. Holt Sebastian takes the seat across from her. I'm about to say something, when he opens his mouth.

However, it's my wife who speaks first. "Before you waste any time, Holt, I just want to say that we took this meeting as a courtesy. There isn't any scenario imaginable that would end in any business relationship between Reach and Sebastian News Corp."

God, I really do want to strangle her. As a reward or as a punishment, remains to be seen.

Holt seems to find her declaration amusing. "Then I'd venture to say that you don't have a great imagination," he says, humor in his tone. "But this isn't about business."

I'm already speaking over him. "Holt has already kindly informed me that this meeting is of a personal nature, dear. No need to put up defenses."

"Oh." She's only thrown for a split second. "Even better that I'm here then. Donovan and I have a very open relationship."

His smile is smooth. "As your husband has told me."

"He has?" She falters here, throwing me a surprised glance.

I cover for her. "Nothing to fear—I didn't give him any of the details of our private life." Leaning back in my chair so I appear more relaxed than I feel, I turn to our host. "With that out of the way, we're very eager to hear what you have to say."

"Are you in a rush? We haven't even ordered yet." Holt flags over a waiter who I now realize has been standing at the bar, waiting to be summoned. Usually, I'd have noticed him right away. Leave it to Sabrina to distract me.

"You already have a beverage," Holt says to her. "Would you prefer something from the bar?"

"No, thank you," she replies.

"I'll take a scotch," I tell the waiter directly, though I have a strong feeling Holt would prefer we order through him. It's a power thing. I get it.

"Donovan," Sabrina chides. "It's only just after noon."

And I still have meetings this afternoon, but I need this drink. "It's Friday."

"The Glenfiddich," Holt says to the waiter, asserting his dominance by choosing the brand for me.

"That would be fine," I reply, as though my opinion had been asked.

Holt continues as if I haven't interrupted. "I'll take a glass of the Château L'évangile. The 2005 if it's still available."

It prices above three hundred dollars a bottle, if I remember right. He's showing off.

I'm tempted not to remark on it and give him the chance to boast, but I want to be sure he knows I'm cultured too. "The 2000 was a good year too. Not as silky as the 2005, though."

"I appreciate the blackberry and truffle notes myself. A knockout nose. I'm stunned every time a new bottle is opened." Holt switches focus to Sabrina. "Are you sure I can't interest you in a glass? If you're a wine lover at all, it's not to be missed."

"I'm actually a very blah wine drinker," she confesses, apparently not concerned with entering the pissing contest. "I can never remember what I like. I always have to ask Donovan."

"Basically, she only likes moscato." I can't resist proving what I know.

"Or a glass of scotch now and then," she counters. "When I want to feel the burn." I don't know how exactly, but I'm sure it's a jab at me.

"Scotch is a far cry from a dessert wine," Holt says, sounding intrigued. "I bet your palate is wider than you realize. You just need some education." He shouts over to the waiter who is gathering our drinks behind the bar. "Bring an extra glass, Bruno."

I start to tell him, *The lady said no*, but Sabrina takes care of herself. "No, really. Even a sip goes to my head, and I still have a busy afternoon."

Holt looks ready to protest. Wisely, he doesn't. "You must smell the bouquet at least."

She agrees, and he continues to talk up the vintage until the bottle arrives, telling her about the velvety tannins and the chocolate and vanilla flavors.

I spend the time staring at my menu, but I swear I don't see any words. Just a blur, as though every bit of my senses' energy is struggling to hear every nuance of their conversation. Is there subtext in her *ah*? Is there innuendo in his *mm*?

Finally, he's sniffing the poured wine and passing a glass to my wife.

"I smell the vanilla," Sabrina says excitedly. "And something like coffee. And, this is going to sound strange, smoked meat?"

"Excellent nose. Most people miss that one. I knew you'd be good at this. I know a born wine enthusiast when I see them."

It's time I inserted myself. "If you want to learn about wine, Sabrina, I can—"

She dismisses me with a shake of her head. "But you don't love wine like Holt does." She didn't even look at me before resuming the conversation. "You're very passionate about the subject. I can tell."

I barely stifle a growl.

"I am," he says, as though I'm not even there. "It makes all the difference. You needed the right teacher, and now you've discovered your talent."

I want to correct him on so many things, not the least of which, that he should refer to her as Mrs. Kincaid, but I'm betting she already told him to call her by her first name. *Sabrina.* I hate the sound coming out of his mouth. It sounds dirty, and not in a good way. Dirty like I want to scrub myself down with rubbing alcohol. Or his expensive wine. Dirty like I want to take him out to the curb.

And what the fuck is this about knowing a wine enthusiast when he sees them and needing the right teacher? He's either flirting with her in front of me because he has balls or he wants to piss me off. Or both. Or he's so privileged he truly believes anything is within his grasp, even my wife.

I'm about to call enough, when Sabrina seems to remember my existence and places a hand on my knee under the table. She's telling me to wait, to trust her, and I do, but it's a battle because I don't trust him.

I suppose it could be called the same thing. So I bite down and bear it. Let her play her next card.

"Like I said before, I'm not a big wine drinker, but I might have been in another life. My mother had the same passion you do."

"Did she?" Holt says.

At the same time, I say, "She did?" This is a tidbit I'd never known. Useless trivia from a time before Sabrina was on my radar, but I treasure those kinds of details, and this one I've never been told.

"Past tense," Holt says before she can answer either of us. "She passed away?"

"Ovarian cancer. She had no chance. Died when I was barely a teenager, so before she could pass her love on to me. But every time I think about her—and my memories are starting to fade, which is hard to stand; harder than I'd imagined because I thought the worst part was losing her, and it turns out that's just one worst part. Anyway, every time I picture her in my mind, she's got a glass in her hand. Not that she was a drunk, because she wasn't. And we were not well-off, so it was cheap wine, but she knew how to shop for a bargain, and she saved her pennies, and when it was a special occasion, she'd open a bottle she'd been saving." She considers for a minute. "I couldn't even tell you what variety she loved most, except that she always had red stained lips."

"Malbec, maybe," Holt purrs. I'm not making that shit up—he fucking purred.

"Oh, maybe!"

Her hand leaves my thigh with her excitement, and I wonder now if I read the gesture wrong, that she had no cards to play, and that she was just enjoying the conversation. Enjoying Holt's attention. His fucking fawning.

Is that why she's sharing stories with him she's never shared with me?

No. I'm done. This is done.

"Or it was a cab sav or a colorino or a durif or a refosco. Or most likely, she was drinking younger wine because she couldn't afford a more mature red." *See? I know wine too, Sabrina.* "This has been a fun little master class, but could we get back to the agenda?"

An outburst is perhaps not the right move, but it feels good. And when I can tell Holt is about to deflect once again and suggest we order our food, I use the momentum to take the reins. "Let's make this a discussion over drinks instead of lunch. As my wife said, our afternoons are booked."

Sabrina purses her lips and pins her gaze on the tablecloth. She's not happy with me. I can feel how badly she wants to scold, but she doesn't say anything.

And you know what? I'm not exactly happy with her at the moment, so I let her pout. This is my meeting. She's the intruder. I'll run it how I see fit.

Holt narrows his eyes, seethes. Hesitates long enough to make sure that all of us know I'm the one who had the tantrum, and that he's the bigger man for not exercising his authority. This is his turf, after all. This is his agenda.

Then he offers a smug smile. "My apologies. I should have been more considerate of your time." He flicks his eyes from the menus to the waiter. "That will be all, Bruno."

With that cue, Bruno gathers the menus and leaves the room, shutting the door behind him so we truly have privacy now.

"Thank you," I say, feeling like I've gained some imaginary control. "The table is yours."

He stifles a laugh, which...fair, because the table always belonged to him. I'm not delusional about that, but I'm also not his pawn. Whatever opinion he has of me, he knows that at least.

"Then I'll cut to the chase." He's serious now, all of the

charm he'd relinquished on my wife is gone, his focus completely on me. "How close are you to your father?"

This has to do with Raymond, then. Surprising only because Weston called it. Easily dealt with because I have a standard answer to requests for help getting an in with the finance legends of Wall Street. "My father makes it a policy not to take any of my advice. If you want to work with King-Kincaid, you have to approach them the old-fashioned way."

I lift my glass, planning to finish it off in one swallow so we can go, but before the liquid hits my lips, Holt clarifies. "I'm not interested in investing. I'm interested in exposing."

I pause, my glass still in the air. "Exposing?"

"As in an exposé." He barely lets that sink in. "You know that your father employs illegal practices in his firm, I'm sure."

"Donovan," Sabrina says, and maybe that's all she means to say. My name, to make me pause, remind me to think before I speak.

"Shh," I tell her, before she can say something she shouldn't. Patronizing, I know, and she'll be hurt. I'll have to deal with that later.

"It's an open secret," Holt continues. "You can't be unaware."

Oh, I'm very aware.

But I school my features. Turn them to steel. "What are you driving at exactly? You want me to know that you're planning a tell-all about King-Kincaid? Is this some kind of friendly advanced notice? If so, tell someone who's on the payroll. I don't work for my father, in case you hadn't heard."

"No, you get me wrong. I don't have anything ready to air." He lets a beat go by. "That's where you come in."

And now I understand. He wants me to be an informant. Maybe it's the whole blood is thicker than water saying, but the idea repulses me. It's one thing to not want to protect my father for his crimes. It's a whole other thing to shout them from the rooftop.

"Whatever you think I might know, I can't help you," I say coolly. This time I get the rest of the alcohol down my throat. Then I set down the glass, and start to stand. The meeting is over, as far as I'm concerned.

"You mean you *won't* help me," Holt says.

"I mean, I have nothing to give you." I get to my feet and move toward Sabrina, planning to pull out her chair.

"Except you do," he insists, as though I'm not actively in the process of leaving. "You have a whole drive full of incriminating information, I'm told."

A lot goes through my mind in the span of a handful of seconds. I quickly dismiss the idea that some unknown player told Sebastian about my drive. The most obvious source is the most likely. Weston didn't just guess Holt wanted to talk about Raymond—he knew. And he knew because he'd already talked to Holt.

No, not Weston..."Elizabeth," I say out loud.

"We're both in the same business," Holt confirms. "Our paths cross."

I would love to walk out now, for no other reason but so I can race over to the airport in time to throttle my partner and his wife before they take off, but first I have to do damage control.

I sit back down. Refusing to jump to conclusions, I give Elizabeth the benefit of the doubt. Perhaps she just hinted at something, and Holt is playing a bluff. The trick is to let him do the talking. "So your paths crossed..."

"Donovan, Elizabeth wouldn't—"

"I sought her out," Holt says, ignoring Sabrina. I would make a big deal about it if I weren't caught up in what he has to say. "She's tied to King-Kincaid through marriage, and from what I'd heard, she's not the type to honor thy father simply because he's the father. I'd hoped she'd have some dirt to share, or at least a lead."

"And...?"

"She said she didn't have anything herself, but that you *might* have a drive full of incriminating documents that you *might* be willing to share."

I swallow, wishing I hadn't finished off my scotch. Spying the wine in front of Sabrina, I reach for it. The scent hits my nose as soon as I lift the glass to my mouth and fuck Holt, because he's right—the bouquet is fantastic. It delivers a hell of a lot of promises, and damn, the taste lives up to it. "This is...really good," I admit, reluctantly.

"Yeah, I know." He thinks it's a win, and it is, but I gave it to him.

It gives me a chance to think. To assess. Elizabeth didn't say anything that I can't walk back. He doesn't have enough to run with. He doesn't know what's on the disk. Its existence is a rumor, that's all.

"You have a good nose for wine," I concede. "But maybe not so good a nose at journalism. Whatever Elizabeth thinks I have, I assure you, it's not useful to you." Because I'm going to destroy it as soon as I get home. Get rid of it once and for all. "This is a dead end. I'm sorry to have wasted your time."

But he's a relentless son of a bitch. "Let me be real with you, Donovan. I could try to bullshit you, let you think I have something to offer, or that I'm doing you a favor by meeting with you today, but we both know you'd see through that in a heartbeat.

I'm in a new position, an extremely coveted position that many of my siblings and cousins fought over, and I have one year to prove myself. Being the network to expose King-Kincaid would be a major coup. You'd be doing me the favor, and I have nothing to offer in return. You don't need my money." He glances at Sabrina. "You don't need what my power can provide. All I can do is assure you that I will owe you one, and if there's one thing you can rely on where Sebastians are concerned, it's that we are loyal to those in our favor."

It's not exactly a moving speech, but it does make me pause. I had to prove myself as well, despite the name that I was born with. Sure, we've had the world handed to us on a platter, but it's not given without expectations. I get that. I get him.

And believe me, there's a part of me that wants to give him what he's after. Not because I'm so affected by Holt Sebastian's plea, but because I resent my father for his sins. For presuming that I'll clean up his messes. That I'll cover his crimes.

Or did I put that supposition on myself?

Wherever the source, blood is blood. I feel the leash pull. The collar tight around my neck for the first time in years.

If I understand him, he has to understand me. "Let me ask you, Holt—if the tables were turned, if I were coming to you asking you to dish on Samuel Sebastian, or any Sebastian, for that matter, on your flesh and blood, can you honestly tell me you'd spill a single word?"

Out of the corner of my eye, I see Sabrina give me a reassuring smile.

Holt's smile, however, is challenging. "Ah, but see, we're in different positions, you and I." He leans back, hooking a shoulder casually over his chair, like he's a young prince sitting on his throne. "It has nothing to do with blood. It's about freedom. I'm completely entangled in the Sebastian empire. Everything I have is tied in some way to SIC. I can't escape.

"But if I could—if I had gotten out, so to say, as you seem to have done—then yes, Donovan Kincaid. I can honestly tell you I'd spill. And I wouldn't just talk; I'd burn the whole fucking thing down."

NINE

SEVEN YEARS *ago*

I SPUN the magic eight ball in my hands while I thought. Cade had given it as a joke when we'd opened the Tokyo office. *For ease in making the tough decisions,* the card had read. Mostly I used it as a fidget toy.

I paused on the current turn to read the reply in the window: *Ask again later.*

Real helpful.

"We don't have to accept every counteroffer that comes in," Cade said from the couch next to my desk.

"But it's a good offer." I didn't have to glance over at him to know he was rereading the contract for the umpteenth time. He was detail oriented like that, poring through the lines looking for something he'd missed.

I tended to absorb all I needed on the first read through. It was easy since there were only two major changes from the marketing campaign we'd offered in our original proposal—they wanted to pay us more than we'd asked for, but they also wanted us to use a targeting list provided by Mason Analytics.

"Is the list from Mason Analytics even legal?"

"It's not *il*legal." The data had been scrubbed from a popular social media site, and while some countries were beginning to lay down laws against the use of such information, it was mostly a gray area.

"It's not ethical."

Now that was up for debate. Reach hadn't been the company that had disregarded customer privacy by collecting the data. We hadn't even been the ones who had purchased the list. It was being given to us by a potential client—a client that wanted to pay us big time if we agreed to use it. Was it unscrupulous for us to accept?

I asked the eight ball. *Better not tell you now.*

"They have to believe that it's unethical or they wouldn't have offered us more money," Cade continued. "They would have hired someone local. They're coming to us because they know no one in the U.S. would get involved in such shitty practices. Didn't we set up an office here specifically so that we wouldn't have to deal with American assholes anymore?"

That was the official story. What we'd told Weston and Nate when they'd asked why we didn't want to stay in New York, and while it was a broad statement, it was based in truth. First and foremost, I was in Tokyo because it was sixteen time zones away from Sabrina in Los Angeles, but the second reason was because Tokyo was thirteen time zones away from my father in New York, and yes, I'd convinced myself that distance would keep him from pulling me into his dirty work.

But there was a third factor about this counter—the mid-size company that had approached us for the marketing campaign in the first place was in the process of being bought out by King-Kincaid. I was fairly certain they wouldn't have been able to offer the amount of money that they had without the backing of my father's empire, and I was absolutely certain they wouldn't have requested such illicit practices if my father hadn't directed them to do so.

And the only reason he would direct them to do so was because he was sure I'd agree.

The thump of Cade tossing the contract aside drew my eye toward the floor where he'd dropped it. "Let's be real," he said. "What would you say if it wasn't your father behind this?"

That was the practical way to approach the matter, though I wasn't sure it led in the direction Cade thought it would. He assumed my hang-up for saying no was some sort of loyalty to Raymond Kincaid.

I wasn't quite ready to accept the truth. "My father is the only asshole who would dare send that counter."

"But just for the sake of argument..."

"For the sake of argument?" I closed my eyes for a beat. Opened them. Shook the eight ball. *Outlook not so good.*

What the fuck did a ten-dollar toy know about anything?

I dropped the ball to the desk, and focused on Cade. "My responsibility is to Reach. We're a new company. We won't be able to charge this kind of money to clients for years without the precedent of a campaign like this. I would not be doing my job serving this company and its owners if I turned the offer down. We should sign."

As I'd expected, Cade was surprised. "You don't need to do

this, D. We'd all stand behind you if you made another decision."

"We should sign," I repeated.

"Signing erases any distance you've created between you and Raymond."

I shook my head, decided now. "Signing puts his money in my pocket, and if I have to erase distance to get that, so be it."

I bent to pick up the contract off the floor, grabbed a pen from my jacket pocket, then added my name on the dotted line.

It was only my imagination that my tie suddenly felt tighter around my neck. This was a good thing. Not just because of the money and not just because we'd get our name on the map, but because if I was tied to Raymond, then he was tied to me. Keep your enemies close and all that.

Maybe that was beyond the scope of my responsibility, but if not me, then who? I didn't bother asking the eight ball.

A notification popped up on my phone with a text from Ferris. I scanned it as I handed the signed contract to Cade. "Can you take care of that? Something just came up that I need to deal with."

"Last I checked, I don't look like your secretary. She has much better legs."

"Yeah, yeah," I said, too focused on dialing Ferris's number to give Cade much attention. "Shut the door on your way out, will you?"

Some part of me registered his sigh, followed by, "Simone? Daddy has a job for you."

The door shut just as Ferris answered. "What do you mean she invited him up?" I asked, without any preamble.

"Just what my message said—he took her to her place after their date, and she invited him up."

A rumbling started in my chest. It made my ribs feel tight, like my lungs didn't have enough room to expand. I rubbed my hand over my sternum, hoping I could massage it away.

It wasn't like I hadn't known this was coming. As soon as this guy had asked Sabrina out for the first time a couple of weeks before, Ferris had told me, and since he knew I'd ask, he'd included a full background check on him as well. Anthony Diaz was his name, a small brewery owner in Santa Monica. He looked good on paper and the tail I'd put on him revealed nothing shady. Son of an immigrant mechanic and a failed actress turned Hollywood makeup artist, he was self-made, decent, hardworking. He went to church on the major holidays, donated to PETA, recycled, gave his mother flowers on her birthday, and never drove more than four miles over the speed limit. He hadn't even tried to kiss her until the third date. He was exactly the kind of man I wanted for Sabrina. Hell, I would have put him in her path if I'd met him first.

But she'd met him all on her own at her favorite coffee shop in Pico. Tonight had been their fourth date, and apparently, that was the magic number as far as my girl was concerned. She'd invited him in.

Dammit, Sabrina.

I picked up the eight ball, needing something in my hand I could squeeze. "Maybe she needed help with something in her apartment. A leaky faucet or a running toilet."

"Could be," Ferris allowed, "but the way they were kissing at the doorstep, it's going to be a while before they get to it."

I brought my fist and the toy enclosed inside it to my mouth and pounded it against my lips, once, twice, three times. It didn't help. I still wanted to scream.

"You have photos?" I asked, through gritted teeth.

"Sending them now. Don't forget you have the live cam."

I never forgot I had the live cam. I'd had it installed in her apartment before the ink was dry on her lease, telling myself it was to keep her safe. I wasn't fooling anyone. I watched her more than I cared to admit. Watched her doing mundane things —dishes, yoga, watching TV. Watched her undress. Watched her sleep. Watching was my guiltiest pleasure. Or maybe it was my favorite punishment, because I certainly left every viewing feeling like the lowest piece of shit to ever walk the planet, and still I couldn't keep myself from returning to watch again.

But as much as I'd watched her, I hadn't ever watched her fuck someone else.

It wasn't like I expected that she'd never have sex after me. I knew she had. Didn't like it, but I knew. Nothing serious yet, partly because I chased away most candidates before she had a chance to "invite them up". So far she'd had only meaningless flings with men she was too good for. She was too good for Anthony too, but at least he would treat her right, and that was why I had let this happen.

Why I was letting this happen.

To be honest, it was taking all my will not to send a fire alarm through the security system, and that was without seeing what was going on. Was it better that I didn't look?

All signs point to yes.

I was already loading up the website as I said goodbye to Ferris. A few keystrokes to enter my password. I hit enter. An array of camera views filled my screen—the kitchen, the living room, the guest bedroom, the master. None in the bathroom; I wasn't a pervert. I switched through the angles in each room, not finding them anywhere.

Then there they were, in the doorway to the guest room.

Immediately, I gave meaning to her decision to take him there instead of the master—she wasn't that into him, she didn't want to share her most intimate space with him—but no excuse I could come up with made me feel better since I hadn't been in her bed myself.

And how could I give any of it much thought when all my attention was pinned on the action in front of me? There was no sound, and the picture stuttered as the stream carried across the world, but I could see it clear enough. He had her pressed up against the frame. Her hands were above her head, but by her choice. His hands were busy elsewhere—one under her shirt, the other cupping her cheek as he kissed her. Slowly. Hesitantly. Leaning back occasionally to ask for consent before resuming the kiss.

This wasn't what she needed.

I knew it like I knew everything about her. Like I knew myself. She needed rough and mean and someone who took without asking. She needed force and dominance. She needed to be scared.

But this was what she wanted. What she thought she wanted, anyway, and that mattered. This was how decent men treated women, and that's what mattered most. Because Anthony Diaz was decent.

Anthony Diaz was nothing like me.

The storm inside my chest intensified, but I forced myself to keep watching while Anthony peeled Sabrina's clothes off, taking care to place them across her chair. I watched as he led her to sit on the edge of the bed. As he spread her legs apart to put his lips on her cunt.

I watched as she threw her head back. As she closed her eyes. I zoomed in on her face, searching for clues in her expression. Did he make her feel good? Good enough or real good? As good as I could make her feel? Better?

She opened her eyes then, and turned her head toward the camera. Coincidence—there was no way she knew I was watching—but it felt like she was looking directly at me.

And in that look I saw the answer I wanted to see least of all. *You gave up the right to know.*

I clicked out of the website, but it wasn't soon enough to stop the cyclone from consuming me. It pulled me to my feet and burst through my upper limbs, sending my computer and everything else on my desk to the floor.

The sound of the crash brought me back to my senses. Enough to acknowledge I'd lost my self-control, anyway, and there was very little I hated more than not being in control.

I had to go somewhere and get a hold of myself.

Ignoring the mess, I grabbed my jacket and headed to the door. Simone was already standing there, likely summoned by the clatter. "Is everything okay?"

"Just peachy," I said as I passed her, because obviously everything was not okay, and that kind of idiotic question deserved an idiotic response. "Have it cleaned up by the time I'm back in the morning," I called over my shoulder.

"You're out for the rest of the day?"

I didn't answer. It was all I could do to get out of the office before another surge of the storm broke through. Simone would figure it out.

I sent a quick text to my driver from the elevator, telling him I wouldn't need his services tonight. If I were in a more patient frame of mind, I could have waited for him. I was his only client, and he was usually able to accommodate me on whim, but my destination was the type I preferred driving to myself.

Once in my Maybach, I sent one more text before I started the car, this time in Japanese, that more or less translated to *My usual. Will be there in thirty minutes.*

Exactly thirty minutes later, I left my car with the valet and walked into the Hotel Empirical, a boutique establishment on the fringe of Kabukicho. Nate had introduced me to the place before he'd gone back to the States. It was expensive, but discreet, and every bit of money exchanged went to the person the money was handed to.

As I'd expected, Honoka was waiting for me in the plush lobby with a glass of Suntory. "All night?" She always addressed me in English, even though I'd told her plenty of times it wasn't necessary.

"Not likely," I replied in Japanese. I took one sip of the drink to take the edge off, then handed it back to her along with a key and a hundred dollars for arranging my request. "Let her know I'll pay for her damaged clothes."

She took my offerings and put them in her pocket. "Not there yet. Be soon."

I nodded then headed to the suite I rented on the top floor. The place was barely used and sat wastefully empty most of the time. Frankly, I could save a lot of money renting by the hour like most clients did, but I couldn't stand the thought of sharing a space. Besides, this way I'd been able to tailor the room to me. The bed had been taken out. Sound absorbing panels had been added to the walls. And I'd removed every romantic touch from the candles to the moody lighting. They weren't necessary. All I needed was a private space.

I looked at my watch when I walked in the room. I'd frequented the hotel enough to know that Honoka's version of *soon* could be any minute now or in an hour. Whichever it was this time, I wanted to be ready. I shut the curtains and turned off all the lights but one lamp in the corner. I took off my jacket, tie, and cuff links. Rolled up the sleeves of my dress shirt.

Then I took my phone from my pocket and pulled up an image I had saved of Sabrina. It was a fairly banal image, a candid pic that Ferris had taken of her at an office gathering. Thousands of images I'd seen of her over the years—public photos for work, snapshots from social media, private screenshots of her in her apartment—and this was the one that got me. She wore a short, fancy black dress with a pair of three-inch heels, and for whatever reason, she was on the floor, on her knees, her legs tucked in at either side. She looked so grown-up and so young all at the same time. Her hair was mussed and her lips pouty, and her eyes—they shone with innocence and trust, and beneath that, filthy desire.

Every time I looked at it, I wanted to be there with her, wanted to rip off her dress and push her knees apart and take whatever she'd give. Roughly, because that was what that filthy desire wanted—to be bullied. To be threatened. To be forced.

I closed the photo less than a minute later and set my phone on a side table, already painfully hard. With Sabrina's image seared in my brain, I found a spot on the wall near the bedroom door and waited.

Hardly any time passed before I heard the key in the lock, and the door opening. I let the woman walk in, let the door shut behind her before I sprang. Grabbing her from behind, she shrieked as I clamped a hand over her mouth and the other around her arms and torso, leaving her hands free.

"Show me your safe signal," I ordered. A safe word wasn't going to cut it today. She needed a signal that could tell me to stop when she wasn't able to speak.

She brought a hand up and snapped three times, a common enough signal among the community that I wouldn't have to think too hard about it. She would still protest, because that's what I was paying for, but everything that wasn't snaps would be ignored. Honoka's money assured me that I wouldn't have to explain any of that to the woman in my arms.

"Good," I said, taking a moment to accustom myself with the stranger. Even in the dark room, I could tell her hair was the right shade of dark brown, as I always requested. Her height was about right too. Her weight felt off, though, and her scent was all wrong.

Because it wasn't her in my arms. It would never be her.

A movie flashed in front of my eyes—Sabrina against the doorframe; Anthony kissing her jaw. He got to hold her, and he didn't even know how to do it right.

Forcefully, I threw the woman to the ground and shook my head free of the image. "Crawl," I told her, but she was already doing it, scrambling to get away.

I didn't let her get far before I was on the floor with her. Her dress was a simple sheath type thing, made out of cotton. Easy to grip and easy to tear. It only took one mean pull on her sleeve to rip down the side and free her breast.

"No, no," the woman begged. Her acting was decent. The tears already streaming down her cheeks were a little much, but I liked the begging.

Holding the material up in an attempt to cover herself, she turned around to face me, though, and that I liked less. I didn't want to see her face. Didn't want to see who she wasn't.

I distracted myself by concentrating on the dress instead. Another yank and the second sleeve broke too. Then I gathered a fistful of her skirt in my hand and waited for her to wriggle free.

This was how Sabrina should have been undressed. How she would have wanted to be seduced.

"Leave me alone!" The woman turned again to her knees. She crawled a few steps then made it to her feet, leaving the dress in my hand as she ran for the other side of the room.

I was faster, catching up to her in three strides. Wrapping a tight arm around her torso, I lifted her in the air so I could wrestle with her panties, ripping them as well before I managed to get them off.

That's what Sabrina deserved. Ripped panties and a hard slap across her cunt.

I slapped the stranger's pussy, watching her bare skin darken in the shape of my palm. Smacked it again, when she didn't get as wet as I wanted her. Sabrina would be dripping. I would restrain her arms and force her to sit on my face, then lap up every drop with my tongue.

Fuck, I was so hard. My cock strained against its confines, aching to be free.

I set the woman back down, quickly so she stumbled and went down on her knees again. Before she could get herself together, I grabbed a fistful of her hair and pulled her to where I wanted her. "Take out my cock," I told her.

"No."

I tugged on her hair. "Take out my cock, and put it in your mouth. If I have to touch my belt myself, you won't like what I do with it."

She didn't argue this time. Hastily, she got my belt and pants undone, then pulled my boxer briefs down. As soon as she'd pulled down far enough for my cock to spring free, I let go of her hair and pinned her arms behind her back, careful to leave her hands free in case she needed to safe out.

Knowing what I expected next, she opened her mouth, and cautiously bent toward my crown. I didn't wait for her to get there—I shoved my hips forward and rammed my cock down her throat, and fuck, yes.

Yes.

Yes.

Her mouth was tight and wet and hot, and I was no longer thinking about what Sabrina deserved or imagining she was here instead of this high price call girl, but instead I was remembering. Remembering her cunt, how I'd had to push through that barrier of her virginity, how she'd squeezed around me. How she'd flooded, and I'd finally slipped all the way in. She'd cried, and I'd kissed away her tears.

She'd opened up for me, and I'd lost myself inside her.

That's who I fucked now, the memory enveloping me as I thrust into her, into Sabrina. In, in, in, over and over, until I felt the tingle at the bottom of my spine. Until the tightness in my chest began to loosen. Until my jealousy unraveled and faded away. Because I was the one with her. I was the one in her bed, in her cunt, in her life. I was the one in her heart.

I came in a violent rush, spilling into her mouth.

Into a mouth that didn't feel right.

I opened my eyes—when had I closed them? And it wasn't Sabrina peering up at me, cum dripping down the side of her mouth. This woman didn't look anything like Sabrina at all.

I stepped back, feeling...dirty. And not in the way I usually enjoyed. To be honest, it was how I always felt after sex at the Empirical. Not because it was paid sex, because I paid at plenty of other brothels. But this was the only place I played the

Sabrina game, where I ordered a girl to taste and didn't bother to find out her name.

The woman wiped her mouth and looked up at me with inquisitive eyes, trying to guess what I wanted next.

All I wanted was to leave.

"You can stay the night if you like," I said, doing my pants up, pulling myself together. I gathered my cell, my jacket, my tie, my cuff links. Then pulled out a thousand dollars from my wallet, which I set on the side table. After a pause, I added another five hundred tip. "Use the shower. Use the phone. Honoka can get you a change of clothes."

She got up to her feet, unsure of herself. "Was that...? Did I...?"

I shook my head. I didn't have an answer for her, not one that made any sense. The only word that sat on my tongue was sorry. *I'm sorry. I'm so fucking sorry.*

But she'd already played substitute for my desires. She didn't need to be the fill-in for my apologies too.

TEN

PRESENT

THERE WASN'T much to say after Holt's bold declaration, certainly nothing that left me with the last word. Still, I consider it a victory. His speech hasn't changed my mind, which means I'm leaving him with exactly what he came in with, nothing more.

I, on the other hand, gained knowledge. About Holt Sebastian and his agenda as well as Elizabeth and her big mouth. There's much to follow up on, but I can't think about any of that as we leave Panache. Not because I'm compartmentalizing or putting it away to deal with later, but because all of my focus is narrowed to one thing—one *person*—and my usual composure is holding together with the barest of threads.

"Well, that was interesting," Sabrina says when we've passed the hostess desk.

"Don't speak," I order, my voice low and guttural. My hand finds her lower back, and I assert a controlling pressure in my grip. There's a conversation that needs to be had, and it's not waiting.

"What do you mean don't...?" She trails off when she glances up at me. There's no misreading my hard expression. She returns it with pursed lips and a narrow glare.

Seems she has things she wants to say as well.

I steer her toward the elevator, then stop when there are people already inside. Scanning the area, I see a woman walking in the women's restroom and an out of order standing sign in front of the men's. Finally, I direct her toward the door marked *EXIT*. We're on the fifty-seventh floor—there's a real good chance no one is taking the stairs.

As soon as the heavy door slams shut behind us, I explode. "What the hell was that?"

She spins around to face me, and for some strange reason, she seems taken aback. "*You're* mad at *me?*"

"You infiltrated my business meeting."

"A meeting I explicitly told you not to take."

I raise my hand up in defense. "I never said I wouldn't take it."

"You think I didn't realize that? You think the whole team didn't realize that?"

It did seem pretty obvious, but since she's apparently angry, it bared saying out loud. "Then what's the problem?"

She flaps her arms in frustration. "The problem is that you don't care what I want."

"That is decidedly untrue." I care about what you want more than I care about anything else period. "Just sometimes you're confused about what you want, and sometimes what you want isn't really in our best interest."

"I'm *confused* about what I want?"

Perhaps not the best moment to point that out, but now that it's been said, I might as well give the proof to back it up. "You thought you wanted Weston."

"You tried to make me believe I wanted Weston."

"You thought you could be happy ignoring your desires."

"I was working through shit."

I'm about to double down—or triple down, at this point—and mention that less than a week ago she told our friend that she didn't want a baby, when she changes gears. "None of this is the point. The point is that I knew that you would go behind my back to meet up with Holt, and rather than just let you do your thing like I always do, I decided that if I couldn't beat you, might as well join you."

Her tone is still terse, but I hear the olive branch in her last words. It's an opportunity to be conciliatory. Commend her for out-witting me. It all worked out in the end. I shouldn't be so worked up.

But my skin itches, and my chest feels stretched, like there's something clawing from the inside, and whatever it is, it's the part of me that's calling the shots.

I take a step toward her. "So what did you do—reach out to Holt yourself and find out when it was happening? Simone didn't tell you."

She sighs and folds her arms over her chest. "No, Simone didn't tell me. She probably wouldn't tell me even if you specifically told her to."

"Then—" A door opens somewhere below us. I pause,

listening to the footsteps as they run down one flight. Two. A second door shuts and the footsteps are gone.

"I know who Ferris Clarke is, Donovan," Sabrina says, bringing my focus back to her. "You gave him to me to level the playing field, remember? You told him to do anything I asked. You think I stopped at that one background check?"

"What are you telling me, Sabrina?"

"Nothing obsessive like you. He gives me a spot check now and then, when I'm feeling curious."

It takes me a second to process. "You're...*spying* on me?"

Her spine straightens. "Oh, don't you dare. Don't you dare say that with so much disdain. Do you even hear yourself?" She shakes her head. "I can't with you right now."

Before I can think to stop her, she stomps past me and pushes through the door behind us.

With a growl, I go after her, following her to the elevator. The door opens as soon as she calls for it. It's empty this time when she steps in.

I walk in right behind her. "I'm reacting to newfound information," I say, continuing the conversation, as she hits the button for the lobby. "Information that puts the ethics of my private investigator into question since he's—" I cut myself off, realizing that I don't necessarily want to finish that sentence.

"Since you currently have him spying on *me*, you mean. One afternoon. I disappear for one afternoon..."

The doors haven't shut yet, and two women in business attire approach. Sabrina leans forward to hold the door open button for them.

We're in mid-conversation, though, so I have other ideas. "Take the next one," I tell them.

Sabrina looks at me, aghast.

Next thing I know, she's leaving the elevator. "Sorry about him," she says, as she passes the women. "He's a real dick sometimes."

I have to take a deep breath.

Then I force a tight grin, holding my arm out to keep the elevator doors open for the very confused women. "It's all yours."

They don't return the smile, and they don't get in the elevator, probably afraid they'll have to ride down with me. Understandable caution, but I don't have the patience for it.

I leave them to figure it out themselves, and trot after Sabrina who is only a yard away from going to the women's restroom. She can't possibly think that I wouldn't dare follow her in there because I most certainly would.

But since I prefer making less of a scene, I grab her by the upper arm and pull her back to the stairwell. This time when the door's shut, I don't let her go. "So what? Ferris tells you my schedule?"

"You mean like how Roxie tells you *my* schedule?"

"Are you suddenly bothered by this?"

"No." She yanks out of my grip, harder than she needs to because I release her as soon as she pulls, and she has to put a hand on the railing to steady herself. "I'm bothered by you being bothered when I call Ferris and ask him to do something for me that he's done for you over and over and over again."

"But you already know what Ferris does for me."

"I didn't always." She lets that hang, and it hits. Yes, I have some guilt about it. But it's very minor guilt, mostly because it didn't end up hurting my chances with her in the end and partly because Sabrina has convinced me to let it go.

I sometimes wonder that she doesn't mean that, though,

particularly when she looks at me the way she looks at me now, like there's something she resents that she hasn't put words to.

She doesn't put words to it now, either, and after a beat, she turns her back on me and starts going down the stairs.

Half a flight down, she continues. "And you should know that Ferris might do it for me because, as I pointed out earlier, it was your idea that I use him."

"That was a show of faith," I say, following after her. "I didn't think you'd really use him."

She turns on the next landing to face me. "Oh, so it was all for show."

"That's not what I meant. Of course I gave him to you for real. I just didn't think—"

She cuts me off. "You didn't think that I cared about what you were up to? I don't, in general. Because I'm not obsessed, and I trust you. I trust you even though I knew that you'd still meet with Holt, and because I care about what you get involved in—because I'm your wife and what you do affects me—I asked Ferris to let me know when you got a meeting. He stopped by my office today before he stopped by yours."

"He's efficient, at least." It's either a bug on Simone's phone or a hack into her computer. I'll have to tighten security up there.

And now I understand Sabrina's playful act before I left the office. She'd known where I was going and had been giving me a chance to change my mind. "You wanted me to cancel my business with Holt."

"And he didn't even want to discuss business in the end."

"You didn't know that at the time."

She spins around on a sigh, apparently not appreciating the excuse, and starts next down the flight of stairs.

I chase after her. "He almost didn't tell us what he wanted because you were there. I had to convince him it was okay without knowing what it was he had to say."

"Big risk for you there, wasn't it? Your wife possibly finding out one of your little secrets. You must have been shaking in your Ferragamos."

"What about you and your secrets?"

She glares over her shoulder. "One afternoon, Donovan."

But her one missing afternoon is not all I'm talking about. "Your mother loved wine?"

She stops on the next landing. "What?"

I wait until I'm standing in front of her to expound. "You told Holt she always had a glass in her hand."

"That's not a secret." She throws half a laugh in, pointing out how ridiculous she thinks I'm being.

And okay, maybe it's ridiculous, but my chest feels like it's splitting in two, and it's not a new feeling. It's just a feeling I haven't felt in some time, and I'm less practiced at commanding the emotion than ever. "It's not something you ever told me before."

"Are you...?" She cocks her head, studying me. "Is that what this is? Are you jealous?"

I cringe at the word. This isn't about jealousy—it's about what's mine. "You practically let him push you into sampling his wine."

"I didn't, and I was being polite."

"You were purring over his compliments."

"Heaven forbid a man says something nice to me. How did you ever survive all the men I dated in the past?"

She's teasing me, using sarcasm to try to get me to see things her way.

But she's struck a nerve, and I am programmed to react a certain way to her taunts. Or maybe it's because I'm so keyed up, because my control has been stretched to its limit, because I'm desperate to prove that I still have claim on her.

Or it's all of those reasons combined. One moment we're staring each other down, the next I have her pinned against the wall, my front pressing to her back, one of her arms wrenched between us. "He used your name like it belonged to him," I murmur into her ear.

Her breath hitches as my free hand pulls up her skirt and slips down her panties. I'm practiced at this. I know she'll be wet before I feel the proof. I know exactly where to press my finger, how hard. "Did you like that? How he said your name? Did you enjoy his effort to seduce you?"

"He wasn't...that wasn't..."

She gasps when I pinch her clit. Another flood of moisture follows, and I lower my hand to draw the fluid up higher. "He ogled you like he had a right."

"He didn't." Her hips buck as I massage a particularly sensitive spot. "Right there, right there."

I pinch her clit again. "I fucking know how to touch you, Sabrina. Do you think Holt would know?"

"No. No one knows but you."

"That's right. No one." I wrench her arm harder, pulling myself to her so she can feel my erection along her backside, all the while stroking her pussy just the way I know she likes. "He would try to fuck you, though. He would get inside your pussy the minute you gave him an opportunity."

She shakes her head. "I wouldn't."

She wouldn't. I know she wouldn't.

But this old torment feels fresh, and every word that comes

out of my mouth is biting and poison. "Did you like knowing that he wanted you? Did you cross your legs for him? Lean forward so he could get a view of your tits?"

"You were sitting right there, Donovan."

"Was that what you liked most? That I was watching? That I was going insane?" Her body jerks, and I know she's close. So close, and I'm desperate for her to come all over my hand. So desperate that I don't even pause when I hear a door open below us.

Sabrina, though, stiffens.

"Don't pay attention to them," I coax. "They're on a lower floor. They aren't coming up. Keep your attention here. I need you to come."

She relaxes, and she's so wet now that I can hear the sound of her juice as I rub her faster, harder. Her body jolts. Her breaths are uneven. Her eyes start to tear. She's so fucking beautiful, and I'm so fucking committed. "I would take a knife to his throat if he touched you, Sabrina. I swear to God. I would tear him in two. You are mine."

The door a floor above us opens and at least two voices are heard as people start down the stairs.

I drop Sabrina's skirt and immediately step away, possibly even fast enough not to have drawn suspicion. It's hard to tell. I turn around in time to see the couple as they pass us.

"Hi," Sabrina says, awkwardly.

I offer a smile, hoping no one happens to look at my crotch. Fuck, I can still smell her cunt on my hand.

We stay still and silent for several seconds after they've gone. Another beat or two and we'll be able to laugh at this.

When I finally attempt to look at her, Sabrina's ready for

me, and she's serious as hell. "I'm yours because I choose to be, Donovan."

I don't have a comeback. I nod, though, because I hear her. Because I know it means she loves me. Because it was not at all what I was hoping for but it's exactly what I needed her to say.

Maybe I'm confused about what I want too.

Sabrina reaches out to straighten my tie, then pats my chest before turning toward the closest door. "I have to get back to the office now. You owe me lunch and an orgasm."

ELEVEN

I'M NOT FOND of the phrase *I'm sorry*. I prefer apologizing with my tongue between Sabrina's legs, which is how I spent my weekend. For two whole days, I pushed pause on her secrets, my father, Holt Sebastian's request, and any talk of children. We both deserved the break.

By Monday, though, I'm back to business.

"I need Weston on the phone and Ferris Clarke in my office before the end of the day," I tell Simone as I pass by her desk on my way to my office.

"At the same time?"

"No. Separately." It's unreasonable to be frustrated that she can't just read my mind, but I am what I am. I'm halfway to my desk when I turn and stride back to the doorway. "You haven't been talking with Ferris, have you?"

"I have been talking to Ferris," she says with an amount of sassiness that requires me to mentally remind myself of all the reasons she's irreplaceable. "Quite frequently, since you've asked me to get him on the phone or in your office several times over the last five years. An inordinate number of times, actually, for someone who runs a straight-up advertising business."

I fold my arms over my chest, and lean my shoulder against the doorframe. "Have you been talking to him beyond that? Outside of work or—"

"I don't have a life outside of work."

I ignore her interruption. "—casual conversation that doesn't relate to what you should be talking about?"

She straightens her back. "I didn't realize there were casual conversation topics that were off-limits. If you're implying that I've broken my NDA—"

I roll my hand in the air, gesturing for her to skip the whole offended routine. "Has he asked you for my schedule, for example. Where I'll be at certain times. Who I'll be with?"

Now she folds her arms over her chest. "As I was saying, I have never and would never share anything confidential with anyone, least of all your creepy PI, including your schedule."

I'd known this was a dead end before I'd even started down the road. Still had to ask. "Good."

I shut the door, but her last words make it to me before it closes. "Do I get an apology?"

How long has she known me? Like I said, I don't like apologies that don't show action, and Sabrina is the only one who gets those.

Not one to let things go, I'm sure she's still ruffled when she buzzes my desk phone a few minutes later. I take my time answering, but when I do, I skip the formalities. "I needed to be sure. It didn't mean I doubted you."

"Glad to know I'm in the circle of trust." It's Weston's voice,

not Simone's. Just like the hellcat at my front desk to skip intro-
ducing the call as payback.

I pinch the bridge of my nose and rest my elbow on the
desk. "Not you. I thought..." I'm not in the mood to catch him
up. "Actually, you're not in the circle of trust right now, asshole.
I have a bone to pick."

"Oh," he sighs. "You talked to Holt."

His comment isn't a revelation—it's validation. Several times
over the weekend, I'd replayed the conversation with Weston
when Simone had told me Holt was on the line. He'd done a
good job at giving nothing away—which was really impressive
for Weston—but looking back, I could see he'd known the reason
for Holt's call all along. I'd been too distracted with Sabrina to
notice.

"Your wife has a big mouth," I say.

"No—"

I'm not ready for his defense. "And you wondered why I
wasn't happy you'd told her. What the fuck is she playing?"

Again, Weston tries to butt in.

Again, I plow over him. "Is this some attempt at an alliance
with Werner Media and Sebastian News Corp?"

"That's so—"

"She obviously has an agenda. And you were aware of it,
and didn't give me any warning. What the fuck, Weston? What
the actual fuck?"

"Would you calm the fuck down for a moment and let me
speak?"

I let a beat pass. "I'm calm." Even though he can't see it, I
lean back in my chair to prove it. "I'm calm."

"Good. Thank you. Okay, first, not everything is about business all the time, dickwad. Elizabeth doesn't want an alliance

with SNC. She certainly doesn't need one. And the fact that you jumped to that conclusion says a lot about your trauma."

"Trauma?" What the hell is he talking about, my *trauma?*

"Second, she had no agenda. She was—"

"She just happened to drop to one of the most powerful names in the world that I had information that could damn our fathers?"

"It was me, you fuckhead. Me. I told her to tell him."

When I'd realized Holt had gotten his intel from Elizabeth, that hadn't surprised me. This, on the other hand, does.

"You told her to tell him," I repeat. Not quite a question. More just so I can hear the words again in my own voice, start to make some sense of why my best friend and partner would stab me in the back like this.

"It wasn't like what you're making it seem like it was. They bumped into each other at an international media soiree thing. He poked around, tried to get a feel of how she felt about her in-laws. Said he'd love to do some sort of exposé if he had the right info. She didn't give him anything, D. Didn't say a word.

"But then last week you brought up the drive again at your house, and later, I mentioned it to Elizabeth, and we got to talking about how you've held on to this information for all this time, and how you haven't been able to make a decision about what to do with it, and it occurred to us that maybe you needed a little push. Kincaid style, so to say. So Elizabeth emailed Holt that night and said that she'd heard a rumor that you might have some sensitive information on a drive, and suggested he ask you about it. Honestly, it was far less than what you would have done in the same situation, and if you're going to be mad about it, I just want to point out all the times that—"

"So you think I should release the information." I wasn't

going to sit through a call out of all my so-called bad behavior over the years—did I need to remind him my interfering got him his wife? None of that mattered right now. "That's what you want?"

"No, I didn't—"

"Why did you tell me that you didn't care?"

"I don't!"

"If you don't care, then—"

"You needed options. I gave you options. I was trying to help."

"Well, don't." This is why I prefer taking care of things myself. When others try to help, it just makes a mess. The people in my orbit generally understand that about me. Why does it feel like I'm losing my grip on all of them?

The silence on the other side of the line tells me I've gone too far. Fucking Sensitive Sally and his puppy dog feelings. "Thank you. I...appreciate it." I manage not to choke over the words. "But no thank you. I'm not handing over the disk to the likes of Holt Sebastian."

"Fine, fine. I'm okay with that." He pauses. "But why not?"

I almost laugh. "You're joking."

"No, I'm not. This could be a perfect answer to your dilemma. Hand over the information anonymously. You won't have to deal with it. It will deal with itself. Your hands are clean."

"How the fuck do you figure that? My hands will be anything but clean. This information is damning, Weston. King-Kincaid could dissolve. Our fathers could be sent to prison. Not to mention what would happen to our own stock."

"Nothing will happen to our stock. King-Kincaid will not dissolve. No one will be sent to prison. Not anyone that matters, anyway. In fact, that's the one downside I can think of—who knows who they'll try to pin this mess on. Knowing them, they'll try to send another innocent man to take the fall."

He's talking about Daniel Clemmons, the man who got sent to prison the last time King-Kincaid got caught with their pants down. "They can't blame this on someone else," I say. "There's no way our dads can refute that they were involved with the crimes recorded on the drive."

"Then the point remains. Nothing will happen to them, Donovan. It never does. They will always get off. The system isn't set up to punish the people on the top."

I know that better than anyone. It was the mantra I was raised with and it's why I've lived my life like I'm untouchable. This isn't new, and it begs the question, "Then why even release it?"

"Because people should know," he says emphatically. "People should know."

It's not how I've been taught. It's not who I am. Money and power mean not having to cater to the wants and shoulds of the general populace. Secrets should remain secrets, and the one responsibility of being untouchable is to protect the secrets of our own kind.

Right?

So why am I so bothered? Why is there a voice screaming in my head that it should matter? These crimes should matter. The drive in my safe should matter.

Weston makes assumptions about my silence, and which way my head is going. "You don't have to do anything with the drive, D. I wasn't trying to force you into a decision. But there was one benefit of all of this—at least, now you know you care."

THE CLOCK on my computer screen says it's four fifty-nine when there's a sharp knock on my door followed by Simone's entrance.

"By all means, come on in," I say, ironically. So much for privacy.

"Mr. Clarke is here to see you. Before I let him in, I wanted to assure you that the only words I said to him were *I'll tell Mr. Kincaid you're here.* I didn't offer him coffee in case that was going too far. If you'd like to offer it to him, you'll have to get it yourself because I'm..." She pauses to look at her watch. When she speaks again, the clock on my screen has flipped to five sharp. "Off the clock."

I refrain from flipping her the bird, but I make sure she reads the sentiment in my expression. To be fair, she hasn't fallen down on her job either. We both know that Ferris doesn't drink coffee and won't accept anything given to him that isn't from a sealed container.

"Oh, and just a reminder that Sabrina's already gone for the day. She's presenting that award tonight at the Banquet for Advances in the Media. Danny drove her home to get ready and will drive her to the hotel later so—"

"So I need to drive myself home," I finish for her. "I remember. Thank you, and you can send Ferris in."

"My pleasure, Mr. Kincaid, and anything for you." She delivers an overdone smile with the sarcasm then turns to leave.

A moment later, Ferris is standing in her place. "Balls on that girl," he says, shutting the door.

"She's a handful."

"Need me to do a spot check on her?"

I actually consider it before shaking my head. "Not necessary. She's proved her loyalty over the years."

"Let me know if you change your mind."

"Always. It's why you're here actually."

He raises a brow. "You changed your mind? Should I sit down for this?"

"Nope. That's the gist of the conversation. I'm dropping the thing with Sabrina. Whatever she was doing last week, I'm letting it go." It was harder to say than I'd thought it would be, but after it's said, I feel a sort of relief. Is that what real trust feels like?

"I'm sorry you had to come all the way to Midtown for that, but I know you're anti-digital communication these days." I can say sorry this time because I don't really mean it. I'm still perturbed about the work he's been doing for Sabrina. Forcing him into this trip to the office feels satisfying, even though I'm sure he'll add the time to his expense sheet.

"No worries." Then, despite me telling him he didn't need to get comfortable, he sits his ass down. And once again, he sits it down in *my* chair. "Since I'm here anyway, maybe you want to hear what I found out."

"About Sabrina?" I hadn't expected that he'd found anything so soon.

"I wanted to have more before I reached out, but I definitely have some of the blanks filled. Interested or...?"

I didn't tell Sabrina I meant to call this off, but still, I hear her voice like she's an angel on my shoulder telling me to drop it. Telling me I don't need to know. Telling me that she chose me because she trusts me, and she deserves her space.

Unfortunately, she's not as loud as the devil who is literally sitting in my office with an open briefcase and a manila folder inside.

Hell, that's not fair. Ferris isn't the devil. It's me with the name that means dark prince and a nature to match and an obsession level of curiosity that is pretty much impossible to ignore.

So the decision is easy.

"As long as you're here..." I get up from my desk and stop at the bar to pour some scotch—dark nature doesn't mean that I'm without guilt; nothing the alcohol won't help dull down—before taking my perch on the arm of the sofa. "Go ahead, Ferris. Tell me what you got."

TWELVE

FERRIS TAKES the folder from his briefcase, opens it, and hands me a black and white image from inside.

"It's a lot easier to keep these things hidden when there isn't physical proof," I say, shaking my head. It's hypocritical because I'm also wary of digital footprints, but I also almost lost Sabrina for good when she discovered the folder where I kept all my "stalking" evidence.

"That's why they invented the shredder," he counters, matter-of-factly.

My attention is already on the photo, a picture of a woman entering a building, taken from an angle that I assume is an outdoor security camera. It's far enough away to make her features fuzzy, but I know my wife when I see her. A glance at the timestamp says it's from last Monday afternoon, exactly the time Sabrina disappeared. "Where is this?"

"Midtown Medical Complex."

"Don't tell me—there's an eye doctor's office there. She was telling the truth all along." I'm a fucking asshole. That's not a surprise, but I don't usually feel ashamed like I do right now.

I throw back my scotch and finish it in one go. I owe Sabrina another round of apologies. Or several rounds.

"Yes, there's an eye doctor there," Ferris confirms. "But when I had my assistant call and pretend to be your wife, they said they had no record of a Sabrina Kincaid being a patient. No record of a Sabrina Lind either."

"I'm surprised they told you anything with privacy laws."

"My assistant can be very convincing."

"Okay. So is there a reason they would lie?" I can't think of any, but I like to walk through all the possibilities.

"She might have paid them not to divulge information or delete her file. Seems unlikely, but it's not out of the question."

Sounds like something I would do, not Sabrina. I almost smile thinking of her engaging in the same kind of behavior. It's not as unimaginable as it was before Friday when she showed up at my meeting with Holt Sebastian.

"There's more," Ferris says. "This wasn't Sabrina's first visit to the complex." He hands me another picture, and this time when I take it from him, I set my empty glass on the coffee table and move from the arm to the sofa, needing to feel less perched and more solidly seated.

Then I look at the image. Same building, same woman. This time in a different outfit. I look at the timestamp and try to recall a random lunch hour on a Tuesday in April. That was more than a month ago. I'm halfway to pulling out my calendar when I remember. "I was with Nate at the Waldorf, wooing a potential client."

It had been on the books for a while, which meant that Sabrina had known I'd be away from the office. Obviously, she'd scheduled whatever appointment she'd gone to then on purpose. I hadn't been any the wiser. Come to think of it, if I hadn't canceled my meetings last Monday, I wouldn't have noticed she'd slipped out then either. "Are there more?" I ask.

Ferris shakes his head. "Not that I found."

"And how did you find this?"

"She turned her phone off last Monday. Just to be thorough, I looked at her GPS history for the last several weeks, looking for anything odd. When I saw she'd visited a complex that had an eye doctor, I accessed the security footage." Without having to be told, I know that *accessed* means bribed someone or hacked into.

"But she didn't see the eye doctor then either?"

"Not that one."

"Are you sure they didn't just fuck up her patient information?" Though, even if they had, why had she gone twice?

"I considered that. Which was why I looked for indoor security footage." He hands over another black and white, this one even blurrier than the others. "They don't keep indoor footage for more than two weeks so I can't see where she went on her first visit, and not all the cameras are in working order, but I found a shot of her coming off the elevator on the fourth floor last Monday. The eye doctor is on the first."

"No other cameras on that floor?"

"None that work. Sad to say, but that's not that uncommon. Cameras are often more scare tactic than anything. The individual practices may have additional security I can look at. That was on my list of next tasks. I only received this information this morning."

I stare at the photo of my wife, wondering what she was thinking. I should be used to this feeling after spending so many years outside of her head. But after having access to her thoughts over the last few years, I've grown accustomed to that privilege. Now this not knowing is ten times more frustrating.

What are you up to, Sabrina?

"So whose offices are on the fourth?" My first thought jumps to a gynecologist. The secrecy, her eluding to not having children. It could all be related. Maybe she's been told she'll have trouble conceiving. Or that she can't have children at all. It's plausible.

After all the pressure I've put on her, no wonder she wouldn't want to tell me. It makes sense.

"Don't jump to negative conclusions," Ferris says, as though he can read my mind.

Okay then, if I'm trying to be optimistic, maybe she's working on getting off her birth control. Maybe she's planning to surprise me with the news. Also plausible.

But then Ferris continues. "There are only a handful of practices on the fourth floor. A couple of dentists, a psychiatric practice, an imaging clinic for a doctor on another floor, a lab— all that fills up one wing. The other wing is dedicated to a women's oncology center."

My heart drops to my stomach. This was why he'd issued the warning not to jump to conclusions, but I can't help myself. "A women's oncology center," I repeat.

"We don't know that that's where she went."

"She'd need to go twice if she'd had suspicious results."

"She could have been getting labs drawn," he reasons.

I hear him, but I don't acknowledge it. "She has a family history."

"She could have had an order for imaging."

"Her mother was forty when she died of ovarian cancer."

"She could be seeing a psychiatrist. Might want to keep that private."

We're having two separate conversations. "Sabrina's thirty now. Ten years before parental onset is a typical recommendation for screenings when you're at risk."

It makes sense. It makes too much fucking sense.

"There are a lot of possibilities, Donovan." Ferris rarely uses my first name.

It works to capture my attention, and I turn a hard stare on him. "Why lie about it?"

"I'm not—"

"Her. Why would she lie to me about getting labs drawn or getting imaging or seeing a goddamn psychiatrist? She already sees a therapist. She knows I don't care. The only reason she'd lie about labs or imaging is the same reason that she wouldn't tell me about an oncologist visit—because she doesn't want me to worry. Which means there's probably a good reason to worry." Too worked up to stay sitting, I stand, throwing the picture down on the coffee table as I do. "Fuck." It isn't satisfying so I kick the table instead, hard, sending the briefcase and the empty glass clattering to the floor. "Fuck!"

Ferris is out of his chair just as fast. "You're making assumptions without facts."

"Logical assumptions." I put my hands on my waist so I'm not tempted to throw a punch at something while I try to string what I know together. "She's been tired lately."

"I'm sure it's exhausting living with you."

I glare at him, but I can't keep up the shade because I'm too consumed with the possibility—the probability even—of my wife being sick. I can't form coherent thoughts past the roaring pain in my chest. All I can feel is how empty my life would be without her. "Fuck. Fuck!"

"Donovan, get a grip," Ferris chides. "We do not have the information. This is not how you process things. We deal with what we know, and right now we do not know enough. I need to tap into other cameras."

It's hard to push through the volcano of emotion to hear reason, but somehow I do. "Okay. Okay, yes."

"Need to see if I can find her in any of the office's databases."

"Yes, right. Yes." I'm encouraged by the to-do list. "We need records. Get records."

"In the meantime, you need to put this out of your mind."

My head snaps toward him. "Are you fucking kidding me? Put this out of my mind?"

He looks guilty for having suggested it. "At least think about this—if it was cancer, they would have started treatment immediately."

My eyes see red when I think about her needing treatment for something serious, but he's not wrong. "It's only been a week since her last visit, though."

"Then if it's as bad as you fear, she'll have to tell you soon."

It's not comforting, but he does bring up a good point. "I'll confront her. I'll make her tell me. Tonight."

Ferris tilts his head back and forth, visually hemming and hawing.

"What? You were pushing me to communicate better before, now you're suddenly against it?"

"What if you find out she was only there to support a friend?" Before I can bring up the point of why would she lie once again he goes on. "Sometimes you can't guess the reasons why a person would keep a secret. They don't always make sense, and they aren't always horrible. If Sabrina's really facing something bad, and she hasn't told you, she probably isn't going to be happy about you forcing it out of her."

I know it's good advice. I even thank him for it.

I also practically push him out of my office, eager for him to get back to digging, making him promise to get back to me with anything he finds. "Anything," I repeat. "And I'm not waiting for this bullshit face-to-face shit. You text or call the minute you find *anything*."

"And you'll stay calm until I do."

I shake my head, emphatically. I tell him I'll try.

I'm sure he doesn't believe me, but I really do mean to try. Waiting for him to get back to me is the most strategic option I have. I've been patient before. I can be patient again.

Maybe.

Once he's gone, I make an honest attempt at pulling myself together. It entails drinking another two fingers of scotch—okay, three fingers—and a brutal analysis of the last five weeks. Every conversation, every encounter. I pour over her schedule, compare it to mine, looking for holes or clues. Anything.

The office is dark when I finally pick myself up from my stupor on the couch. My watch says it's past six. Everyone's gone.

I grab my phone and consider calling Sabrina, not caring that she's at an event. Not to confront her. Just to hear her voice.

But if she answers, what will I say?

Not knowing makes me feel deflated.

Then it makes me angry. Or brings out the anger that I already feel. It's the easiest of the emotions that are pulling for my attention. Fear? Grief? Fuck those emotions. If I let those in, I'll drown.

But anger is easy. Anger is justified, no matter what she's hiding, because she shouldn't be hiding anything at all. She's mine. She chose to be mine. And being mine means no walls. It means letting me in—all the way in. It means I should never ever have to wonder what to say.

And it most definitely means that whatever she's going through, she goes through it with me, especially if it means her days could be numbered.

Another burst of fury has me striding out my door and down the hall, toward Sabrina's office. That's the other thing about anger—it provokes action. Not necessarily wise action, but as I unlock her door and then start a thorough sweep of her things, I tell myself this is better than forcing her into a confession.

I know immediately that that's a lie.

So when I'm opening her locked drawers with the extra one I have on my keyring—the one I'm not sure she knows I have—I tell myself that she brought this on herself.

Also a lie.

So when I'm logging into her computer and checking her search history, looking for anything that might give a clue to what she's going through, I tell myself she knew what she married.

That one's true.

But it's also an excuse. And when I've searched every folder, both digital and physical, and opened every drawer and found nothing informative at all, I sit back and hate myself for it. For what I'm doing. For the excuse. For the truth.

There's nothing here. And that's as angering as anything. I feel shut out, and in many ways, further away from my wife than I've ever been. Which is saying a lot, since I spent a few years on the other side of the world. Why is there distance between us? Am I losing touch? Am I losing her?

Spiraling, my eyes wander to the picture of us she keeps on her desk, a black and white candid captured at our wedding. I'd surprised her with the affair. Didn't give her a chance to think about it. Didn't even ask. She'd told me it was incredibly romantic at the time. Does she have regrets?

I reach over to pick it up, and when I do, something falls out, the back apparently not on tight. I pick up the paper, expecting it's probably the commercial image that is usually packaged with photo frames.

That's not what it is. Though the paper feels similar, when I turn it over, my pulse starts to race. I check the date in the corner—last Monday—and the name typed underneath—S. Kincaid.

Then I let myself stare at the image—a black oblong bubble in a sea of white noise.

And while I've never actually seen a prenatal ultrasound before, I'm dead certain that the large headed alien figure inside the bubble is a baby.

THIRTEEN

I'M NOT what you'd call a "feely" man. Touch, yes, I'm into that. Without all the gooey stuff attached. I generally find that shit tedious.

That said, I'm blown over by a strong gust of emotion as I sit at Sabrina's desk and hold that flimsy film paper in my hand. There's a lot I should be feeling, I suppose. Shock, confusion, elation, overwhelm—it's a storm with a complicated eye wall.

It's the emotion at the eye itself, though, that gets me. An emotion too big to name. I stare at that little bean of a figure, and my vision clouds, and my body starts to shake, and that tight spot in my torso rips open, and it feels like my chest is making room for a whole new planet under my skin. There's poetry that describes this phenomenon, I'm sure. Loads of it. Probably with phrases about hearts growing in size and never knowing so much love was possible, yada yada bullshit.

That's me right now. All those cliché sentiments suddenly seem less trite.

And it's so much more than the relief of knowing Sabrina isn't carrying a terrible cancer inside her, though I know that's a good part of it, and it doesn't even seem enough to say it's the joy of finding out I'm going to be a father. Honestly, I find that fact a bit terrifying at the moment, despite how much I've wanted it. Fuck, I really wanted it.

I want it.

Him. Or her. I'm not particular about gender. It doesn't matter. What matters is that I made this. *We* made this. Sabrina and I, together. With a relationship that I had written off as doomed from the moment it began. That we are together at all is due to some chance and a whole lot of bad choices, and yet here we are, strong enough to have created this tiny person—an honest-to-god person. Okay, it's just a bunch of cells right now with a heartbeat, fine, but it's ours. It's mine, and some puzzle piece I didn't know had been missing clicks into place, and I'm complete.

Jesus, I sound like a Hallmark card.

I actually have to reach over and snag a tissue from the box on Sabrina's desk. I'm not even going to pretend it's allergies. Call it what it is—I'm fucking *moved*.

But the seconds of staring turn into minutes.

My brain can never stay silent for long. I start to wonder about the size of my baby—another rush of emotion at the words *my baby*—I don't have a lot of experience with this shit, but I pay enough attention to know that a first ultrasound usually looks more like a tadpole than a human. Not that this image is very baby-like, but there's definitely a head and a belly and sprouts for limbs. I remember what I learned from Ferris—that last Monday was a second visit to the medical complex. She must have been going to the imaging for an ultrasound—this ultrasound—not the oncologist. I put together that the notation 10w 6d likely means our baby was measuring at ten weeks, six days old and then I can't help wondering—how long has Sabrina known? How long was she planning on keeping this from me?

Maybe more important is the question of why. Was she waiting to see if it stuck? Was there a complication that made her worry it wouldn't? Is there something wrong with our child?

Whatever the reason, I can't come up with a suitable justification for keeping this from me. Not one.

Now other emotions start to enter the mix. I'm not going to be pissed, I decide, until I know more. I'm not going to be resentful. I'm not going to feel betrayed.

Except you can't really tell yourself how to feel, can you? If that were possible, I wouldn't have spent a decade stalking the woman who bedeviled me. And so deciding what I feel right now does nothing to alter the fact that I am pissed. I am resentful. I do feel betrayed. I'm worked up to where I want to track down my wife right this minute and ask her what the actual fuck.

Then I look at that baby again—*fuck, I'm going to have a baby*—and I'm once again washed over with that immenseness. How can anything else have meaning next to this? This feeling dwarfs every other, and I need Sabrina right now, not to rail against or interrogate, but to share with. If she was meaning to keep this as a surprise, too fucking bad. I'm bursting with this news, and there's no way I'm not talking to her right the fuck now.

I pull out my cell phone, and six rings later, when the call goes to voicemail, I remember she's at that goddamned event. Most likely with her phone silenced because she's polite like that.

I scrub my hands over my face. I should go home and wait for her there. I check the time. It's only seven o'clock. She won't be home for hours. Gives me time to set up a celebration. Flowers, her favorite takeout, wine.

Not wine, you idiot. She's pregnant.

Sparkling cider then. Danny's supposed to be her ride home in the Tesla, which means I'll have the Jag. Plenty of time to collect what I need.

With what I can only call excitement, I put the ultrasound away where I found it—after snapping a pic of it on my cell—tidy up her office, then shut the rest of the floor before locking up and heading down to the garage. Thank God I'm the only one here. If Nate caught me whistling, I'd never hear the end of it.

Within fifteen minutes, I'm in the car and headed home.

Except I'm not actually headed home. My car is pointed toward the Financial District. And I can't even pretend I'm looking for a flower shop or going to Okazu to pick up dinner because I most definitely put the Broad Street Ballroom into my GPS. After all the years I spent watching Sabrina from afar, I am practiced at patience, and yet the idea of waiting three whole hours to see her sounds like a death sentence. I have to see her now.

Traffic, in typical New York fashion, does not respect my eagerness, and I arrive at my destination forty-five minutes later. Then it's another twenty minutes finding parking and walking back to the event space. When I arrive, I'm hot and sweaty and regretting not having called Danny for the ride over. I don't generally make bad decisions where Sabrina is concerned, but I did not think this through.

The extent of my lack of forethought is apparent when I'm standing in front of the check-in desk at the banquet.

"I don't see your name on the RSVP list," the hostess says, searching her laptop.

"I didn't RSVP." The Annual Awards for Advances in the Media are focused more on production companies than the advertising sector, and they're boring as shit. I try not to attend unless I have to. Understanding wife that Sabrina is, she specifically told me not to come when she accepted the invitation to present.

"I see," says the hostess, smiling so she doesn't seem like she's judging, which she most certainly is. "Do you have your ticket?"

Somewhere. Filed away in one of Simone's drawers. Just as likely, in the trash. "Look, I'm not here for the banquet. I just need to speak to one of the presenters."

"I'm sorry—what did you say your name is?"

"Kincaid. Donovan Kincaid."

"I'm sorry, Mr. Kincaid. I can't let anyone in without a ticket."

"I have a ticket. Just not on me." I peer around her, trying to find someone I know, but the ballroom's doors are shut and all I see are a dozen or so strays mingling in the lobby and using the restrooms. "My wife is here. Does her ticket have a plus-one? Look up her name and add me with that."

"Everyone has to have their own ticket," she insists. "One for the attendee and one for their plus-one."

"For fuck's sake," I mutter. Then I pull out my wallet. Next best thing to a ticket is usually cash.

The hostess glares before I can make an offer. "I hope you're not thinking of trying to bribe me."

"Well, not now." Why is nothing easy? I find her name tag. "Like, I said, Alysse, I don't want to eat dinner. I just need to speak to my wife, who is presenting here tonight. I'll be in and out. It really shouldn't be a problem."

Considering that's all that needs to be said, I start to circle past her.

But then she stands up and the motion signals a security guard to take a step toward me, his hand on the gun in his holster.

I put my hands up in surrender. "It's all good." Jesus, what kind of celebrities do they have attending? "I'll just step aside to make a call."

I pull out my phone as I walk to the wall, out of the way while I try to decide how to play this. Again, I try Sabrina. This time the call goes to voicemail immediately, which means she probably turned her phone off when the event started. I scroll through my contacts, trying to see who I might know who would be inside. Someone less likely to turn their cell off. My hand hovers over Hudson Pierce's name when applause drifts from the ballroom, suddenly louder as though someone opened a door.

I lift my head at the sound and my luck kicks in—I see someone I know. "Simone," I call out.

She freezes at the sound of her name. When she sees it's me, I swear her face pales. *Yeah, I'm not usually keen on seeing you after hours either.*

Right now, however, I can truly say I've never been happier to see my brassy-mouthed secretary.

"Uh, Donovan," Simone says, blinking rapidly. "I'm...hi. You're here."

I wave to the security guard then point at Simone indicating

I'm only walking far enough into the lobby to talk to her. He lets me pass, though I can feel his eyes on me, which is annoying, but hopefully this will be quick.

"Hey, I'm looking for Sabrina. Do you...?" I trail off, suddenly realizing how odd this encounter is considering Simone is my secretary. "What are you doing here?" And how did she get in? There's no way she was invited. "Did you use my ticket?"

"No!" she exclaims, quickly. Too quickly. "No. Of course I didn't do that. I just. I'm, um, here—"

She's cut off suddenly by a scruffy faced man in a tux. "She's here with me," he says smoothly, wrapping an arm around my secretary's waist. "It's okay, Simone. We don't have to keep it a secret."

She gives him an odd look. I suppose I would too if my date had suggested that their coupling should be hush hush, which must be the case for that remark.

Though, I keep pretty good tabs on the employees that work close to me. Not like Sabrina, but I prefer to know who I'm dealing with, and I can't for the life of me figure out how Simone would land a date with someone like the man in front of me. He has money. I know a Brioni tux when I see one, and they are not cheap.

The man's face is familiar too, I realize. I haven't met him, but... "You're a Sebastian," I say, seeing Holt in his features.

"Steele," he says, offering his free hand for me to shake. "And you are?"

The condescension coats his words as thickly as they'd coated his brother's. Or cousin's? The Sebastian family is a big bunch. I'm guessing the former based on how close the resemblance.

I extend my own hand, squeezing extra hard just to be irritating. "Donovan Kincaid."

"That's my boss, Steele, honey," Simone says, and I don't know who cringes worse at her use of the endearment—me or her. She's as foreign to the feely shit as I am. Obviously, that's why I hired her. "Be nice."

"Ah, right. Your boss. At that advertising agency you work at."

"Uh-huh." Her smile is tight. If this is how uncomfortable she is on a date, she really needs to date more.

Again, I wonder how in the hell she ended up with a Sebastian. And why the hell he'd bring her to this snooze festival. And why something feels so off about the two of them.

But I drop it because honestly I don't really give a fuck. All I care about is finding my wife. "Yeah, yeah, nice meeting you. Hey, Simone, I left my ticket at the office, and I can't get inside without it."

"If I'd known you were—"

I cut her off short. "I wasn't planning on coming, Just something came up, and I need to talk to Sabrina, but this fine lady" —I give a tight smile toward the host who is keenly watching us from the check-in desk—"won't let me in without a ticket."

"Still can't let you in," she calls.

"You need me to get you in?" Steele offers, as if he's better at pulling strings than I am.

"No." Too sharp. "Thank you. I just need Simone to try to find her for me, have her come out for a second." Just thinking about why I want to see her brings back that ready-to-burst feeling from earlier. It's weird how I want to pull out my phone and show off the ultrasound pic.

Somehow I manage restraint.

"An emergency?" she asks, her tone edged with concern.

"Not an emergency. But important. And urgent. But not anything to worry about. Make sure she's not worried." I hear how I sound. Sabrina's going to think I've lost it. Hopefully, she finds all this exuberance charming.

"Uh, sure." Simone looks toward her date then toward the ballroom. "I'm not sure where the presenters are seated..."

"In the front, sweetie. Do you want me to come with you?"

"No," she says quickly. "I've got it."

She heads toward the ballroom with her usual no-nonsense stride, leaving me alone with Steele Sebastian. I almost tell him he doesn't have to wait with me but then realize he's waiting for Simone.

And for some reason that takes me back to those questions I'd had before that I hadn't thought I cared about.

I was wrong. I do care. "This is about that stupid request from your brother."

Steele's brow furrows. "Pardon?"

"Holt—brother, right?" I don't wait for him to confirm. "What, does he think he can get me to change my mind by getting close to my secretary? First, good luck with that. Simone is a damn good assistant, but she's telling it straight when she says I'm the boss. There's not getting anything from me, especially not on the Sebastian behest. Tell me you understand so I can get on to number two."

"You can go on," he says flatly.

"Number two, this goes beyond the pale. I said no. I mean no. I understand he's still trying to fit in at the top of the food chain, but sending his brother to seduce my employee for his benefit is not only low level, but it can get him canceled before he even has a chance to make his mark." I mean, I can be persistent when I want something, but there is a code of conduct, even among rich men.

Huh. Seems I have some ethics after all.

"Third, you hurt her, I'll hurt your face. Got it?"

Steele's expression is stoic. When he doesn't respond, I nudge him. "I said, do you understand?"

"Ah, just making sure it was time for me to speak."

God, I hate these asshole types. "Please."

"Well, Mr. Kincaid. Donovan? I feel like a good berating deserves a first-name basis."

"Sure, Steele. Whatever floats your boat." Honestly, I'm mostly focused on the ballroom doors where Simone disappeared. Why the fuck is she taking so long?

Meanwhile, this dickwad is still talking. "So then, Donovan, first I'd love to tell you that I know what you're talking about, simply because it sounds like it's a good story. I wish I had the dirt. Unfortunately, Holt keeps his espionage tactics to himself. Most of his non-espionage as well. In other words, he's closed-lipped about his dealings. I assure you, I'm not part of whatever scheme you think I'm part of."

I tilt my head, doubtful.

"Second, that said, you're right to watch your back where Holt's concerned. He may be new to his position, but he didn't get it by being a pussycat. My brother is known to be brutal."

Brutal wasn't the word I'd use. Unpolished. Immature. Out of his league. Those are better descriptors. "I've been warned," I say.

"Third..." He steps closer to me, and I'm not sure whether it's meant to be conspiratorial or a threat. Either way, I make damn sure to hold my ground. "I'm not going to seduce Simone because she's your secretary. I'm going to seduce her because she owes me."

"What the fuck did you just say?" I prefer my battles to be with the pocketbook, but I wrap my hand into a fist at my side, certain this Steele guy is a breath away from being punched. "She *owes* you?"

But then the devil herself is back. "She's not here," she says, somewhat out of breath. As though she clipped it to bring me the message.

My fist tightens, along with the rest of my muscles. "What do you mean she's not here?"

Simone shrugs. "I don't know. I talked to the stage manager. Said she was here but she left. Rushed out, actually. Before the award she was supposed to present."

Ferris warned me not to jump to conclusions, but I can't think of any reason that Sabrina would walk out on an obligation. Not any that was good, anyway.

I exchange a glance with Simone, who seems to share my concern. She might not care much for Sabrina, but she knows this isn't like her. "You tried to call her?"

My phone is already in my hand. Before I can dial, though, it starts ringing. I check the name on the screen and answer when I see it's Danny. "What happened?" He would only be calling if there was something urgent. It has to be about Sabrina. "Where is she?"

It takes him a second, his prepared speech probably thrown by the way I answered. "Uh, New York Presbyterian emergency room," he says finally. "I can come get you."

All that worry I'd felt when I'd thought she'd had cancer returns with a tsunami. "Don't leave her side. I'm on my way."

FOURTEEN

THE NEXT THIRTY minutes are the most harrowing of my life. I should have asked Danny more questions. I consider calling him back, but at the same time I don't want to know.

I don't want to know because I already *know*. Deep in my gut. It's the baby. It has to be. She wouldn't have left the award show suddenly for any other reason. And since whatever happened landed her in the emergency room, there is a very good chance that the situation is bad. I'll deal with it, and I'll be who and what I need to be for Sabrina. But knowing this might be the last half hour where I can be excited about fatherhood, then I'd rather stay in the dark.

Who knows? Maybe it will be something else entirely— appendicitis or a kidney stone or chest pain or a seizure or a severe allergic reaction—

I refuse to think more about the possibilities or else I'll spiral. Instead, I concentrate on weaving my way through traffic, pretending my only reason for rage is the road.

Finally, I'm at the hospital. I leave my car parked in the circle drive without talking to a valet. If it's been towed when I return, so be it. I'm too desperate to find my wife and be at her side to care about something so trivial as an automobile.

Inside, I consider blowing past the emergency room desk and searching for her myself, but one look at the stern-faced security guard on duty, and I decide I'd better play by the rules. Thankfully, the ER is only moderately busy, so it's only another fifteen minutes—fifteen long-ass minutes—before it's my turn at the desk.

"It doesn't look like she'll be admitted," the receptionist tells me as she reads her screen.

Somehow, I manage to keep myself from reaching over her desk and turning the monitor toward me so I can read along with her. "I need to see her," I demand.

"I understand. I'm just looking to see if she's authorized you to go back."

I almost lose it right then and there. If she's suggesting that Sabrina doesn't—

"Ah, there you are. Donovan, you said, right? She's asked to let you back when you arrive."

I let out a slow breath, feeling a relief that's hard to acknowledge considering how fucking tense I still am.

"Let me get someone to take you back."

I stop the receptionist before she picks up the phone. "Just tell me where she is," I practically beg. "I'll find her."

She has pity on me, and a few seconds later, I'm buzzed into the secure area. I don't even have to look at the numbers outside each curtained area to find her because Danny is standing in the hallway.

I practically run.

"She's okay," he says as soon as he spots me coming toward him. "I should have said that on the phone."

The knot in my chest loosens ever so slightly. "Why aren't you in there with her?"

"She's...it's..." He shakes his head. "It's private."

My knees weaken. It's as I'd thought then. Without thinking, I reach out to something—anything—for support. My hand lands on his shoulder.

He places his hand gently over mine. "The doctor's with her right now. You should go."

I nod. "You can go home now. Thank you for being here." My hand drops from his shoulder as I take a step toward the curtained room. "Oh, um, I left the Jag in the circle."

Understanding, he pulls out a valet ticket from his pocket. "Let me deal with the Jag. You take the Tesla."

I hand him the keys in exchange for the ticket and send him on his way. With another deep breath, I step past the curtain.

She's looking at the doctor, and doesn't glance at me, probably thinking I'm just another attendant or Danny checking on her. It gives me a chance to study her. Her face is ashen, and she looks small in her hospital gown. Her fancy dress is draped over a chair, and when I see a spot of blood on the peach-colored fabric, my stomach drops. I quickly scan the monitors for any information I can find, looking for a sign of hope, but the only thing she's hooked up to is an IV drip.

"...very common. Highly unlikely because of anything you did," the doctor is saying.

"Are you sure?" asks Sabrina.

And even though I'm walking into this blind, with no information or certainty, I'm quick to jump in. "It's not your fault, Sabrina."

Her eyes quickly find mine, and when they do, her face crumbles. "I'm sorry, Donovan. I'm sorry. I should have told you."

I rush to her and squeeze myself onto the side of the tiny bed so that I can take her in my arms. "Don't worry about that."

She's crying now, but still trying to explain, her words muffled by her tears and my shoulder. "It started last night. And I didn't think anything. They say sometimes you can have spotting, so I didn't worry. And then when I was getting ready for tonight, I kept getting these cramps. And they got worse and worse and then I was waiting to present, and I could barely stand up, and someone told me I had blood on my dress, and then when I got here...in the bathroom...I'm so sorry I didn't tell you. I know how much you wanted this. I'm sorry. I'm so sorry."

"It's okay. I'm here." I stroke her hair, and murmur assurances in her ear. And all the while, I'm grateful that she's not looking at me, that her face is buried in my jacket because I don't want her to see how much I'm struggling to not ask questions, to not grill her. To not break down along with her.

What I need is something to do. A concrete way to care for her to get the rest off my mind. "Are you in pain now?" I look to the doctor, a young woman who's probably just out of med school. "Has she been given anything?"

"She's had morphine," the doctor says at the same time Sabrina says, "I'm just cold."

She's shaking, in fact, though her skin feels warm.

"She's probably in shock. I'll have a nurse bring a heated blanket." The doctor starts to leave.

I stop her before she's gone. "Morphine—isn't that bad for...?" I don't know how to ask what I'm asking. The answer is already obvious, but I have to hear it for myself. "Is there nothing that can be done? No chance? An ultrasound to see...? Anything?"

Young as she is, the doctor is sincere and tactful in her response. "Your wife passed fetal material. There isn't anything left to do now but let it run its course."

Sabrina's body racks with sobs in my arms, and I am helpless. So I hold her and rock her, and when the nurse returns with the heated blanket, I wrap it around Sabrina then wrap myself around her to keep the heat from escaping.

The doctor returns soon after with discharge papers. "I can admit you, if you'd like. Let you stay through the night."

"I want to go home," Sabrina says. Her tears have reduced to hiccups and heavy sighs.

"Is there any reason we should stay?" I ask.

"No. As I said, there isn't anything to be done at this point. She's far enough along that we might want to perform a D&C to make sure the miscarriage is complete, but that's a personal choice."

"I just want to go home," Sabrina repeats.

"I'll give you a prescription for any lingering pain. Just follow up with your regular OB/GYN in a couple of weeks to make sure there weren't any complications." She goes over other discharge information—no sex until she sees her doctor, use pads instead of tampons until the bleeding stops, take iron pills for the next month. It's all on the papers she hands us, which is good since my head feels like it's in a fog.

A short while later, a nurse comes in to take out the IV. I move to get Sabrina's clothes off the chair and remember the bloodstain. My jacket would cover it, but the dress is formal. I'm sure the fabric and style is uncomfortable, and asking her to wear something right now that's meant for special occasions seems cruel.

Cruel to me, at least.

I pull out a fifty from my wallet and hand it toward the nurse. "Is there any way you could round up some scrubs or something?"

He waves away the money. "Let me see what I have in my locker. I'll be right back."

When he returns with a clean set of scrubs, I try to feel like I've done something significant. I thought of Sabrina's comfort, I took care of her needs.

But Sabrina looks at the clothes and shakes her head. "Can I wear the gown?"

"Sure thing," he says, and all my usefulness is thrown out the window.

I give her my jacket to wear to keep her modest, but even that's unnecessary since they insist she leave in a wheelchair. I'm not even allowed to push. I walk ahead so I can give the attendant the valet ticket, and I slip him a twenty to incentivize him to bring the car up fast.

Eventually, we're in the car. Sabrina is quiet on the ride home, but she keeps her fingers laced in mine the whole time, and I somehow manage the drive with just one hand.

Once we're in our apartment, I feel more sure-footed. I'm on my home turf. I have things I can do, things for Sabrina. I leave her soiled dress by the front door, making a mental note to have the housekeeper deal with it as soon as possible.

"Did you eat anything? I can heat up some soup." The offer is out of my mouth before I know for sure that we have any cans in the pantry. "Or I can order something?"

"I'm not hungry." She peels off my jacket and hands it

toward me.

"I can draw you a bath. Make you some tea."

She shakes her head and kicks off her heels. Wordlessly, I follow her into the living room. I'm ready to grab a blanket from the closet if she wants to get cozy on the couch. I'll turn on the TV, find a show to make her laugh.

She doesn't sit, though. Instead, she turns back to me. We stare at each other, and there is so much I want to say, so much that is burning a hole in my chest, needing to be expressed. I want to ease her pain. I want to tell her that I hurt too. I want to ask her why she kept it secret. I want to tell her that it doesn't matter, that I don't care. I want to lie and make everything better.

But every subject feels like barbed wire. There isn't a way through to her without someone getting scraped, and if it's only me, then that's one thing, but I can't do that to her. I won't.

And so what do I do? What do I say? "I can..." I don't even know how to finish the sentence.

"I'm really tired," she says.

I'm a fucking idiot. Of course, she's tired after the morphine. "I'll carry you up."

"I can walk."

She lets me help her up the stairs, despite not needing me. When we get to our room, she disappears into the bathroom. I turn on the lamp next to the bed. Turn off the overhead. Find her a tank top, clean panties, and sleep shorts and then spend an entire minute trying to decide if I should knock or just walk in.

What the fuck with that? I never hesitate about these things. I do what needs to be done. I go where I need to go. I don't ask.

Finally, I walk in and set the clothes on the counter. She's on the toilet, and she avoids eye contact—or maybe it's me who's avoiding—but for the first time ever, it feels like I'm invading her privacy. Like I don't have a right. Like there's not a place for me here.

I rub my finger along the lace of her panties. "There's fresh clothes for you here," I tell her. "Are you sure you don't want me to start a shower."

"I'm sure."

I leave her and go back to the bedroom. I pull off the extra pillows, and turn back the covers before stripping down to my boxer briefs. I throw on a pair of running shorts, and I'm looking for a T-shirt when she comes out of the bathroom.

"Are you going for a run?" she asks, in a tone that suggests that's exactly the wrong thing to do.

"No," I lie, suddenly feeling heartless for considering it. I wouldn't have left the building. We have a treadmill in the next room, and there is a Newton ton of energy inside me that needs to be burned off. And if she doesn't need me, I definitely need the distraction.

But if she *does* need me...

"No," I say again. "I'm not going anywhere."

"Okay."

She just stands there, and I hate myself because I think I should know what I'm supposed to do, and I just don't.

"Can you...can you hold me?" It kills me that she has to ask.

"I was planning on it," I say, and then to prove it, I get in the bed and scoot over, leaving a space for her. Then I hold the covers up and invite her in.

I reach past her to turn off the light, then spoon up behind her. Wrapped in my arms, she falls asleep fast, and I stay awake beside her for hours, wondering just how much I've lost tonight, and if I'll ever have any of it back again.

FIFTEEN

TWELVE YEARS *ago*

THE KITCHEN LIGHT CAME ON, and I winced. To be fair, it was easier to read the newspaper than it had been with just the thin rays of sun that managed to penetrate through the overcast sky and reach through the window, but the overhead was hell on a hangover.

To make it worse, the asswipe who had turned on the light had moved on to slamming cupboards followed by slamming dishes. When the refrigerator door closed soundlessly, Weston kicked it before slamming the beer bottle he'd removed on the counter.

"What's your problem?" I really didn't care. I just wanted the noise to stop.

"What's *your* problem?" he snarled back.

Okay, touché. I'd been a bitch to live with the last few days.

Scratch that, I'd been a bitch to live with the last year, since Amanda had died in a crash that had essentially been my fault. My moody disposition had been tolerated by my friends, if just barely, since they understood the circumstances.

Then this week, I'd become insufferable, drinking the minute I got home from class, barking at everyone and everything. I'd been especially cruel, which was saying something since I was pretty good at it when I wanted to be in the first place.

I looked over at him, for no reason in particular, and saw guilt fall over his features. I knew what he was thinking—that he shouldn't have pushed me, that he already knew the answer, that of course I'd be moody coming up on the year anniversary of Amanda's death.

And now I felt guilty, because although Amanda was always in the back of my mind, my foul mood the last few days had a different name attached to it—Sabrina Lind.

Not that I was discussing that with Weston.

With a measured sigh, I looked back at my paper. "It's complicated."

"No, I know. I know."

He didn't know shit.

We stood there in silence—him brooding, me pretending to read the finance section. I knew he wanted me to ask, but I hated that passive-aggressive bullshit, so I refused to play into it.

On the other hand, the silence was heavy. "Beer for breakfast?" I asked instead.

"Cereal too."

So that was the crunching sound. Weren't we out of milk, though? I peered over to see if he was eating it dry.

Nope. He'd poured the beer on his cornflakes. *Nasty.*

Another tense minute went by before he went back to slamming things, which was infinitely worse than the silence.

As though to show that I could compete, I slammed my coffee mug on the table and set down my paper. "Out with it."

"Out with what?"

"You obviously want to tell me what got you in such a pissy mood this morning, and since it seems you won't go away until you do, just get it over with."

He scowled at me, and for a second I thought he was going to make me pull it out of him now, out of spite.

Thank God, he'd never been that patient. "I was stood up."

Well, that explained why there hadn't been the usual T-shirt-only clad freshman following him into the kitchen this morning.

"Last night?" I'd spent the night drunk on scotch in my room, but the weekly Saturday party seemed to be going as strong as always. "Wasn't there a plethora of other women to choose from or had you already slept with them all?"

He gave me the finger. "I'd made plans this time with someone special."

I raised an eyebrow. Weston didn't do special. Or more accurately, every woman was special to him in the moment. But he was always over them the next day, which was why this was almost intriguing.

"Oh, you know her, actually. She's in Ethics. Sabrina. Or maybe you don't know her, know her. She's kind of missable."

"I know her." I eyed my mug, wondering if it would do significant damage if I flung it at his face. Sabrina Lind, missable? Like I said before, he didn't know shit.

I also knew that she was supposed to have been his date, but after what had happened on Thursday—when things had gotten out of hand, and I'd let my jealousy and desire lead me to steal her virginity in Mr. Velasquez's office—I'd expected that she'd cancel. Not because I thought she had grand ideas about the two of us, but because coming to Weston's party would have meant seeing me, and there was no way she was ready for that. She'd skipped class on Friday too, and I was betting it was because of me.

I hoped that was why she was staying away, anyway. When I'd basically thrown her away afterward, I made her think the incident had just been transactional on my part. A reason to change her grade, nothing else. None of that was true, of course. That moment had been everything, which was exactly the reason I needed her to stay away. Before I made *her* my everything.

I'd done that before. It hadn't ended well. I wouldn't do it to Sabrina too.

So Weston's news should have been validating.

"She's actually got something about her, once you notice it." Jesus, he sounded almost dreamy. "I don't know. It's weird. I really thought we connected, but she didn't call or anything. Didn't answer my texts, either. I've just...I've never been stood up."

"Poor baby." But I was concerned now. The fact that she hadn't given Weston the courtesy of an explanation, even if it were a lie, didn't sit right. That wasn't like her. She was too polite, too conforming to formalities. And it seemed she genuinely liked the guy, much to my chagrin.

Had I done more damage than I'd imagined? Already?

"Fuck you very much, bumblefuck." Shit. His feelings were hurt.

"Look, I didn't mean—" Actually, I had meant to imply he

was a privileged player who got every girl he'd ever wanted. He didn't need me to soothe him.

With my luck, he'd decide to double down on Sabrina, which was the last thing I needed.

I turned my chair to face him. "Like I said, I know her. And she's not for you."

"What's that supposed to mean? I'm not good enough for her?"

"No, no, no." *Yes, yes, yes.* "She's a scholarship girl, Weston. She's not of our breeding. She doesn't fit in here with us. With you."

He chuckled. "Man, D. Never knew you were such a classist."

"I'm being practical, that's all. If you're looking for something serious with this girl, it's not likely going to happen. She is out of her league. And if you were only in it for a fuck, then I can't feel sorry for you because you have a surplus of beautiful women ready to give you just that."

He hollowed his cheeks then puffed them out as he considered. Then he took a slow pull on what was left of his beer. "Okay. Yeah." He nodded, as if trying to convince himself. "Barely know her. Not serious. And yeah. I can fuck someone else. Totally."

"That's right."

"You know? I feel better, surprisingly. And there will be other Saturdays. I'll get Sabrina in my bed eventually."

Not what I'd been going for, but the future was a worry for another day. Right now things were just as they should be— Sabrina out of the picture and Weston's thoughts elsewhere.

Now to get my own thoughts to do the same.

TWO HOURS LATER, I found myself standing outside of Sabrina's dorm. So much for getting her out of my head.

This wasn't the first time I'd been here, either. The first time in the light, yes, but I'd spent plenty of nights leaning against the lamppost with the broken bulb—not my doing, for once—staring up at the third window on the fourth floor, wishing I could get inside. Wishing I could know everything she was doing at any given minute of the day or night.

It had been like this with Amanda, too, though then my obsession had been driven by fear. She'd been the only woman who had seemed to care about me for me, not because I was a blue-blooded heir to a financial empire like all my other dates, and I'd known I was losing her. Desperate to keep her, I'd become possessive. I'd followed her. I'd hired a PI to track her when I couldn't. She'd discovered what I was doing and understandably broke things off.

Still, I couldn't stop myself. I'd sent the detective after her again, and when she'd tried to lose him, she'd ended up in a fatal accident.

My love had done that, and I'd vowed never to feel that way again.

Then Sabrina showed up. And it wasn't like Amanda because this time my obsession was driven by something I couldn't name. Intrigue? Desire? Fate?

Shit, it didn't matter the reason behind it. The point was that I was toxic. That I was unworthy. That I was fucked up.

And still.

And now that I'd had her, I was consumed like never before. I could smell her on the wind. I could taste her on my tongue. I could feel her pussy clutching around my dick. Phantom sensory input, like I'd lost a limb and still imagined it in place.

I had to figure a way out of this. A way to sever her from me for real. What would that take?

The door opened to her building, and I quickly started walking, pretending that I hadn't been idly staring like the creepy stalker that I was. My luck, she was the one coming out. It wouldn't matter if I didn't look in that direction. If I didn't look, she wouldn't see my face, and she'd never know.

But as I've said, I couldn't help myself—I looked. It wasn't Sabrina.

However, it was her roommate, and while I had the feeling they weren't that close, it was probably a good idea to play it safe.

"Sheri, right?" I asked, the words coming out of their own volition as I stepped onto the sidewalk in front of her.

"Uh..." Sheri looked over her shoulder, as if hoping to find back up somewhere. Smart, I supposed, but it was barely noon on a Saturday. Was that really the hour for predators?

Yes, I saw the irony.

She clutched her bag. Probably had pepper spray inside. "Yeah, that's me."

I put my hands up in surrender. "Didn't mean to startle you. You're Sabrina Lind's roommate."

It wasn't a question, but she answered. "Yeah. You know Sabrina?"

What the fuck was I doing?

Too late to stop it. I was neck in now. "I'm one of her teacher's assistants. She missed class yesterday."

"Yeah, she did. She probably hasn't had a chance to tell her teachers yet. She had to go home. Family emergency. Dad's in the hospital. Stroke, maybe? Something serious. She was all in tears while she was packing her bag. I couldn't make it all out. When I hear from her, I'll let her know—"

"She went back to Denver?" I should have been worried that she'd tell Sabrina I'd come looking. If she thought I cared, she would think it gave her permission to care, and I could not give her that.

But that was the last thing on my mind. The only thing I was thinking about was Sabrina and what she'd been through this semester, and how she'd already lost her mother. Sabrina trying to be strong for her father or her sister. Sabrina all alone.

"Is that where she's from? Colorado, right." She laughed. "You know more than I do about her, I guess."

Yeah, because Sheri was a crap roommate. I walked away without another word. She wasn't getting any more of my time or energy, especially not when I had other pressing things to attend to now.

I pulled my phone out as I walked toward my part of town and only hesitated briefly before dialing.

My father answered on the second ring. "What's up?"

Usually, I hated asking him for favors. That wasn't how our relationship worked. I was the one who did and he was the one who demanded.

But this time, I didn't give it a second thought. "Who do you know in the Denver medical system? I need information on a patient."

Fortunately, Raymond Kincaid being known as connected. "Hmm. I think Saul Eliman is still on the board at UCHealth. He might know someone, and he owes us one."

I wasn't sure if "us" was King-Kincaid or if he was including me. Either way, I could use it to my benefit. "Can you get me in touch ASAP?"

"Maybe. Maybe. This isn't about that scholarship girl, is it?"

I stopped walking. Denver was too big for him to think that Sabrina was the only reason I could have interests there without a reason. "Why would you think that it was?"

"Brandi forwarded an email from her saying she'd had to go home to deal with her father's heart attack. She's not expecting to be back this semester. You think she's playing us?"

If he'd read Sabrina's application essay, he'd know how amusing the question was. I'd had the added bonus of seeing her work in Ethics. She was the type who believed in fairness. She worked for every stitch of money she received from The MADAR Foundation. It seemed like she didn't want to be in the world of the rich—in *my* world—unless she belonged there.

Funny how she thought that belonging meant playing by the rules.

But my father didn't know that about her, and as I'd been taught self-preservation above all else, I unashamedly latched onto his suggestion. "I didn't want to say anything until I was sure."

"You have her in class—is she not cutting it?"

It was like a window had opened. An opportunity to end all of this. I saw it clear as day, how this would play out. How I could fix the future with just a bit of misdirection.

God, I was going to destroy her, wasn't I? Did I have any other choice?

I rolled the lie around in my head once before I said it out loud, before I set the severing into motion, as if that would make it hurt less. "She's struggled a bit." I cleared my throat, gaining confidence. "She met with me during office hours on Thursday. My impression is that she didn't walk away happy."

"So she could be trying to cover bad grades with a fake emergency."

"Yeah. Yeah. Something like that." I shook my head, shook my entire body with it, trying to shake off the cold. "Get me in touch with your guy. I'll see what's what."

"You do that. Report back as soon as you find anything." He was giving the orders now as though he'd been the one to call me. "There were other strong candidates. Give it to a man this time. They tend to work out better."

I let the misogynistic asswad accept my silence as agreement. It was really a wonder the committee had selected a woman in the first place. It was a wonder Sabrina had shown up in my life at all. Where could she have ended up instead?

This was better for her. It would be painful, but it would be less painful than what I'd do to her if she stayed. She'd find her happy ending.

It was better for me, too. It had to be.

I SPENT the better part of the next two hours on the phone. The rest of the afternoon was spent on a plane.

I landed at Denver International just after five and by six-thirty, I was covertly lingering in the lounge outside ICU, on the lookout for a tall white man with a thick mustache, if he still resembled his driver's license.

Being so close to Sabrina and hoping not to be seen was a risk, and I knew it. A calculated risk. I was betting that she would stay true to her character and never leave her father's side. Or at least not until I had a chance to do what I'd come for.

The minutes ticked by. Each time the doors swung open, I went on alert. It was almost eight o'clock when a man matching the image I'd been given walked out and headed toward the vending machines.

Bingo.

I came up beside him as he studied his options. "You can go ahead," he said. "I'm trying to decide between Doritos or trail mix."

"Why choose?"

He laughed, but he stepped out of the way, making me room. I stepped up to the machine and put in my money, trying to decide how I wanted to play this. I'd gone through a bunch of different options in my head, but now that I'd seen who I was dealing with, my gut told me the best choice would be as straight as possible.

Or I could just leave it.

I already had enough information to pull the scholarship. Sabrina's father had had a massive heart attack and was in a coma, but the doctors were recommending that life support be pulled. She could have the funeral over with by the end of Thanksgiving week and be back in time for finals.

That's what my father would say, anyway. He could maybe be convinced she needed more time, but no one would try besides me, and I wouldn't try. I had everything I needed to walk away from this and never look back.

Yet here I was. Worrying about her.

Wordlessly, I chose Doritos and trail mix, then when they shot out of the machine, I handed it toward the man. "Monty McGill, right?"

His back straightened. "That's me. Do I know you?"

My face appeared of an ambiguous age. I could have been twenty or I could have been thirty—no one ever could tell. The fact that I was wearing a suit made the distinction even more difficult. Made it easier to dance around his question. "We haven't met. But I know the situation you're in—you're the medical power of attorney for George Lind."

"Yeah. He's my neighbor. You from the counseling office? The nurse said they'd send someone if I needed help with my decision, but I'm just going by the advice of the doctors. They said if he didn't wake up after seventy-two hours, there wasn't any hope, and it's been that now. The medical bills are already piling up. I wouldn't want the girls to have to deal with any more than they have to."

It was obvious he'd been thoughtful about it, and my own research had suggested that throwing money at the situation wouldn't lead to a better outcome. Inserting myself further only increased the risk of Sabrina discovering my involvement.

Problem was, I knew what Sabrina needed, and I knew that I was the only person who would be sure that she got it.

"That's very considerate of you, Mr. McGill. Thinking of Sabrina and Audrey." I gestured again to the snacks in my hand. "Please, take them. My treat." He accepted the offering, and I let that give me permission to go on. "Shame, though, isn't it? That Sabrina still has a month to go before her birthday. If she were eighteen already, this decision would have fallen on her."

Monty shook his head. "I'm glad it's fallen on me. I wouldn't want Sabrina to have to make that decision. And she understands the situation. She knows there's no chance he'll wake up."

"Again, very considerate. Very thought out. Just..." I

scratched my chin, deliberately inviting him to push me to say more.

"Just...what? You think I should keep him hooked up another day? The doctors are quite certain—"

"No, no, you're right. He's showing as brain dead. Just, there's a certain closure that comes from being able to make that decision." Not for everyone, but Sabrina would want it. I knew that like I knew the back of my hand. "It seems like a lot to put on a teenager, I know. Sabrina isn't an ordinary teenager. Graduated high school a year early, went away to an Ivy League school on full scholarship—she's smart enough. She's strong enough. She'll make the same decision, but if it's *her* decision, she will feel better about it in the long run."

He seemed unsure. "You think I should ask for her input?"

"I think you should tell her the decision is hers. Whatever she wants to do, that's what you'll do."

"Okay, I see. Except if she says she doesn't want to shut off the machines—"

"She will."

"But if she doesn't, the bills will add up."

"Like I said, she's smart. She knows how expenses work. She should be the one to decide how much of a financial burden this decision is to her." I already planned on paying down as much of the hospital bill as I could without being caught. "Let her choose. Trust me. It will help her let go."

He only hesitated a second. "I hear you. Good advice. Thank you. I'll do that." He held up the snacks. "And thank you for these. I should probably get something for the girls, too. They've barely eaten."

I tried to bite my tongue.

I failed. "Peanut butter cups. Get those. Always a favorite."

Sabrina's anyway, considering how often she'd brought them to class.

Monty turned to the machine to put his money in. "I guess I shouldn't have said no to the counseling. I didn't realize you'd have useful advice."

I didn't hear what he'd said because I was already walking away. I wanted to be gone before he started asking more questions about my "position" at the hospital. Before he got a good enough look at me to cement my image to memory.

It had been the right thing to do, even with the risk. A small detail that would make all the difference in how Sabrina handled her father's death. It was what she needed, and I took pride that I'd been the one to give it to her.

And I knew it wouldn't make up for the rest. For how I'd treated her. For taking away her scholarship. For not giving her a choice where Harvard was concerned. Where I was concerned.

But it was for the best.

It was for the best.

SIXTEEN

PRESENT

SABRINA GIVES me a quizzical look as I pull into the driveway in front of the log cabin. "Do we own this?"

The tone of her voice says she'd be very surprised if the answer was yes, and reasonably so. It's luxurious but rustic, and even despite the style, I can't imagine ever acquiring a property that is so far from civilization.

Under the circumstances, though, I thought it might be exactly what we need. Or hoped, anyway. "It belongs to Hudson." Pierce Industries is one of our biggest advertising clients. When I canceled a meeting with him—as I've canceled all our meetings this week—I felt obligated to explain our situation. He's not the kind of man you reschedule without good reason. "He said no one's using it right now. Offered it through next weekend if we want."

I study her profile while she studies the landscape. Her face is drawn, and there are bags under her eyes, even though she's barely left her bed the past few days, and I realize that this getaway isn't going to fix anything. There's no escape from this, and I'm a wreck without the ability to make it go away.

When she turns toward me, her smile is forced. "That was generous of him, but I need to get back by Monday. We're already behind—"

"The office can run without us," I interject. Words no one ever thought would come from my mouth, including me.

She pierces me with a stare that says everything. She married a meticulous and controlling asshole who doesn't know how to take a weekend off let alone a whole week. She thinks this is killing me, and it is, just not for the reasons she believes.

"We're fine," I insist.

"*I'm* fine," she counters.

We're both lying.

I take a deep breath when really I feel like banging my fist against the steering wheel. *It's been less than four days*, I remind myself. It will get better. Time just needs to pass. That's all.

Right now, small goals seem like the best way to handle things. Yesterday, she got out of bed. Today, she got in the car. "Let's see how we feel on Sunday, okay?"

I can see the argument behind her eyes, but she either decides to placate me or doesn't have the energy to refute. "Okay."

We busy ourselves for the next half hour with unloading the car and getting settled. Hudson's generosity extended to having the fridge and cupboards packed for us so after Sabrina's situated on one of the oversized leather sofas with blankets, pillows, and a heating pad, I put together a charcuterie board and bring it to the coffee table. Then I open one of the pricier bottles of wine that I find—*Thanks, Hudson, I owe you*—and pour two generous glasses.

"No, thank you," she says when I deliver it to her. "I'm..." Then she thinks about it, lets out a small sigh. "I guess there's no reason not to. Now." She takes the glass and looks away while she sips from it.

I stand there like an idiot, staring at her, realizing how fucking out of touch I've been. How long has she been staying away from alcohol? How did I miss that? How did I miss that she skipped period cramps for two whole months? What else didn't I see?

"I hid it all," she says, reading my mind. "I didn't want you to know."

We've tiptoed around that fact, but it hasn't been neglected completely. Since she's the one who brought it up this time, I take the opportunity to ask, "Why not?"

She closes her eyes against tears. Bites her lip. Shakes her head.

She's not ready, which has basically been the response she's given every time it's come up before. "We'll talk. I promise."

But not now. The subtext is clear.

I'm torn up inside with the desire to know, but I'm not about to push her. "I'm not going anywhere. Take your time."

I gesture for her to move over so she can lean into me while still having space to stretch out. We eat and drink wordlessly, which is pretty much what we did at home, but the insulation of our high-rise apartment made the silence thicker. Now, the sounds of birds and nature dot the quiet with a pleasantness the city lacked.

"It's relaxing," Sabrina says eventually, and I'm not sure if she's following my thoughts and talking about the environment or if she means the wine until she goes on. "I mean, we would never choose this style, but it's homey."

I glance around at the open floor plan of the cabin. There's a stone fireplace and floor-to-ceiling windows that overlook the deck and the lake. The furniture is all oversized and the space is littered with decor that reminds you you're in the woods, in case you might have forgotten, like a wooden plaque that says *Cabin Sweet Cabin* and dish towels with the silhouette of a moose. The ottomans all hinge open to reveal quilted blankets and the bookshelves have as many board games as they do things to read. Honestly, it's not what I imagine Hudson Pierce's style to be, either, and I wonder if the playpen in the corner and the basket of kid's toys are the reason why. He's not just the powerful CEO of an uber successful industrial firm—he's also a father. Does parenthood really take over a life like that? Changing priorities and preferences until you don't recognize yourself in your surroundings? Could I ever be that?

Honestly, the jury's out. What do I even know about being a parent? My mother's a cold fish, and my father thinks conspiring together is equivalent to love. Without a decent role model, could I do any better? Do I want to?

Yes. I do.

I still want it. I want *this*. Not a cabin maybe, but what it achieves. That homey feel that Sabrina's talking about—it's the kind of space I've never had in my life, and one she most likely feels nostalgia for. It doesn't have to be in the Poconos. We could have it just as easily in our own apartment. We'd need to make some adjustments, but we have plenty of room. We'll carve our own path. We've done it before. We can do it again.

Too late, I wonder if I should have come in first and hidden away all the proof that children belong here. I can't see Sabrina's face the way we're sitting, so I can't see if she's noticed or if she's bothered. "I'm sorry," I say, assuming both. "Maybe coming here was the wrong choice."

She takes another sip of wine before she answers. "No. It's a good change of scenery."

I'm certain she's saying it to appease me, and that only makes me more frustrated. I'm the one who's supposed to be comforting her, not the other way around.

But I'm at a fucking loss. All week, everything I've tried has been wrong. I bought her chocolate that she barely touched. I hired a massage therapist that she sent away. I practically had her sister on a plane when Sabrina aborted that plan. She zones out when I turn on a movie. She doesn't want to talk. She doesn't even cry. What else am I supposed to do?

I resign myself to being silent with her, so I'm surprised when she picks up the thread again. "Would you ever want to own a place like this?"

I take the empty plate from my lap and the one from hers and set them on the coffee table. It gives me a chance to think before I speak, and I wonder if the question she's really asking is the one I'd asked myself earlier—if I could become a man who would own a place like this. While I still think I'd prefer to be that kind of man in the city, I'm eager to make her happy. "If you want a place like this, let's do it. Should I call a realtor? We could look over the next week."

"Don't call a realtor. I just wanted to know if you would want this."

"If you do, then yes." Too blatant. She twists her head to glare at me for it. "Well, what do *you* want?"

She doesn't speak until she's facing away again. "I want to know what you want."

For you to be happy. It hasn't changed in the twelve years that I've known her. That's always what I've wanted most. Then I'd gone and gotten greedy and wanted a baby too. Now I just want to know that Sabrina will be okay again. I want to make her okay again.

"I don't know," I tell her, unable to voice the truth without sounding trite.

She huffs in frustration, and once again I feel like I'm fucking it all up.

I try again. "Are you not happy with the apartment?" We own apartments all over the world, but most were purchased before we were together. "We could change cities, if you want. Or buy a country home." I'm glad she's not facing me because I cringe with that last suggestion. It was how I grew up, and I hate anything that feels like a replica of that.

"You want a place in Connecticut?"

I can't go so far as to agree to that. "Maybe upstate New York?"

She turns so her entire body is facing me. "You want that commute? Would you take it every day or just on the weekends?"

"Whichever you want."

"What?" I say when she glares again. It seems that's the look I get the most from her lately, and fuck if I know how to respond.

"Quit placating me."

"I'm not." Well, I am. I'm searching for what she wants to hear, which is so not how we usually operate. Usually, I don't have to search. I don't have to ask. I just know.

"You are. And when you're not, you're walking on eggshells. Treating me like I'm fragile."

"You're not fragile," I tell her. "You're the strongest person I know."

"Then why are you acting like I'm made of glass?"

I run my hand through my hair. "Look, Sabrina, I'm trying. I can't seem to say the right thing. Can you tell me what I should be saying?"

She lifts a shoulder in a shrug. "I don't know. Nothing, I guess."

"Nothing. Okay. Nothing." I recognize my frustration turning into irritation, and yet I can't stop the words that follow. "You obviously want to do this alone. Might as well have stayed in the city."

Standing up, I grab the empty dishes as an excuse to walk away to the kitchen. Her eyes follow me, her expression confused. "Why did you bring me here, Donovan?"

I slam the plates down on the counter. "Because I thought you'd like the escape." No, that's not true. "Because I don't know what to do, Sabrina. I don't know how to make it better, and it's killing me, okay? I don't know what to do for you."

She continues to stare, like she can't understand what she's looking at. Like she's looking at a stranger. After a beat, she says, "You know what I need."

Like hell I do. Isn't that what I've been explaining? Hasn't she been listening?

Except, she's right—I do know. In the past, when she needed an outlet, I knew exactly how to give it to her. Even when she didn't know how to ask for it.

She can't be talking about that. Can she?

"Donovan..."

I shake my head. "We can't."

"Why not? I'm not bleeding heavily. Only spotting now."

"The doctor said two weeks before—"

She cuts me off. "I don't care what the fucking doctor said. You asked what I need, and I'm telling you that you already know. You know, Donovan."

She's pleading, and I'm torn. Am I willing to risk her physical health for her emotional needs? It was so much easier making difficult decisions for her when I didn't have to face her afterward. It was easier to stand my ground.

I hesitate too long thinking about it. "Whatever," she says, slipping on her All Birds. "I'm going for a walk." She knows what I'm about to say, and she counters before I can open my mouth. "I'm going alone."

It takes all I have to let her walk out without running after her.

SEVENTEEN

ONCE THE DOOR CLOSES, my exasperation overtakes me, and I spin, looking for somewhere to land a throw. The refrigerator ends up the unlucky surface. My palm crashes against the stainless steel. Unsatisfied with just one hit, I strike it again, again, again.

After five blows, my hand is feeling it. I shake it out, trying to halt the pain by confusing the nerves, and actually, despite the throbbing of my palm, my head does feel clearer.

Or maybe it's because she's not standing there in front of me, her big brown eyes glossy with tears she hasn't been able to shed, not since that first night. It hurts to see her like that. Hurts so much that the pain blinds me. Hurts so much that it makes me stupid.

Fuck, she's right. I've been treating her like glass. How can she process what she needs like that? She's too tough. Too thick skinned. She'll stay numb until she's forced to feel otherwise. I know that. I've known it far longer than she has.

And I'm smart enough to know how to give her what she needs and keep her safe at the same time.

Without thinking too hard about it, I start collecting what I need to make things right. I find a ski cap in a drawer in one of the bedrooms, along with a scarf that is thin enough that it can be tied. Possible blindfold? Or gag. We'll see.

It takes longer to track down something suitable for securing her wrists. The fishing wire in the garage seems like a possibility until I find the duct tape.

As for a choice of lube, I have plenty. There's olive oil in the kitchen and I find both Vaseline and coconut oil in the master bathroom. I settle on a tube of aloe vera, easy to fit in my pocket and less messy than the oil-based products.

My supplies taken care of, I change out of my khakis into jeans, and pair them with a black pullover. It's summer and still early in the day, but I like the idea of armor. As I lace up my Ferragamo boots, I think about that night so long ago, when Theo had assaulted her outside my window, and I'd watched from above. I wasn't going to get involved. That's what I'd told myself. I was not going to be the one to save her. I had not signed up for that role. I didn't want to get involved.

But I'd laced my boots as I'd watched, and I told myself, *if she looks up, then I'll go down. If she sees me, then I'll rescue her.*

She never looked up, and I knew I should have just shut my blinds and forgotten about her. But it didn't matter that she hadn't seen me because I'd seen her, and I could never unsee her, and the magnet that pulled me down those stairs to face her would-be rapist didn't care what I wanted, didn't care that I was heartless, didn't care that I was already dead inside.

I saved her then, and though it took years to see it, she saved me right back. She gave me meaning when I'd had none. She gave my life a purpose. I live for her, and I'll save her again today because there's no point to my life without her.

No point at all.

Knowing the stakes, I grab a couple of water bottles, and head outside.

The hardest part is figuring out which way Sabrina went since I didn't watch her when she left. The driveway is visible from the kitchen, and I didn't see her out the window while I was beating up the fridge. The lake is on the west side of the house, so she didn't go that way. Walking the trail that follows the shore would eventually take her through marsh, which she would have wanted to avoid. South is a possibility. There's a clearing that could be easily walked, but my gut says she took the trail going north. It cuts through the forest, twisting and turning so that I can't see farther than a hundred feet or so down the path. She wanted to get lost for a while—this trail provides that.

Certain as I am of which direction she went, I decide to stay near the house, in case she comes back another way or in the unlikely event that I'm wrong. So after following the pathway for about five minutes, I find a thick evergreen to hide behind.

Then I wait, crouched and silent. Like I'm on stakeout. This can still work if she sees me—I can definitely outrun her, and maybe she wants the chase—but I'm conscious of the state of her body. If we're doing this, I want to limit her exertion. I'll take the pain instead, and I do. My thighs start to cramp after a while, but I only straighten long enough to shake my legs and get some blood to my feet before I stoop again, hiding in the thicket.

For nearly an hour, I perk up at every crack of a twig, every rustle of branches. Lots of squirrels and chipmunks scurry around these woods when it's quiet. A variety of bird songs fill the air. I spent a lot of time in the woods outside our Connecticut home growing up, but I'd forgotten how noisy nature can be.

It's actually when everything gets suddenly quiet that I know I need to be ready. I put on the mask and strain my ears, thinking something must have scared all the creatures off. Sure enough, the silence is followed by the rhythmic pad of footsteps.

Carefully, quietly, I circle the tree in the opposite direction, ending up on the trail after she's passed. She's so into her thoughts that she doesn't hear me as I come up behind her. When my arm hooks around her waist, she gasps, but my other hand clamps over her mouth before she can scream.

"This will go better for you if you don't make a sound," I say into her ear, clear enough that she'll know it's me. She's still on alert, but I feel her shoulders relax letting go of fear before her muscles tighten again with excitement. I can smell it on her, her adrenaline and pheromones putting off a scent that I'm wired to respond to.

This is about her, but I'm instantly hard.

I pull her tight against me. When she feels my erection along her backside, her breath hitches.

Then she draws her elbow back sharply into my rib cage. "Fuck," I wheeze, my grip loosening enough for her to jerk away.

I'm quick though, and could overtake her again in an instant, but I give her a few yards before chasing after her. Just to make it sporting. Just to make it fun.

This time when I grab her, she's kicking and fighting all the way. "Let go of me, you fucking bastard. Let go."

"Not a chance." I get both her wrists in the grip of one hand then reach for the duct tape tucked in the waistband of my jeans. Holding the roll, I pull at the end of the tape with my teeth until I have a decent length.

When I go to put it around her wrists, though, she manages to get one free and, twisting around to face me, she uses it to smack across my jaw. I barely feel it through the ski mask, but it throws me enough off-balance, and I drop the duct tape. It goes rolling out of reach.

Shit.

Well, I still have the scarf. Maybe it can work.

I had planned on securing her wrists behind her back, but with some quick maneuvering, I'm able to grab her free hand and get the scarf wrapped around both her wrists in front of her body. It won't hold, though, and it's not ideal because, as she soon proves, she can still fight back with them in this position. She raises them both together then buries her fingernails into the exposed skin at my neck, digging in so deep, I'm sure she's drawn blood.

Her hands, though, are just a distraction so she can get me with her knee. She doesn't get my crotch, but only because that wasn't where she was aiming, and turns out a bony kneecap in the hip is still noticeable discomfort.

It's also more of a fight than she usually puts up. Wilder, maybe. More brutal. She's feral, the way her fingers make their way under my mask to claw at my jawline. We always play rough, but the extra fight feels like she's asking for more, and if she needs the pain, I'll give it to her. She just needs to know how to ask.

"You hurt me, I hurt you," I tell her, an invitation more than a threat.

She stills, though, and I realize I was wrong. She wants the fight, not the pain. She wants to hurt, not be hurt. She's already hurting. She doesn't need more.

I amend the invitation. "Do your best. It's not going to stop me."

She understands the message and follows the first knee with another, this time getting me in the kidney. And fuck, that almost hits as hard as being punched in the nuts. I can't help but bend over with the blow.

She takes the opportunity to get loose from the scarf—I knew it wouldn't hold—and then she runs. But she stumbles over a tree root, and I use her fall to my advantage and wrap my arms around her thighs, tackling her to the ground. She falls hard on her tailbone, crying out on impact.

The pain doesn't stop her from lashing out. She kicks at my shoulder, and when I climb up her body, she elbows me good in the jaw. Her next attempt to get me with her knee brushes the side of my erection. Thankfully, she didn't have enough force behind it to hurt. Though, now I'm in pain from how hard I am. When she goes to slap my face, I grab her arm. A handful of seconds later, I have both wrists above her head, and her body pinned under mine.

She uses her capture to catch her breath. I watch the fall of her chest as it slows and evens, then when it seems she's calmed, I arrange her wrists so they're held down with my forearm, and I use my other hand to slip inside her shorts.

She's wet. Wet enough that I don't have to slide my fingers lower—her clit is already soaked. When I press my thumb against the nerves, she lets out a hollow cry.

There're no tears, but the sound hits me between the ribs, and I close my eyes, pressing against the liquid gathering in them. Not that she could see what's going on with my face since I'm still wearing the mask.

But then that beautiful nymph of mine uses my moment of weakness to get a hand free and manages to push the mask up to my forehead. My eyes pop open. If she sees the tears, she doesn't acknowledge them. Instead, she digs her nails once again into my skin, and this time scratches down my cheek.

"Not going to stop me," I say again, increasing the pressure on her clit.

She whimpers then changes her tactic, using the heel of her hand to push against my neck. I'm glad I didn't manage to secure her wrists because she needs to be able to fight, but honestly, her hands are becoming a nuisance.

Without pausing the massage, I wrestle her to her stomach. Her arms are free, but she can't do much damage to me with them now. I cover her body with mine, my arm snaked around her waist to continue the assault on her clit. She kicks and flails, and digs into the ground with her fingers, but soon her body goes still, and she grunts as an orgasm ripples through her.

It's not enough. I know that before she's finished coming. Not enough for her, and not enough for me. I move to work on getting her shorts down, which is a battle, and when I go to undo my jeans, she succeeds in crawling a couple of yards. I grab her by the ankle, and drag her back toward me. She manages to smack me good across the same cheek she scratched, but then I get her pinned again.

I press my bare cock against the slit of her naked ass. With my mouth at her ear, I say, "You get what you ask for, bitch. And you were asking, weren't you?"

I'm surprised by how mean the words come out. But not really surprised. Because all the time she was building up to

needing this, I was building up to needing it too. I need to call
her names. I need to fight. I need to be mean and cruel the same
way the world has been mean and cruel to us, and I need to
share that meanness and cruelty with the one person who
understands what I've lost.

"Fuck you," she says.

"Oh, I will." Awkwardly and with one hand, I work the aloe
vera from my pocket and somehow get the liquid on my cock.
Some drips onto her ass, and I slide it between her ass cheeks,
making sure not to neglect the tight bud hidden there. I stick my
thumb past the tight rim, and the assumption she makes renews
her will.

"No, no, please no." No safe word, yet, and there won't be
because while that had been my plan, it changed when I
decided she didn't need more pain.

But the threat works the way I hope it does. She thrashes
underneath me. Her hands become fists that she punches
against the ground like a child having a tantrum. She twists and
turns, trying to buck me off of her.

Leaning my elbow firmly across her back to keep her as still
as I need her, I use my other hand to guide my cock between her
cheeks, sliding along the length of the crease, letting out a groan
as I do. I'm focused on her, but damn, she feels good. Just like
this, skin to skin. It's best this way. Even besides the restriction
the doctor gave for vaginal intercourse, it would feel wrong to be
inside her right now. But this is good. This feels right.

With my cock in place, I wrap that arm around her waist
and find the swollen bundle of nerves. Her breath draws in
ragged when I press against the spot, but she doubles down on
her attack against the ground, as if the idea of more pleasure is
even worse than the threat of pain.

Her body feels differently about it and is already primed for another orgasm. I increase the pressure on her clit, and at the same time, I begin to thrust, up and down, my cock cocooned between her ass cheeks. Already I feel the build, the buzz at the bottom of my spine, the tightening of my balls as I fuck, fuck, fuck. As I take out my emotions on her body. As I pour out my anger and my resentment and Jesus, my grief. So much fucking grief. I want it gone. The word repeats in my head with each thrust. Then I'm saying it out loud. "Gone, gone, gone, gone, gone."

I'm on the verge of release when Sabrina's body goes rigid. Her fingers claw into the ground. Her torso lifts as a moan rips slowly from her throat, a sort of bleating sound. Like a lost lamb crying for its mother. Like the mother in return crying for her child.

Then she's shivering and shaking, possessed with the power of her climax, and in fact, it feels like an exorcism the way it tears through her body. As though she's casting something out. As though she's retching up her pain instead of succumbing to pleasure.

And maybe that's why it's no surprise that her quivering turns to heaving and then she's sobbing. Wailing, really. A sound so unsettling that I'm instantly crying with her.

Abandoning my own orgasm—I've lost all interest, even if my dick hasn't—I roll off Sabrina then pull her into me, wrapping my arms tightly around her, wishing I could hold her tight enough that nothing could ever get to her without going through me first. Wishing I could guard her from any kind of harm and every kind of pain.

She clutches onto me in turn, burying her fingers into my sweater. We rock like this, back and forth, two drifters in a treacherous ocean, alone except for each other.

I kiss her face, my tears mingling with hers, never urging her to hush. "We're going to be okay," I tell her instead, and maybe even mean it. "We're going to be okay."

EIGHTEEN

I KEEP my eyes peeled on the elevator to the garage. As soon as I see Sabrina, I open the car door and scoot over to the other side of the backseat. She doesn't even slow her gait when she sees me. I guess she's not surprised.

"You're coming with me, I see," she says, when she climbs in the car.

"I didn't ask. That's not—"

She finishes for me. "Not how we do things. I know."

Yeah, she remembers. It was just me who fucked up and forgot. Since our weekend in the Poconos, I've been back to myself—making decisions for us, being assertive, crossing my usual lines. I didn't even think of asking if she wanted me at her doctor's appointment today. I'm going, and that's the end of it.

Instead of arguing or pouting, she laces her fingers in mine. "I'm glad you're here."

We still haven't discussed her reasons for keeping her pregnancy secret. She hasn't volunteered the information, and I haven't brought it up. We'll get there eventually. Her hand in mine feels like we're headed the right direction. *Baby steps.*

Without the baby.

My chest tightens and I squeeze her hand. "We're ready, Danny."

"You don't have anything this afternoon?" she asks after we're on the road.

"Nothing important." But I am still playing catch up. She made the right call, going back to work this week instead of spending another weekend in the mountains, but I insisted that neither of us stay at the office past six. And even though I cheated and have slipped in work at home after she's gone to sleep every night, I'm still behind more than I like to be.

"I could be caught up by Monday if I'm allowed to do a little work this weekend." She doesn't have to bat her lashes. Her tone gives the same effect.

She's getting back to herself too, it seems.

"We'll see what the doctor says." I lean in to kiss her, and she meets me halfway. I'd meant it to be a peck, but somehow our tongues start tangling and pretty soon my pants are feeling tight.

When my thoughts refuse to stop wondering what color panties she's wearing today, I force myself to pull away. I miss her though. Physically. I scoot an inch away, reducing temptation, and adjust myself.

She notices and smiles like she's holding a trump card. "Maybe we could negotiate. You let me work a bit, and then we...*don't work* for a bit."

"Or...we *don't work* a lot."

She laughs. "That's a change of tune. I thought you'd turned prude on me."

Did she really not notice all the long showers I'd been taking this week? It's nice to know that I'm not the only one suffering from the no-sex-while-she-recovers advice. Sure I've pampered her with my mouth and hands, but it's not what we both need. And our adventure in the woods, fulfilling as it was, understandably didn't scratch that itch.

"Soon," she says, reading the countdown in my eyes. She guesses my response and says it with me. "We'll see what the doctor says."

"Exactly."

We're still holding hands, and I don't want to break that connection, but I also don't want to walk into her OB/GYN office with a hard-on. So I use my free hand and open my voicemail text messages on my phone as a distraction. There are only a dozen unheard, since I've managed to make my way through most of them already. The first two are follow-ups to issues that have been resolved. The next is regarding creative, so I forward it to Nate. The fourth one is from an unknown number.

Hey, it's Holt Sebastian. Heard your wife was in the hospital. Just checking in to see if you're both fine.

I'm not surprised that Steele talked to his brother, but I am more than a little curious how Holt got a hold of my private number.

Sabrina must see the question in my expression. "What's wrong?"

"Oh...it's just that Sebastian guy again." *It was probably Simone.* In all the hubbub, I haven't given much thought to how I found her at the awards event. Or rather, who I'd found her with. Whether or not that relationship was an attempt to get close to me, it's probably a good idea that I remind her about her NDA.

"He's still badgering you for information?" Sabrina asks.

I'm still thinking about Simone so I don't think through my answer. "I'm sure that's what he really wants, but he's using you as an excuse. Wants to know how you're doing after the hospital."

Sabrina turns to look at me. "He knew? How did he know that?"

I hadn't told her where I was when I'd heard she was in the hospital. That would require explaining why I'd gone looking for her that night, how I'd found the picture of the ultrasound. If we weren't on our way to an appointment, this might be a good lead into the conversation that needs to be had.

As it is, I'll have to find a way to deflect.

Fortune smiles on me when my phone starts buzzing in my hand with an incoming call.

Then I check the caller ID. **Raymond Kincaid.** So maybe it's not fortune smiling.

"You could ignore it," Sabrina says, seeing the name over my shoulder.

I could, but I do need the excuse not to answer her question. Though, considering my luck lately, there's every chance he's calling to say he heard about Sabrina's visit to the hospital as well since he runs in the same crowds as the Sebastians. How likely is that?

I debate back and forth and finally decide to answer on the fifth ring. "Make it quick. I'm on my way to an appointment."

Getting to the point is a skill I learned from my father, so he does just that. "I need you to make an investment."

"Investment?" Sabrina whispers. She must be able to hear him as well.

I repeat her question into the phone.

"Temporarily, if you prefer. I'm about to land Manova Tech."

King-Kincaid has been trying to get Manova Tech to invest with them since I was in college. In other words, this is a big fish. The stakes of this call are high. "That's fantastic," I say evenly. "What's that got to do with me?"

"He's never liked our ratio of high to low risk stocks in our portfolio. You know how some people get about our aggressive position."

"Yes, I know." Aggressive is actually a gentle term. It's one reason why I don't personally invest in King-Kincaid myself. The excuse I gave when we started Reach, though, was that it was best to diversify. I already have stocks in my father's business. I've kept the rest of my money elsewhere. Weston has too, though I think his reasons have more to do with his morals than with his business acumen.

"But recently we had another player wanting to invest big in low-risk stocks. Not the kind of deal we usually take, but it was a sizable amount and the man has a name. When we realized how our portfolio would balance out with his money, we went to Manova Tech, and they're finally on board."

"Let me guess. The other player changed his mind. Who is it?"

"Eh, he's dragging his feet anyway. A Sebastian, believe it or not. One of the kids. Holt."

"Holt Sebastian?" I glance at Sabrina to see if she's still listening.

"He's poking around," she whispers. "No way he's serious about investing."

My thoughts exactly. Which means Dad will lose Manova Tech too without finding someone else to make the same sort of investment. "So you're looking for me to put in some money to make the portfolio look pretty for your new potential client."

"We might have told Manova that the money was already invested," he admits.

Of course he did. Because that's the kind of shady dealing my father's into.

"How much did you say was invested?" I'm not saying yes. I'm just curious.

"Twenty."

"Million?" I glance again at Sabrina. Not because I need her permission or her advice, but I don't know. I'm curious what she thinks.

She mouths, "Yikes." But then shrugs, leaving the problem to me.

It's a problem that shouldn't be so complicated. It's a lot of money, but it's low-risk, and my father lacks scruples, but he's good at what he does. It wouldn't take much work on my part. A quick call to my finance guy, and he'd get it done. And I already have money with King-Kincaid. It's not like this is a radical financial move.

Probably the most compelling reason to say yes is that it's easier than saying no. There would be drama. There would be arguing. It wouldn't be said out loud, but he'd take it as a personal rejection. This is how love works for my father. Favors. Back scratching. Quid pro quo.

I guess I've learned that from him too because him asking me feels like affection.

But I can't help thinking about what Holt said the other day, maybe only because his name came up in the conversation and his message is sitting on my phone, but it's blaring in my head all the same. How I'm not entangled with my father's business like he is. It feels like a lie. The drive in my safe, the stocks in his company, the shared DNA—they may be all the connections I have with Raymond, but they have the weight of an anchor. How much heavier will it feel if I do this favor for him now?

"Look, I'm in a hurry with this, Donovan. We're meeting with Manova first thing Monday. I'd like to wrap this up by end of day."

The car slows, and I realize we're pulling to the curb at the medical center. Saved by our arrival. "I'm at my appointment," I tell my father. "I'll have to give you a call back."

I hang up without giving him a chance to talk. Then I turn my phone off and slip it in my pocket before turning to Sabrina. "Ready?"

"Yeah. Let's go."

We hold hands on the way to the office, and I even remember to let her lead the way so she doesn't realize I've already seen both a map and videos of the center when Ferris brought her previous visits to my attention. The check-in process is tedious, and the waiting room full of women—many of whom are visibly pregnant—is unexpectedly sombering. My gaze lands on a mother cooing at a baby so tiny it can't be more than a few days old. I stare for a handful of seconds, wondering what it feels like to be responsible for something so small. What it feels like to be so unconditionally loved.

There's a pinching in my chest, and I look away only to find Sabrina's also watching the new mother. I can't read her expression, but I know this can't be easy for her. This whole situation is cruel. She shouldn't have to wait out here, a witness to all these happy endings that weren't hers.

"I'm getting us into a room," I say, standing up.

Sabrina pulls at my jacket. "No! Sit down."

Ignoring her, I make my way to the desk, ready to complain. Sabrina follows on my heels. "Donovan! Stop. It's not our turn. This is fine. We'll be called soon."

"Yes, hi," I say when the receptionist asks what she can do for us. "My wife has just been through a traumatic experience. Waiting out here with, um..." I turn to gesture to the scene behind me. "It's unacceptable. Can we get into a room? The name's Kincaid."

At least the receptionist—Bonnie, her name tag says—looks mortified. Whether it's on my behalf or Sabrina's, I'm not so sure.

"Kincaid, you said?" She types on her keyboard and studies her computer screen then smiles with relief. "She's actually next. They should be calling you back any minute."

Before I can argue that that minute needs to be now, a door opens and a scrub-clad technician steps out. "Sabrina?"

"See?" Sabrina hisses as we walk toward the technician.

I'm not so sure it wasn't because of me that we've been called back, but I keep my mouth shut, just happy to be out of that waiting room.

The next few minutes are spent with the normal doctor office shit. They take Sabrina's weight and temperature and check her blood pressure. The technician gets a brief account of the reason for our visit then gives Sabrina a gown, promising the doctor will be in shortly before she leaves.

"Hot," I say when Sabrina's changed, mostly to lighten the mood. It's heavier than it's been the last few days, which seems strange considering the worst has passed. Maybe it's being forced to face what happened instead of sidestepping it as we have been. Maybe it's fear that there's more bad news to come.

The humor seems to work. She smirks in my direction. "Behave."

"Or what?"

"Or I'll send you back to the waiting room."

I manage not to shudder. "You might have the power here, Sabrina, but just remember who's in charge when we're out the door."

She actually does shiver, and since that's the exact moment that the doctor walks in, she blushes as well. "Hi, Sabrina," the doctor says, her tone solemn. "I've read the reports from the hospital. How are you doing?"

Sabrina takes a deep breath. "Hanging in."

The doctor turns to me. "Radhika Khatri."

"Donovan Kincaid." I take her outstretched hand.

"Glad you can be here today to support Sabrina." I try not to make anything of her statement. Try not to assume she's chiding me for not being here on previous visits. I don't exactly succeed.

But she's moved on from me, and she's focused entirely on my wife, as she should be. She gets another recount from Sabrina, briefer than before since Dr. Khatri has already read the tech's notes as well as the hospital notes.

"Let's do an exam and see how you're healing. Since you've stopped bleeding, I'm sure everything is fine. Miscarriages in the first trimester are very normal, unfortunately. Any questions before we begin?"

Both Sabrina and I answer at the same time. "How soon can we start—"

"Having sex," Sabrina says while I say, "Trying again."

Same thing, I suppose. I glance at her, but she doesn't return my gaze.

"It's probably safe to resume sex again now," Dr. Khatri says, "but I recommend using condoms until you have your next period. Longer, if you feel like you aren't ready emotionally. It's also very natural to need some time before trying to get pregnant again." She looks at me. Pointedly? Not sure. "How about I look at you, and we can go from there."

Dr. Khatri starts by feeling Sabrina's abdomen. "Uterus is still enlarged," she says. "Which is normal."

Once again, I'm surprised how I missed my wife's changing body. It's obvious looking at her now, how her belly is slightly swollen, how her skin is tight across her midriff.

"I'm going to do an ultrasound. You didn't have one at the hospital?"

Sabrina shakes her head. "Only one I've had was with you."

She's still not looking at me, and I realize now that, if I had asked, she might not have given me permission to come today. Here, she can't hide how much she knew about her pregnancy before the miscarriage.

And as much as I hate myself for it, there's a sour taste of resentment in my mouth. For me, the baby was gone before I had a chance to love it. I didn't get to be excited while Dr. Khatri poured ultrasound jelly across Sabrina's stomach, waiting to see life on the screen. Now the doctor has the screen facing only her, which feels like a kindness. Sabrina denied me the good part.

Fuck. I don't want to be this way. Not right now.

I swallow the emotion down and reach out to take Sabrina's hand. She's still only looking at the doctor, but she bends her fingers around mine. We're still good.

"You said you bled for several days," Dr. Khatri clarifies. "And you passed fetal material?"

Sabrina nods. "At the hospital."

"The doctor had a chance to examine it?"

There's something she's trying to find out, something she's blatantly not saying. My entire body goes tense. "What's wrong, Dr.?"

She doesn't answer me, waiting for Sabrina's answer instead. "Yes, the doctor, um, retrieved it from the toilet. Is there something wrong?"

"No, actually. I think, Sabrina, that you might have been pregnant with twins."

Finally, Sabrina looks at me. Just to exchange a glance before we both look inquisitively toward the obstetrician. "What are you saying?" Sabrina asks.

But I think I already understand. That cloak of darkness that's pressed down on us for the last two weeks starts to lift.

"I'm saying..." Dr. Khatri turns the screen toward us, showing rather than telling. There right in front of us, is a tiny form with a large head and dancing toothpick limbs. "You're still pregnant."

NINETEEN

"YOU DIDN'T SEE both babies on the ultrasound the first time?" Cade asks, the exact same question Nate asked when I called him.

"Nope." I gloss over the fact that I wasn't present at the first ultrasound. "Apparently, it's not uncommon. Especially when the ultrasound is performed before twelve weeks, which it was. The doctor thinks that the other baby was probably not thriving, and may have even already passed by the time of the first ultrasound, which was why they didn't hear two heartbeats. She said sometimes one twin absorbs the other and people don't even know they were ever pregnant with more than one baby until one day someone discovers they have an extra kidney."

"Damn. That's weird." He lets the news settle. Clears his throat. "That's...wow. I don't know what to say. Congrats or I'm sorry?"

"I know, I know. It's a lot of up and down." I try not to dwell on the negative. "Anyway, the doctor thinks there isn't any risk to the surviving baby, but she'll treat this like a twin pregnancy and do extra monitoring to be sure. Everything looked really good today. Strong heartbeat, development on schedule. Due a couple of weeks before Christmas."

"And Sabrina's okay?"

I glance toward the stairs just as the woman in question walks down them. "Yeah, she's...good."

Realizing she's being talked about, she smiles, though it doesn't quite seem to reach her eyes.

"Tired, I think. Like I said, it's been a lot." I move the phone from my mouth. "Cade," I whisper in Sabrina's direction.

"Ah. And yes. I'm tired." She plops down on the couch, mirroring her sentiment.

"There's a lot more of that to come," Cade says. "For both of you." His daughter Devyn is now a year and a half old, so he's speaking from experience. "Worth it, though. You might even feel moved to get a tattoo."

"No fucking way, and you cheated." He's talking about the bet he lost. My prize was getting to choose his next tattoo. I chose *I Love D*. Then the asshole changed the D into Devyn, and now the joke is totally ruined.

Fucker.

But I'm not really annoyed. Not right now. I'm walking on air, cliché as that sounds, literally pacing back and forth because I'm so buoyant. For once, I understand what the statement is trying to express. My body feels lighter than it's ever felt. The normal everyday burdens, old baggage, heartaches that never fully healed—all of that weight is negated by the joy of today's news.

Cade hears it in my voice. "You sound really happy, D. Congratulations."

"Thank you. I am." I take a beat to think about all he and I have gone through and how far we've come. When we first met back in Tokyo, we'd both been running away from the women we thought would never love us the way we loved them. And now we're fucking family men.

I'm not getting teary-eyed or anything, but I do have to swallow before I speak again, and it's definitely time to get off the phone.

I wrap things up quickly, then go behind the couch so I can bend down and wrap my arms around Sabrina. "Good talk with Audrey? Was she surprised?"

While I'd been in the living room, making my calls, Sabrina had been upstairs on the phone with her sister. Audrey is her only living family, and she's also a recent mother, so of course that was the first person Sabrina wanted to talk to. She went directly upstairs as soon as we got home.

"Yeah, well. Yeah. She wondered if twins run in the family."

"Hm. Hadn't thought of that." I prefer thinking that it has something to do with the strength of my sperm, but considering that Audrey has twins, maybe Sabrina's genetics makes more sense.

Nah. I like my reasoning better.

I kiss Sabrina on the cheek, then nuzzle my face into her neck. "Are you hungry?"

"Eh..." She shrugs.

She's probably not in the mood to have to decide what's for dinner. Luckily, I've already taken care of it. "I thought something celebratory was in order, but since you can't have sushi, I ordered from Gaston's." I straighten and start for the kitchen, calling over my shoulder. "I can make you a plate. Oh, and I have sparkling cider since you can't have alcohol."

"Is it okay if we wait? I'm not hungry yet."

"Sure. I already have it in the warmer. Are you feeling sick?" She'd told the doctor that she hadn't had much morning sickness, but that sometimes she got a little queasy in the evening if it had been a long time since she'd eaten. "I'll get you some saltines—"

"No, not sick. Just not hungry."

I turn back to her, ready to remind her that she shouldn't go too long without eating, but she beats me to it. "I snacked on trail mix while I was talking to Audrey. I'm fine."

"Okay, okay." I let it go but make a mental note to fix her a plate in half an hour or so.

Meanwhile...

"Audrey wasn't surprised about the twins or that you're still pregnant? Weston actually guessed we'd have twins." He rightly assumed I was virile. This was the first he was hearing anything about it, though, since I'd been too wrapped up in Sabrina to reach out and tell him about the miscarriage when it happened. "Nate, on the other hand...I could practically hear his jaw drop." He, of course, had known everything since he was the one who covered us at the office when we took time off.

"You already talked to both of them? And Cade?"

"Oh, shit. Did you want to tell them together? We can call them again, if you want."

"No, that's fine. I just wondered if we should wait."

"Why wait? We're already three months along."

"Yeah. Good point." Her eyes land on a bottle of water on the coffee table. I grabbed it earlier, planning to take it up to her, and never got around to it.

Before she can reach for it herself, I get it and hand it to her, sitting next to her as I do. "Did you get to talk to Dylan?"

She takes a sip of the water. "No, just Audrey."

"Oh, good. I get to tell him." I pull my phone out from my pocket—I swear it still feels warm from my last call—and open up my contacts.

"Donovan, it's late there."

"Right, right." Weston had already chided when I'd called him, because it was approaching eleven in France, and that was half an hour ago now. I should have called Dylan right then and waited on Cade and Nate.

Still, if Sabrina just got off the phone with Audrey, maybe Dylan's still awake too.

"He's asleep," she says, likely realizing where my thoughts are since I'm still holding my phone. "And sleep is precious with babies, so let him have it."

"Okay, okay. Tomorrow." I'm just about to put my phone away again when it rings. I glance down, excited about who else I might be able to share the news with, until I see it's my father's name on the ID. "Raymond."

"Might as well tell him too." I'm probably imagining the sourness to her tone. Then she seems to remember. "Oh, he's calling about your investment, isn't he?"

I waffle about answering. "That's all he'll want to talk about, and I'm not interested right now."

"You don't have to take it."

It feels strange sending my father to voicemail, but I do, and strangely the world doesn't shatter. Knowing he'll call again, I turn my phone off and pocket it.

Then I lean to the side so I can look at my wife, truly study her, for the first time since we arrived home. She said she's tired, and she looks it. She's growing a human being inside her, so that's to be expected.

But something else is going on that I haven't quite put a finger on.

She was quiet when the doctor told us we were still pregnant, which I attributed to shock. On the car ride too, now that I think about it, but I was excited enough that I hadn't noticed. Then she went upstairs immediately to talk to Audrey. Now that all the news sharing is on pause, I can see that she's not just tired—she's somber.

Fuck, of course she's still somber.

Immediately, I feel guilty. This is a happy occasion, yes, but there's still grief. We're having a baby, but we lost one too. One doesn't cancel out the other.

I take her hand in mine. "We'll make sure this baby knows about their twin. We won't forget. I promise."

"I know." She squeezes my hand and gives me that same smile she gave earlier, the one that doesn't reach her eyes.

There's something else.

I'm about to ask, but then it hits me. All the puzzle pieces from the last couple of months come together—why she'd been secretive. Why she hadn't told me. Why she told Elizabeth we were still deciding about children when she was already pregnant. Why she's so white-faced and solemn. How did I not see it before?

"You don't want it."

Her head whips in my direction, her face even more pale. "Donovan..." She shakes her head ever so slightly, and I'm not sure if she means to refute my statement or acknowledge it, but I know as sure as I've known anything that I'm right.

I withdraw my hand from hers. "You can't say it, but you can't deny it, can you?"

"It's...complicated."

Complicated.

Actually, it's quite simple. Plain as day. I just didn't see it because I didn't want to see it.

Now I can't see anything else.

Sabrina places her hand on my thigh. Her usually warm touch feels cold, and I pull away. "Donovan," she says again.

"Don't." My name is not what I want to hear from her. I stand because I need distance, and I'm too upset to sit. Specifically, I feel mad and betrayed. There's so much red in front of my eyes, I can't see straight. I should take this feeling and go upstairs. Hit the treadmill. Take a shower. Anything other than pursue this conversation while I'm in this headspace. Because I know Sabrina. I know her heart. I know the things I'm thinking are tainted with this anger. Any questions I have will come out mean, and she deserves my patience. Deserves a chance to explain.

But haven't I been patient? Hasn't she already had a chance to explain? There's too much emotion built up inside, and the accusation comes out on its own accord. "Were you planning to get rid of it?"

She stands immediately in defense. "No! Never! Are you seriously asking me that? How could you ever think that I would do that?"

I don't want to think it. I don't want to think any of this, but her silence has given little guidance on what's going on in her head, and now that the thought trail has begun, I can't stop myself from following it all the way. "So you were just waiting and hoping something would happen on its own then." I feel the razor on the words as they pass my lips. "You must have thought you got lucky for a minute."

She looks like I've slapped her in the face. "That's cruel. And not true. My heart's broken."

The quiver in her voice hits me in the gut, but I refuse to feel the pain. Like when I'm in the office, and I press the button to turn the clear glass opaque so I can hide myself away. I hit that imaginary button inside me now and shut myself off from her emotions, intent on getting to the truth. "That's why you didn't tell me."

"I was going to tell you. I just needed time."

"To what? Make sure you had to?"

"Time to process."

"You needed ten weeks? Ten whole weeks, working beside me, sleeping beside me, letting me stay in the dark while the clock ticked on." It's the first time I've let on that I knew before the hospital. "That's right, I knew. And I know you kept it secret for that long."

She sets her jaw, her lips pursed together, and crosses her arms over her chest protectively.

"Yeah, you thought you covered your tracks. Surprise. Ferris clocks your first doctor visit at the end of April. That's when you found out you were pregnant, wasn't it?"

"This isn't fair," she says.

But I'm chasing this theory to the end. "And you didn't say a thing. You went back a month later for an ultrasound. You saw our child, heard its heartbeat for the first time."

"You don't know what you're talking about, Donovan."

"By yourself," I say, ignoring her.

"I wanted you there."

"And you didn't say a goddamned word. Because you needed to *process*? You want to tell me why, Sabrina?"

"Because this!" Her hands fly out in front of her, open in my direction. "Because you!"

A beat passes, and all I can say is, "Me."

"This...this stuff you do. The controlling and the stalking and the obsessing. How you decide everything that happens. You moved me in without asking. You sprung a wedding on me with no proposal. You decide." She's throwing the last two years of our relationship at me, and I'm still trying to figure out how to react, when she lands a real blow. "Tell me the truth—did you switch out my birth control with placebos?"

"What? No. Is that what you assumed?"

She shrugs. "Why would I have any idea?"

"Is that what this has all been about? You should have just asked."

"I shouldn't have to ask." Animosity seeps from every part of her. It's in her tone, in her stance, in her eyes.

And wall up or not, it hits.

It hits, and it hurts, and it fucking pisses me off. Because the issues she's bringing up aren't just confined to an incident or two. She's talking about the very nature of our relationship. She's talking about shit that I tried to protect her from when I pushed her away. "You know who I am, Sabrina. You knew when you married me."

"Yes, I did. I do."

"And all of a sudden it's not what you signed up for?" I laid everything on the table for her when she found that folder in my desk drawer. And now she's acting like she was blindsided?

"I didn't say that. I didn't. Are you listening to me?"

I'm pacing, walking out this energy before I slam my fist through a wall. Turning back to face her, I give her the floor. "Go ahead. Talk."

"This works for me." She takes a step toward me. "Okay? I'm not saying that it doesn't. This is what I wanted. *You* are who I wanted."

Her use of past tense doesn't go unnoticed. I steel myself for the rest. "But...?"

She swallows, and her face contorts like she's trying to make her next words gentle. Like she's trying to cushion a blow. "But I never considered what this arrangement would be like for someone else. For a child."

I somehow manage to stay standing. "Good enough for you, but not a child. I see."

"Do you?" Her gentleness is gone. "Have you thought it through? Are you going to have our kids' schedules memorized too? Will you have a PI follow them when they come home too late? Will they only realize you love them when they find you have a fucking file on them in a drawer?

"And what about the example our relationship will give to our kids? Will our son think it's okay to install cameras in his girlfriend's apartment? Will our daughter think that her husband gets to dominate every aspect of her life? Because that's not okay, Donovan. None of this is normal."

Ouch.

Like a motherfucking grenade going off in my heart.

"Wow." My voice comes out flat, surprising considering how wrecked I am inside. "I didn't realize you've been harboring such resentment about our marriage. Guess that's another secret you've been keeping. You're really racking them up."

Sabrina covers her hands with her face, and it's only now I realize that she's crying. "I'm not resentful. That's not what I'm saying."

"You just said we aren't normal. You just said the way we are is not okay."

"I didn't mean for *us*. I meant..."

"...what? Say it."

She sighs. "I consented to this, Donovan. Our children did not."

The truth is out now, her secrets and doubts out in the air, and if I were another man, I could tell her what she wants to hear, that we can fix this. I can be what I need to be for our kids. I can change. I can be who she needs me to be.

But I'm not that man. Which is the whole problem. Which was always the problem. If I'd been born to a different family, if I'd had a different dad, if a different swimmer had been the first one to my mother's egg... "I feel fairly positive that children rarely consent to being born."

"God, you're so frustrating," Sabrina says, throwing her head back. When she lifts it again, she tries pleading with me. "I just needed time. I needed to figure out what our lives looked like with a baby. That is all."

Part of me wants to pull her in my arms, tell her we'll work it out, that I'm on her side.

The other part of me is too fucking devastated.

Guess which one wins?

"So you decided to figure it all out on your own." I take several steps until I'm right in her face. "We're married, Sabrina. You're supposed to share these things with me. We're supposed to figure it out together."

She straightens, tears trailing down her face. "Really? I guess I forgot the rules are different for me than they are for you."

"For someone who isn't resentful, you sure have a lot of

biting comments at the ready." Hypocritical, I know. Everything that comes out of my mouth is loaded, and I don't see that changing anytime soon. To steal her words, I need time to process.

I decide to do what I should have done to begin with. "Dinner's in the warmer," I remind her as I button my jacket. "Don't forget about it. I'll be home late." I head to the foyer.

"Where are you going?"

"The Grand Havana," I say over my shoulder. "Nate's there. I'd like to smoke a cigar with someone who thinks our news is worth celebrating."

Then asshole that I am, I leave, slamming the door behind me.

TWENTY

THIRTEEN YEARS *ago*

I SAT down on the bench, setting the bottle of bourbon at my side, and leaned back against the building. The metal was cold against my skin, even through my pants, despite the electric heaters. First weekend of December in New York. It was to be expected. Probably why I was the only person out there, which worked for me. To be alone was the entire reason I'd come up to the roof in the first place.

Now that I was out here, though, the quiet was deafening. Inside, at least, the noise of people delivering well wishes and sympathies drowned out the thoughts in my head. Both options were torture.

Trying not to think anything at all, I pulled the pack of ciga-rettes and lighter from my suit jacket pocket and lit one up. The first drag settled me. Weird how I'd already gotten used to them when I'd only been smoking for a total of a day and a half. I didn't even cough anymore. The taste, on the other hand, was still nasty as fuck.

But what was worse? Focusing on the dirty ashtray in my mouth or thinking about Amanda. What I'd done to her. Why I'd done it.

Because I couldn't stop.

No other reason. I was a monster. I deserved to feel like it, and boy did I. Already halfway to drunk, I picked up the bottle and took a swig. Then I poured out some on the rooftop next to me—a glass for the dead, even though Amanda had never touched anything harder than a wine cooler. It was the thought, anyway.

To the right of me, I heard the door open. *Fuck.* So much for being alone.

Maybe whoever it was would want solitude as well. I refused to look over, hoping that the law of no eye contact means no invitation to talking would hold true.

But alas.

"Thought I'd find you out here," Dylan said. Dylan was Amanda's stepfather. He probably thought he had more right to being mournful than I did, and I didn't have it in me to pretend at the moment, so I still didn't look up.

At least it wasn't Weston. He was both eager to comfort me and also to avoid all talk of emotions, which basically meant all he'd done all week was try to get me laid.

How fucking lucky to be able to lose yourself in sex.

As for myself, I didn't think I'd be able to lose myself in anything—or anyone—ever again.

"Mind if I join you?" Apparently, ignoring him hadn't been a big enough hint.

I poured back another swig, then capped the bottle. "Suit yourself."

He stood next to the bench, doing who the hell knew what. Staring into the distance like I was, perhaps. I really didn't care, as long as he was quiet, which he was.

Until he wasn't. "Cold out here. I told Ellen that the heaters wouldn't be enough."

I shrugged. I hated small talk even under the best of circumstances, and I definitely didn't want to small talk about the mother of the woman I'd basically killed. If Ellen knew my involvement, she'd never be able to look at me again.

"I don't know how you can stand it," Dylan went on.

I shot him a glare. "You could go back inside."

He almost smiled. "Fair enough." A beat passed, and I went back to staring at nothing, back to willing the buzz in my brain to shut the fuck up. Then Dylan piped up again. "Do you have a light I can borrow?"

I passed over my lighter without looking at him, half expecting to ask if he could bum a smoke too, since as long as I'd known him, I'd never once seen him with a cigarette. Granted, I'd known him for less time than I'd known his stepdaughter, and that had only been a couple of years. Maybe he was the type who smoked under stress.

Maybe I was that type too.

Except he didn't ask for anything else. I heard the flick of the lighter, then a minute later, the scent of cedar and cranberry wafted past me. The Marlboros I had certainly didn't smell like that.

I glanced over to find he had a cigar, not a cigarette. When I did, I made the grave error of making eye contact.

Fuck my life.

"I didn't realize you smoked," he said, because of course he took that as permission to have a conversation.

I considered another shitty retort, but honestly, at this point, it was easier just to talk. "Just started."

"Enjoying it?"

I stared at the cigarette in my hand that was now really just a butt, then tossed it to the ground. "Not really."

It had been an impulse, grabbing the full pack that someone had left at The Keep, along with the bourbon before getting on the train into New York for the funeral. If someone had left a bottle of oxy, I probably would have nabbed that too. I was willing to try anything that had the potential to stop the thoughts and dull the pain. Maybe I'd even get shit faced enough to try Weston's method of escape.

Or maybe not.

I started to pull out another cigarette, but Dylan reached his hand toward me. "Try this."

Not really interested, I took the cigar from him and brought it to my lips.

"Don't pull it in like you do a cigarette. Just bring it into your mouth, let the flavor settle, then blow it back out."

I did as he said and had to admit it was a much more pleasant experience than the cigarettes.

He must have read the look on my face. "Keep it. I have another."

I watched as he went through the business of lighting a new cigar, then I passed him the bottle of bourbon. One offering deserved another and all.

He took a swallow and passed it back. "I heard you tell someone in there you were engaged?"

No. I did not want to talk about this.

Again, Dylan read me. "Sorry. You don't have to—"

"Not officially," I said, cutting him off. "Your wife has the ring. I gave it to her earlier today."

"Ah, she hasn't mentioned it yet. But I guess it's been hectic." The funeral and the grief and all the friends and family and a two-year-old to take care of on top of it—hectic was an understatement. "Are you sure you don't want to keep it for yourself?"

"I'm sure." No way did I want to see it again. Amanda and I chose it together months ago. I'd planned to give it to her for Christmas, in front of her family, because it was mostly for them. As far as we'd been concerned, we were already engaged.

Well, until recently, anyway.

But then we'd started drifting apart. It was her second year at Harvard. I'd chosen to stay there for my master's, despite the benefits of going elsewhere, so we could be together, and yet it felt like things had shifted. She'd pulled away. The more it seemed like I was losing her, the more I'd tried to hold on.

Then that fight, the one we'd had only two weeks before. *You're invasive. Like black mold. A disease. If there's any hope for us, you'll stop.*

Stop obsessing, she meant. Stop hovering. Stop invading. Stop trying to keep her.

But I couldn't stop. I'd had her followed, and when she'd realized it, she'd driven into the opposite traffic lane in an attempt to lose the PI.

Now she was dead, and it was all my fault.

Part of me wanted to admit it to everyone, wanted to take

the blame for what I'd done. The smarter part of me knew how to keep shit quiet. The PI had accepted the substantial payment I'd given him, and I didn't intend to ever work with him again. In time, maybe it would be easier not to think about it all the time.

"It gets better," Dylan said, as if he could read my mind.

Rage surged through me, an almost pleasant reprieve from the mourning. "Fuck you very much. Look, what Amanda and I were to each other doesn't mean it's your responsibility to play father to me. You can take your cigar back if that's what this was about."

"I've got ten years on you, Donovan. That's all. I know you're grieving, but that doesn't give you permission to be an asshole." In truth, he'd been more big brother than stepfather to Amanda too. She'd never have taken him seriously if he'd tried to pull off anything else. "Anyway, I was saying it for myself."

I wasn't going to apologize.

But after a beat passed, I asked, "Do you believe it?"

"That it will get better?" He glanced toward the building, and I wondered what specific details were going through his head. Ellen, as to be expected, wasn't taking her daughter's death well. She was cold and distant, barely even acknowledging her toddler's existence, leaving Aaron's care all to Dylan and the nanny. Not that I blamed her. And it had only been a week. That wasn't enough time to decide how things would be in the future.

Yet I'd already decided, hadn't I?

"No, I really don't think it will." Apparently, Dylan had decided as well. "Is that overly morose?"

I pulled on the cigar, considering. "Might just be realistic."

"Right? Because a week ago, I lived in a world where the

worst thing that could happen had never happened. Sure, I'd think about it on occasion. But it was a passing worry. More like a game. 'What if something happened to someone I loved?' And then I'd mentally plan what I'd say at the funeral and what songs I'd want played, and I'd feel vindicated about everyone who had ever done me wrong when they showed up and said how sorry they were for me. Then I'd feel terrible for imagining such a morbid scene and making it all about me, but that was the luxury I had because the worst thing had never happened before.

"And now the worst thing *has* happened. It's real. Now I live in a world where the worst things happen, and it's like discovering there's no Santa Claus. It's not something you can ever unknow. The magic is gone. No one is safe. There is no happily ever after. There just isn't."

"That's, um. Really fucking bleak."

"Mm." He exhaled, the cigar smoke amplified by his warm breath in the cold air. "Sorry, I suppose."

He was right though. More right than he even knew because, for me, it wasn't just one worst thing that had happened, but a culmination of worst things. Amanda's death, that it was my fault, and then before that, when she'd practically ended things. When she'd given the ultimatum. When she'd said, *No one can live like this, Donovan. This isn't love.*

I was the worst thing that could happen for Amanda.

My love was the worst thing that could happen.

So Dylan was wrong too. The bleak world he spoke about was one that believed we were powerless to bad shit happening, and maybe there was some truth to that, but there was something I could do about it.

"I'm never going to love anyone again," I said, now drunk

enough to speak my vow out loud. I held up the bourbon to enunciate my declaration, then took another swig to seal the deal.

Dylan studied me thoughtfully. "Yeah, maybe. You're young yet, though. You might change your mind."

"Keep saying shit like that, and I'm going to go back to insulting your age."

"Touché."

"And I'm not changing my mind." I wouldn't, and it wasn't about fear of a broken heart or that bullshit. I would not inflict my damage on another person like that. I'd already proven that I couldn't change who I was, so this was the answer instead. I wouldn't let anyone close. I would not be the worst thing that happened to somebody else.

It wasn't like anyone could love a man like me, anyway. Wasn't that what Amanda had meant?

"Okay, then." He didn't even sound like he doubted me this time. "But you can't say I'm the only one who's bleak."

"I accept that." We fell back into silence, and as much as I'd wanted it earlier, it felt heavier now. Felt like I'd made it heavier for Dylan as well, and maybe that was just how things would be from now on. I'd make life heavier for everyone around me. Maybe I always had.

Motherfucking bleak.

"These cigars, though," I said, holding up the one bright spot in a very dark night.

"These cigars," he agreed. "See, you said you wouldn't fall in love again, and I venture that you just did."

"Yeah, yeah. Whatever you say, old man."

He chuckled, then immediately stopped. As if he'd been

surprised. "I didn't know I could still do that," he mused. "Maybe things do get better."

He still had a wife and a kid and a solidly settled life, so for him, maybe yeah.

For me, though.

Well, like I'd said, I wasn't changing my mind.

TWENTY-ONE

PRESENT

MY HEAD IS POUNDING when I wake up the next morning. Or maybe it's closer to afternoon since the sun seems awfully high in the sky when I peel back the curtain in the guest room. The lights had been out throughout the apartment when I came home last night, and as much as I had wanted to look in on Sabrina, it felt like I was proving something by leaving her alone. I'd even considered not coming home at all, sleeping instead on Nate's couch or getting a room at the Four Seasons, just to show that I could do it. That I could give her the space that a "normal" husband could give a wife.

Whether I was trying to prove it to myself or her, I'm not sure.

I'd come home, in the end, because I'd run away from her before, and I'm not allowed to do that again. My rule, not hers.

We can fight, but I'm here to deal with it. Going out with Nate may have bordered on breaking that rule, but there has to be room in that agreement for cooling down. For her sake as well as mine.

All that to say, it wasn't that long that I was away from her, and probably didn't prove anything. Honestly, the only thing I think last night determined is that I'm getting to an age where my body feels the scotch in the morning. Not that I usually indulge like that, but it's good to take note.

It's also likely that the reason I feel like shit this morning has nothing to do with the alcohol and cigars. My head is definitely suffering from a hangover, but it's more than that. My insides feel twisted and there's a weight on my chest that seems immovable.

And why wouldn't I feel like shit? The reasons are numerous.

My wife is conflicted about her pregnancy with our child.

She thinks I'm not fit to be a father.

And my great fear that no one could love a man like me feels once again validated.

No one *should* love a man like me, anyway. Especially not someone as deserving of happiness as Sabrina.

On top of all that, it's been at least twelve hours since I've checked in on her via any method including physically, surveillance camera, text message, or the app that tracks her on my phone. There's a very good chance I'm going through withdrawal.

There's also a very good chance that Sabrina doesn't know I haven't run. The door's shut, and I'm a fairly light sleeper. If she'd come looking for me in here, I think I would have heard her.

It's for her sake that I sit up, carefully since my head is spinning, and reach for my cell on the bedside table. I'd turned it back on when I'd left the apartment, then turned on the Do Not Disturb, which took more strength than I knew I'd had, and now I'm a bit antsy to check all my messages.

As to be expected, it's dead.

Note to self: buy extra phone chargers for the guest room.

I reach next for my watch and find that it's after ten. I can't remember the last time I slept that long. It was fitful sleep, and I probably needed the extra hours. But now I definitely need to track down my wife so I can fix all of this, if it's even fixable—by promising that I'll be someone different, that I'll be the man she needs me to be, that I'll change. Whatever it takes to make her feel like this baby isn't a mistake.

Because it can't be a mistake.

And I can't lose her. I can't lose either of them. I *won't* lose them.

Committed to my decision, I drag myself out of bed and out of the guest room. In the hall, the apartment is just as quiet as it was last night, and I wonder if Sabrina also slept in. Now I feel guilty. She probably tossed and turned as much as I did. Maybe not checking in had been the wrong decision.

But when I get to our bedroom and open the door, she's not there. What's more, the bed's made, and God love that woman, but Sabrina has not once, since I've known her, made her bed.

Guilt turns to panic. *No, no, no, no, no.*

My hangover is instantly pushed to the bottom of my awareness, and I go into detective mode. A quick inspection of our room and closet doesn't seem to indicate anything's gone, which makes me feel marginally better, until I discover her toothbrush isn't in the bathroom.

If she left, she would have told me. There's no note anywhere. Did she call?

Fucking dead phone.

I plug it in by our bed, then grab the cordless, and after I dial her number, take it with me so I can search the rest of the house. While it rings, I check out my office. No note there. I head downstairs just as I get her voicemail.

God fucking dammit.

I hit redial and do a sweep of the main floor. Her purse is gone. Her house key. Still no note, and my call again goes to voicemail.

Back upstairs, I find my cell has enough charge that I can turn it on, as long as I keep it plugged in. After an eternity, it's on. I turn off the Do Not Disturb, and while I wait for text messages to come in, I scan my visual voicemail. There's one from Nate that I save for later. Several from my father that I flat out ignore.

Then finally, one from Sabrina. Left shortly before midnight.

I, um. I need my sister right now so I got a red eye to London. We're good Donovan, okay? We are. But I could use some space to...I don't know. Get used to our new reality, I guess. Please consider waiting until Monday to come after me.

I listen to it after I read it. Twice. To see if I can hear anything in her voice that isn't present in her words, but the sound of her voice just makes me feel more desperate.

And pissed.

"So I stick around, and you're the one who runs away?" I'm talking to her like she's still here. "No, no. That's not how we do things." I dial her again, from the cell, and this time the call goes straight to voicemail.

I hang up, and immediately call Dylan. Four rings go by, and I'm beginning to think he's going to ignore me too.

But then the rings stop, and in place of hello, I hear, "She needs space, Donovan. I know you get separation anxiety, but when a girl needs space, you give it to her."

It's not Dylan. It's his wife, and she's way too perky for this time, well, for any time of the day. Really, she always is.

"Hello, Audrey." It comes out flat, which is an achievement, considering. "This isn't your business. Just put her on the phone."

"I will not. But I will tell you that she's fine. She's feeling fine. She looks..." She pauses, as if she's assessing Sabrina before she goes on. "Tired, but not terrible."

"Audrey!" Sabrina scolds in the background, and that brief evidence of her existence is enough to drive me mad. It's like one hit of my favorite drug. Always leaves me wanting more.

"Put her on the phone, Audrey," I say through gritted teeth. "Put. Her. On. The. Phone."

"Like I said, not going to do that." A baby cries, and Audrey sounds like she's moving toward that sound—away from Sabrina? "If you have any message you need me to give her, now's the time to tell me because I need to feed the babies, and I'm telling you now that no one is going to answer if you call again. Do you hear me, Dylan Locke?"

"Take the baby," Dylan says, sounding exhausted. "Should we trade?"

"No, Donovan and I are wrapping up. Right, Donovan? Any last words?"

I close my eyes and take a breath. This phone call has only frustrated me more. I'm tempted to hang up, but I recognize that anything I say or do will be relayed to Sabrina. "No, Audrey. No last words. Thank you so very much."

I don't manage to hide the sarcasm. Honestly, I don't really try.

"Anyti—" I click END before she completes the word.

Seething, I throw the phone to the bed and spin around, running my hands through my hair as I do. *What next, what next, what next?*

Ready the plane for my own flight to London, obviously.

I pick up my phone to make the arrangements, and then pause, remembering Sabrina's message. *Please consider waiting until Monday to come after me.*

FUCK.

It's a test. It's a fucking test. She wants to see if I can be the man that I was planning to promise her that I can be. A man that will listen to his wife's request and give her the space she needs and...fuck.

What if I can't be that man?

The impulse to call and get my jet ready is so strong that my muscles ache from the restraint.

Maybe it's not a test. Sabrina's not that calculating. And if it's not a test...

No. I can't. I have to prove this to her. I have to prove I can be this for her. For our baby.

With a groan, I throw it down, and leave the room. Out of sight, out of mind. If only that were a truism I understood.

I take a run to distract myself.

Then a long shower.

Then another run.

What do people do when they aren't able to be with the person they love most? Google tells me to get a hobby.

Sabrina *is* my hobby.

So what now?

The baby. I should focus on the baby. There's so much we'll need. Furniture, car seats, baby proofing the house.

I have several things in a cart on one of those Everything Baby sites, but I second-guess actually making a purchase. This is something Sabrina will want to be part of, won't she? The new man I need to be would at least check with her.

So then I decide I'll just do some research, starting with what to expect during pregnancy and all that jazz.

But every article makes me antsy. Makes me miss Sabrina even more. I end up ordering some paperbacks to read later and close out my browser.

After that, I work. Or try to. It's impossible to concentrate on anything. Every five minutes, I'm logging into our accounts, looking for her activity, imagining what she's doing. I email Dylan who replies instantly with an *I'm out until Monday* message. Liar. It's his personal account. Has Audrey taken over every method of communication? Is that what kind of relationship I'm supposed to have with Sabrina?

I only make it a couple of hours before I'm back in the bedroom, checking my phone. I dismiss more notifications about missed calls from my father and open the app that tracks Sabrina's phone. She hasn't disabled it, which is validating, but seeing the dot flash in the middle of London, England doesn't make me feel any better. I consider calling Ferris. He could get there by tonight. Or maybe he knows someone already in the UK who can do some surveillance.

Except if I send a PI after her, I'm not really trying to change.

Which leads to the question, do I really have to change or just make her believe I've changed?

I'm berating myself for even considering such a thing when the phone rings. I glance hopefully at the ID, but it's only Raymond.

And he'll keep on calling until I deal with him.

I answer and immediately start talking before I've figured out what excuse I'm going to give. "Look, Dad, I'm not going to be able to make that investment. I'm just—"

He cuts me off. "Forget that. The deal with Manova Tech is on hold. I've been trying to reach you all morning."

"Yeah, it's not a good—"

He cuts me off again. "We're in a crisis, Donovan. I'm being blackmailed."

Well. That's distracting. "Blackmailed?"

"Some files from a few years back. Some screwy accounting. It doesn't matter all the backstory. Point is we had someone clean our books, but apparently the guy we hired kept copies. Now he wants to charge us to make them go away permanently."

I don't even need the backstory. These have to be the same files that I already bought copies of. Supposedly the *only* copies. The opportunist asshole must have decided he could double dip. Triple dip, more accurately.

"This could ruin us." He sounds desperate. As desperate as I've felt all morning. "I need you on this, Donovan."

My body starts to buzz, the way it does when my brain starts strategizing. It's like my thoughts are too big to just be contained in my head, and my entire being vibrates with the neurons that are firing. "How much do they want? What have you told them? What's the timeline?"

I get the details from him, discovering most importantly that we have until Monday night to respond. "I'll take care of it," I say then hang up before he can say thank you.

Not that he was going to.

And no, I don't have a plan to deal with my father's situation, and I don't really care about his mess except that, if I did care, there's only one person who I trust to help me figure it out —I mean, if I were to trust anyone at all—and that feels like a valid excuse for what I do next.

I make another call.

"Simone—" She starts to bitch about the weekend and time off, but I interrupt. "Stop whining, you'll get overtime. I need you to do something ASAP. Arrange for the jet to take off as soon as possible. I'm going to London."

TWENTY-TWO

I'VE KNOWN Dylan for a long time now, and yet the version of him I see when he opens the door is a first. He's barefoot and scruffy, wearing a stained Deep Purple T-shirt and boxers. His hair is standing up in places, there are circles under his eyes, and the baby fussing in his arms is only just barely louder than the fussing baby in the background.

"Oh. It's you. Of course." He turns away from me, leaving the door open at least.

I walk in, shutting it behind me, and set my travel bag on the floor. "Hello to you too."

"I suppose the luggage means you're staying with us as well," he says, knowing I'm following him without looking over his shoulder. "Should I ask how you got past the doorman?"

"Doorman?" Like I didn't watch him for a good twenty minutes through the front glass until he got distracted by helping an elderly woman to her car. Then took the opportunity to sneak past, just in case Audrey's orders extended to the building staff.

Though, two crying babies and Dylan answering the door in his shorts... It sort of seems he might be alone.

"I've lost the wager now, thanks to you." He stops in the kitchen, in front of what looks sort of like a small crockpot. He shifts the baby to his hip, takes a baby bottle out of the appliance, and drops some milk onto the inside of his wrist.

I take the opening to scan the room. There are dishes piled in the sink—many baby-sized with pureed food stuck to the surfaces—and Dylan's usually spotless counter is cluttered with latex nipples, pacifiers, and bottle parts. I'm also very aware of the still crying baby in the other room. Should someone take care of that?

But his kids, his business. "There was a bet?" I ask instead.

"Are you surprised?" Really, I'm not. Between us men at Reach, there's always a bet. "I had more faith in you than the women did. I placed your arrival at eight a.m. tomorrow. You're a full twenty-four hours early."

I should feel guilty but all I want to know is, "What did Sabrina bet?"

He glances at his watch. "You're thirty-four minutes late, according to her prediction. Seems she's the winner." He shifts the fussing baby again, cradling her this time so that he can thrust the nipple in her mouth. Finally, the noise is cut in half.

"And what's the prize?"

"You, I suppose." He smiles, but I'm not sure if it's for me or the child in his arms. "Okay, Bianca, now that you're happy, should we see what we can do about your sister?"

He's walking again, so again I'm following. The second

baby's fussing gets louder as we approach, but Dylan just raises his voice to be heard. "They aren't here, you know."

It doesn't take a genius to know which *they* he's referring to. "Will they be back soon?"

"Nope."

We enter the den where there's a duplicate baby in a low to the ground swing. Though swing seems like a generous label. It moves in more of a rocking fashion, back and forth, back and forth, with hardly any swing to it at all. The ottoman has been moved right in front of it, which is where Dylan plops himself. He repositions Bianca on his lap and angles the way he holds the bottle in her mouth.

Then he reaches out his foot, sets it on the swing, and pushes it back before letting it fall, creating more of a genuine swing motion.

Within seconds, baby number two also calms down.

I perch on the arm of the sofa, watching Dylan as he balances the care of his twins. He can't seriously mean that he's going to be alone with them for long. "They're *not* coming back soon?"

Obviously, my real interest is in when I can see Sabrina.

He knows this, and the look he throws me tells me he clearly thinks I'm pathetic. "Audrey was sure you'd arrive last night. So the two of them got a hotel. They'll be back tomorrow."

"Tomorrow?" Not going to cut it. I stand up. "Which hotel?" I've already pulled out my phone, intending to call a cab.

"No idea."

I'm half sure he's playing with me until I see the seriousness in his expression. "You can call her."

"I don't want to call her. She'll hear the babies crying and think I can't handle it."

"Text then." I remember his hands are full. "Tell me where your phone is and—"

He interrupts me with a yelp. "Sorry, leg cramp." He stops pushing the swing and balances the bottle with his chin so that he can rub his shin.

...and then baby two starts crying again.

"Is it broken or something?" I nod to the swing.

"No, Maya is just more adventurous than the manufacturers think is safe. She takes after her mother, clearly."

I bend to push the swing myself, mostly so that she'll be quiet enough that I can continue this conversation. "Is your phone nearby?"

"She's not going to tell me where she is, Donovan."

Right, right. That was probably the whole point of her not telling him in the first place. "Okay." Sabrina won't have used her credit card to book the room. "So let's look up the charges on her card. We can see where they are that way."

"Look up the charges on her card?" He sounds like he doesn't understand what I'm talking about.

"Yeah. You log in, see where the charges are coming from. It should mention the hotel or at least the umbrella corporation. Narrow down the search from there."

He studies me strangely. "I don't have access to Audrey's credit cards."

"Why not?"

"I'm not someone who stalks his wife's every move, I suppose."

I want to respond with something snarky in response— something indicating the measure of my love for Sabrina versus his love for Audrey—but Maya starts fussing again. "What's wrong with her? Am I swinging her wrong?"

Dylan heaves a sigh. "She's probably hungry. Her breakfast is late since her sister's breakfast was late." He glares at me. "Or she needs her diaper changed. Or she wants to be held. Or she's just bored."

I stop the swinging—it's not working, so what's the point?—and stand up straight. "Do you not have a nanny?"

"On the weekdays, yes. We might have planned for one this weekend as well if we'd known Audrey wouldn't be here, but even then it would be later in the day. There's no way in hell my wife would leave me alone overnight with another woman in the house. And before you start forming judgment on the matter, it's not me that she doesn't trust—it's any other woman alone with her man."

"How very modern of her." My annoyance can't possibly be registered over the sound of Maya's wailing. "Can I...do something?"

"Are you offering to take one?"

I pause. Generally, I'm not that into kids. I hear it's different when they're your own, and I believe that in my bones. The baby in Sabrina's stomach is the only one I've ever been interested in, and I'm aggressively interested in it. But other people's kids are loud and complicated and don't come with instructions.

"You could use the practice," Dylan says when I hesitate too long. "Trust me."

"Fine. Yes. Sure." I start for the baby in the swing, but the buckle looks confusing, and anyway I'd prefer the one that isn't crying, so I change direction and reach for the one in Dylan's arms instead. "Hand her over."

"All right." He stands up to bring her to me, then tries to micromanage the exchange.

"I got it, I got it. I can hold a baby." Except it's not exactly as easy as it looks. She's light enough, but she wiggles, and I'm not exactly sure how to hold her head.

Dylan moves his attention to the other one, but he looks up when mine starts fussing.

"I got it," I say again, not very convincing. "She wants the bottle, is all. Just, how do I—" One hand is under her and the other under her butt. How the hell am I supposed to hold anything else?

"Move your arm." He's trying not to laugh as he helps me adjust my arm so that I can cradle her against my body and hold the bottle in the other hand. "You got it."

"I said I got it."

He doesn't hide back his laugh this time, but he leaves me with her while he attends to her sister.

I stare down at her. Big blue eyes stare up at me. Eyes that share the same shape as her mother's. As Sabrina's. She sucks greedily at the bottle for several seconds, but then stops, as though distracted by what she's looking at. Distracted by me. Then goes back to sucking before repeating the cycle.

Then she reaches her hand up to my face.

"Oh." It's startling how such a soft touch can be felt throughout my body. "You're a cutie, aren't you? What's her name again?"

When no one answers, I realize that Dylan has left the room.

Hurriedly, not in any way remotely panicked about being left alone with her, I search him out and find him in the kitchen. Because I suddenly remember that I'm not here for baby bonding. That's why. "I didn't come to London to—"

Dylan cuts me off. "Angle the bottle," he says, putting a second bottle into what must be a warmer.

"Excuse me?"

"Hold it at an angle. So she gets fewer gas bubbles."

I adjust the angle as I talk. "I didn't come chasing after Sabrina like you think."

"Your presence says otherwise."

"I know how it looks. But I came because I need to—" I cut myself off this time. "She doesn't seem like she wants it anymore."

"So put it down." He waits until I set it on the counter. "And now you need to burp her. Put her over your shoulder and—"

"I'm not an idiot. I've seen people burp babies." I move her upright, but Dylan goes on instructing me as if I haven't spoken at all.

"Rub her back. Or you can pat it, if you prefer."

"I got it." I choose patting because it feels more natural. "I need to talk to Sabrina about a matter that can't wait until Monday. Personal matter. Urgent. Which is why I need to find her."

Dylan shrugs. "Don't know what to tell you, Donovan. Maybe try texting her? She might reply if you explain."

"Her phone is off." I pretend I don't see the judgy way he looks at me for being so sure. It's not like Sabrina doesn't know about the app that tracks her. Nowadays. "Besides, it's complicated. Easier said face-to-face."

The warmer beeps, apparently saying the bottle is heated. He takes it out, tests it on his wrist the way he did the other one, then positions the baby to feed her. "Could I help you with this personal, urgent matter?"

"No, it's..." I mean, maybe he could. It's not like I don't trust Dylan to have good ideas. Or rather I don't distrust him specifically. But there's really only one person that I want to voice in on this. "It's complicated. And like I said, personal. And it's—"

"Sure, sure. You need the wife." His baby doesn't seem to want the bottle he's trying to give her, and he puts the bottle down and repositions her so he's holding her the way I'm holding my twin. "Just like this one needs her momma. Substitutions won't do." He bounces her as he sways back and forth, which doesn't seem to be doing much to calm her.

Meanwhile, I haven't gotten a single hiccup out of the baby I'm holding, and it occurs to me that taking care of them is hard. "How the hell were you trying to do this alone?"

He chuckles. "It's not that bad. Try massaging instead of patting. I think that's what Bianca likes better."

I switch to massaging. "This one's Bianca?"

"Yep. Her mouth is crooked, and she already has her front tooth. That's how I tell them apart."

I study both of their faces. "Ah, I see it."

"Bianca likes things gentle on the whole. Maya is more adventurous, as I said earlier. And pickier."

"Like that—there's so much to remember. So much to learn. How do you do it?"

"Just like with any new relationship. And they aren't newborns anymore. They've been around for six months, remember. Two is harder, I admit. But definitely worth it. I couldn't imagine not having the both of them."

He sombers immediately after saying it. Maybe because he's realized what he said. Maybe because he can tell that it has suddenly hit me that I was supposed to have two of them too. That one of them is gone. That one of them will never fuss on my shoulder and refuse the bottle and cry when the swing doesn't have a strong enough motor.

"I'm sorry," he says. "About the miscarriage."

"Thank you. I'm still..." I borrow Sabrina's word, "processing it, I think."

His back and forth starts to look more like a dance. "Ellen had a miscarriage. After Aaron. Then we lost Amanda right after that...but even before that, she was torn up. We both were. It's especially difficult to mourn something that was only ever potential. The *what could have been* is so magnified when you never got a chance to glimpse any of it at all."

My throat feels tight, so I don't try to say anything.

"Anyway, give yourself time, and don't be surprised if the grief sneaks up on you now and again."

He lets an appropriate beat pass. "And congratulations! Donovan Kincaid is going to be a dad. My whole idea of reality has been thrown off-kilter."

"Thanks." It's less sincere this time. "I'd say you're an asshole, but—" Finally, Bianca burps.

And then throws up all over my button-down shirt.

"Fuck. Seriously?"

Dylan can't contain his laughter. "You're going to have to start dressing down."

My sleeves are rolled up, and I'm not wearing a tie or a jacket. This is casual in my book.

"You'll at least want to not buy everything at Armani." He wipes a tear from his eye. "Come on. Let's clean you two up."

"HOW THE FUCK does this much shit come out of something so small?" It's been almost four hours since I got here, and this is the third diaper I've changed. The first two were deceptively easy to deal with—whoever invented changing table straps is a genius since both these girls wiggle—and I had fooled myself into thinking I was a natural.

Then Bianca delivered what I can only call a shitplosion. It even leaked down her leg. Thankfully, the T-shirt and sweats I borrowed from Dylan seem to still be clean.

"No wonder she's been so grumpy." He hands over a wet wipe in exchange for the messy diaper. "Make sure you get everywhere." He supervises as I do cleanup. "Everywhere, Donovan. All the nooks and crannies, not just the backside."

I work the wipe around baby lady parts and grimace. "Is this weird? Can I get arrested for touching my niece's privates? I don't know how to feel about this."

I seem to have been a major source of amusement for him all morning as once again he laughs. "As long as you're not turned on—"

"—No, hell no—"

"Then you're good."

"I don't know." I finish with the job and hand them to Dylan, this time in exchange for a clean diaper. "I thought I was a feminist, but I'm completely comfortable with calling this women's work."

"You, a feminist?"

I glare.

Okay, I've said some fairly shitty things to women, particularly Sabrina, but that was because I was in love with her so it doesn't count.

"You better not ever let your wife hear that anything baby related is women's work. Or mine. She'll divorce me just because I call you a friend." The diaper's on now, but he reaches past me and tests his finger in the leg hole. "It's too loose. This was why it leaked. Tighter this time."

I growl in frustration. "Do I need a new one?"

"Nope. The adhesive is meant to be adjustable." He seems to know what I'm thinking. "Not just for the new-to-nappy folks, but also because, as you've noticed, babies squirm."

I fix it and feel ridiculously proud when I'm given a seal of approval. "What next?"

"Back to trying to put them down for a nap."

I preferred tummy time. Then we moved to the nursery where we've already been trying to put them down for half an hour. Chances of success seem to be as unpredictable as the magic eight ball sitting back in New York on my office desk.

He gives me a consoling pat on the back. "Bianca might be ready now that she's gotten all that out of her. Or would you prefer to trade?"

And risk the other one shitploding on me as well? "No thanks. B and I have a thing now, don't we, bug?" I have no idea where the nicknames are coming from, but it seems a different one comes out of my mouth every fifteen minutes. She's just so little and adorable and amazing and I want to cover her in kisses and eat her up, and I seriously don't even know who I am right now.

"Just wait until it's your own."

Fucking Dylan. Assuming I'll go soft.

I put Bianca on my shoulder and turn my back to him while I walk the room, as if that might keep him from seeing that I'm already a gooey cinnamon roll.

Behind me, I hear Dylan retrieving Maya from the baby bouncer. She's apparently just graduated to the chair since she can keep her head up on her own, a milestone Bianca has yet to reach, and she's obsessed. Predictably, she starts fussing as soon as he has her out.

Dylan coos to her, and when I look over, he's dancing with her. Soon, he starts singing as well. "Na na na na na. Hush, hush."

The man always surprises me with how well he can carry a tune, though it isn't exactly the most pleasant of voices to listen to. Also, despite the lyrics, the song seems to be upbeat, and I highly suspect it's one of the rock songs that his cover band plays.

"Don't you know any ballads?"

"Easy for you to complain. I don't see you giving it a go."

I'm tempted to ignore the challenge, but there's something moving inside of me. Like something's opening up and breathing inside my chest, and it makes me feel light and present and maybe this is how people feel when they're living in a musical, because out of nowhere, a tune slips out of my mouth.

"By the light of the silvery moon
I want to spoon
To my honey, I'll croon love's tune
Honey moon, keep a-shinin' in June
Your silvery beams will bring love's dreams
We'll be cuddlin' soon
By the silvery moon."

I slow dance as I sing, and when I finish, I realize Dylan's staring at me. Not with disgust or surprise, but the same way I looked at him when I arrived this morning and saw a side of my friend I'd never seen standing in his open door.

Where the hell did it come from? Was it just buried inside us waiting to come out?

I think about how I even know a song like this. "My father's father used to sing to me," I say. Not that Dylan asked. "He died when I was really young, but his singing must have made an impression because I still remember a couple of the songs. This is the only one I know all the words to except *Yes! We Have No Bananas*, which is not one I feel comfortable singing. Apparently, in retrospect, Papa Kincaid might have been a bit racist."

"Definitely no bananas then."

We continue dancing in silence, the rhythm entrancing to the girls. Maya has finally stopped fussing, her head resting on Dylan's shoulder the way Bianca's is resting on mine. When I look down at the baby in my arms, her eyelids look heavy, and she's sucking her thumb.

It's tedious and tiring, how long this is taking, and at the same time, I don't mind at all.

Who the fuck am I?

I glance again at Dylan. "Who the fuck are you?"

He understands the question. "Still the same person I was before the babies. Still work with you dimwits. Still like beating you at billiards. Still play bass with the band. You'll still be you too."

I'm pretty sure he thinks that's what I want to hear, and maybe there are parts of me that do.

But there are other parts of me that would prefer being told that having a baby magically transitions you into someone else. "What if the person you had been was bad for them?"

"Well." He carefully moves to one of the rocking chairs, switching one rhythm out for another. "I try not to swear around them so much. I'm drinking and smoking less these days."

Are you fucking kidding me?

Those were not the parts of me I'd hoped would magically change.

I don't have to say it aloud. Dylan reads it on me. "It's not a loss. You pivot because that's what they need. You love them the way they need to be loved. You don't even think about it a lot of the time. Your priorities just change."

I think about this as I sit myself down in the other rocking chair. *You love them the way they need to be loved.* "Then you *aren't* the same."

"I suppose not." Dylan considers. "You're better."

I could be okay with being better. "Think how fucking amazing I'm going to be then."

"Cover your ears, Bianca," he teases.

Thoughts drift in and out of my head as I rock back and forth. Memories. Connections. Emotions I haven't felt in years. Secrets I've held too long.

"Dylan..." It's not the right time. It's never going to be the right time. "I should have told you years ago. Amanda was your stepdaughter. I should have told you that it was—"

He doesn't let me finish. "I know."

My head turns sharply toward him. I can tell by his expression that he's rightly guessed that I was about to finally tell him that Amanda's death was my fault. But... "How?"

"Hired my own PI. Back then. You think you're the only one who has investigative access?"

I'm stunned. He knows. He's *known.* Since back then. Thirteen years ago now. "Why didn't you say anything?"

He exhales. "Because no matter the circumstances, it was an accident. And you obviously already blamed yourself. If you thought I knew, you'd bend over backwards to make it up to me, which you couldn't, and you wouldn't need to. I preferred our relationship without that burden."

I rest my cheek against Bianca's head and concentrate really hard to stop my eyes from watering.

When I think I can speak again, I lift my head and look at my friend. "You're a good father, Dylan."

A beat passes. Then his brows furrow. "Are you...? Do not father figure me, Donovan Kincaid. I am not nearly old enough to—"

I bite back a smile and nod at Maya. "With her. She's asleep. You're good with her."

"Oh." He returns the smile. "You will be too."

"But how do you know?"

"I just do."

TWENTY-THREE

"WELL, LOOK AT THAT." The familiar voice interrupts a sweet, dreamless sleep.

I stir, but I'm not ready to wake up.

"Two men, sleeping with babies, almost makes it impossible to be mad," Audrey continues.

"Yeah," a second voice agrees. "Almost."

I blink my eyes, adjusting to the light, and see Sabrina standing in the doorway with her sister. In cut-off shorts and a tank top with her hair in a messy bun at her nape, she's a vision. "Hi," I say.

She has her arms folded over her chest, but I'm pleasantly surprised when her reply is more smile than scowl.

"Audrey, love. You're home early." Dylan is awake too now. He gets up from his rocker, baby on his shoulder, and crosses to his wife. "This is because you didn't trust me, isn't it?"

For a second, I think she's leaning in to kiss him. Instead, she grabs Maya from his arms. "This is because I missed my babies."

I look down at Bianca. She's smacking her lips, but she's still asleep.

When I look up again, it's to find Sabrina is watching me. "You look good with a baby in your arms, Mr. Kincaid."

A knot releases in my chest. Not all the knots, but a big one. "Maybe there's hope for me yet."

"Is there?" Audrey asks. "Because my sister told you to not come here until Monday. Monday, Donovan. It's Sunday."

"But it's not Saturday," I counter.

Sabrina brings her hand to her mouth, and I know she's covering a laugh.

"That is correct," Dylan says. "He got here this morning, and that means you lost the bet, my dear."

Audrey smirks. "Not to you."

"No, but at least you lost too," he teases. "And that means Sabrina knows Donovan best of all. Congrats on the win."

"Oh, no." I stand up too fast, or talk too loud, causing Bianca to rustle in her sleep. Everyone holds their breath until she rests again. When I speak again, it's in a near whisper. "Sabrina absolutely did not win the bet."

I have more to say, but Audrey interrupts. "I don't see how you can say that when you're standing right in front of us."

"Yes, that's true. But I'm not here for the reason you all think I'm here. Something's come up."

Sabrina's expression grows serious. "What is it, Donovan?"

I look to the others and back to her, indicating that the matter is private. "Is there somewhere we can go to talk?"

"My room?" Sabrina suggests as Dylan moves to take Bianca from me. "*Our* room, I guess, now that you're here."

She doesn't sound completely disappointed about it, which should be encouraging, except that now that she's here, and she's all right, and she's not mad, I'm feeling a little guilty about the intrusion.

"Well, we'll see about that. Let's just..." I gesture toward the hallway.

Concern knits her brow, but she nods. "Okay."

It's the same apartment Dylan's had for years, so I know my way around, but I let Sabrina lead the way to the guest wing and follow her into the room she stays in whenever she visits.

I shut the door behind me, and she turns to face me. "Is everything okay? You have me worried, Donovan."

"Yeah, yeah. I mean..." Funny how I've said this issue with my father is the impetus for my arrival, and yet I haven't thought at all about what to say about it.

Okay, I was using it as an excuse. I admit it.

But the reality is that my father does have a problem that is time sensitive, and whatever needs to be worked out between me and Sabrina needs to take a backseat. "My father's being blackmailed."

"What? By whom? Over what?"

I'm almost surprised that she cares, which is fucked up because why wouldn't she care? Seeing her concern validates my need to see her and makes it easier to go on. "The same information I have in my safe. Probably the same guy too."

"Ah, he kept a copy." She kicks off her flip-flops then sits at the head of the bed and leans against the headboard. "For a minute, I thought you were going to say it was Holt Sebastian."

I'd actually considered it. "The fucker does seem like he'd go to incredible lengths to get a story, but no. There's no way he knows what's on the disk, and the blackmailer gave Dad visual proof that he has what he says he has."

"So what are you thinking you should do?" I wish that she

didn't have to assume that my father's problem was also mine, but she knows me, and I'm here, so it's obviously the most reasonable conclusion.

I sit on the edge of the bed and rest my elbows on my thighs. "It's a lot of money—much more than I paid out. The guy must have finally realized what he's holding."

"Or he just got greedy."

"Or that. Raymond won't want to pay it. And he shouldn't. It'll never end if he does. There's nothing to stop him from asking for more. The smartest play is to flat out tell the guy no. What's the guy going to do? He could release it to the press, but he doesn't get anything out of that unless he takes it to one of those tabloids. But those outfits don't deal in cash. Someone dealing with illegal materials like this won't want a transaction that's traceable. So chances are nothing will happen."

"Holt would probably pay in cash."

I nod in agreement. "Yes, but—"

"Unlikely that the blackmailer would know that."

"Right." Something sparks in the back of my head, the beginning of an idea, but I ignore it. "Problem solved, then. I reach out to the guy and tell him no deal."

"Except...?"

I turn to stretch out on the bed, facing her, and prop my head up on my elbow. "Except I don't want to be involved with this. I don't want to be my father's henchman. I don't want to help him get out of his dirty situation."

"Donovan," she says, sounding proud. "What happened to the main responsibility of a stockholder is the bottom line?"

It almost hurts to say this. "Turns out there might be other considerations as well. But before you get too smug—there's a problem."

Her eyes glaze as she tries to see what I see. "You're already involved. If you let your father deal with it on his own, he could find out you bought the information before. Would that cause issues?"

"Possibly."

"Or when your father turns him away, he could come back to you to ask for a second payout."

"That too. And I don't want to interact with men like this." My eyes drift briefly to her belly. "Not anymore."

"Okay."

"But the thing is...I've been holding on to that disk for a reason. You said that before. Weston did too. It wasn't to protect his ass."

"Okay," she says again.

"It wasn't to hand it directly over to SNC either. It will have my fingerprints all over it. I don't want to do that to us. To our family."

She nods and her hand goes to her stomach, consciously or not, I'm not sure.

"And, this is harder to articulate, but I don't want him—don't want *Raymond* to, um." I stop to gather my thoughts. "I've been thinking about legacy. What I want to leave behind, what I want..." I'm trying so hard to keep our baby at the periphery of this conversation. Because she asked for space, and I don't want to force her to address it before she's ready.

But the truth is this baby is reframing everything. This baby is the heart of why I'm here. Sabrina challenged me to consider what kind of a parent I'll be. I don't want to be the kind of parent that covered up his father's scandals.

For that matter, I don't want to be that kind of son.

"I would want my kid to expect better of me," I say, finally. "I want to give him the chance to be better *for* me."

She takes a breath in. Lets it out. It's as hard for her to ignore the elephant in the room as it is for me. Harder, maybe, since she's never been able to compartmentalize the way that I can.

In the end, she manages just fine. "So then what do you want to do instead?"

"If I knew that, Sabrina, I wouldn't have had to rush across the ocean to talk to you."

A smile spreads across her lips. "It is refreshing to be needed instead of just obsessed over."

"There's a difference?"

She reaches a red painted toe out to poke at my chest. "There's a difference, and you know it. Tell me what you're thinking. I know there's something spinning in that head of yours already. I see the steam."

I grab her foot and hold it in place, for no other reason than that I love touching her. "Yes, I have a thought. But for the record, Sabrina? Contrary to what you seem to believe, I have always needed you."

Her eyes are shiny when she responds. "Okay, then. Let's figure this out, super couple style then, shall we?"

"*Super couple style.*" I think I like the sound of that.

TWENTY-FOUR

"IT'S A PLAN," I say an hour later.

"It's a good plan," Sabrina assures me.

I sit up, perching on the end of the bed, and shrug, not so sure I'd go that far. It keeps my family out of it, anyway. *This* family. The family that counts.

And while I know all the details of the plan are mine, it's only because of her that I've been able to organize it. My back is to her now, so I peer over my shoulder in her direction. "I couldn't have done this without you."

"I know."

"It wasn't just an excuse to get on the plane."

She smirks. "Uh-huh."

Fuck, I love her. For that reason, I push myself up to my feet, with every intention of getting out of her hair.

Really. That is one thousand percent my plan.

But I'm not perfect, and I'm not ready to leave her, so I linger. "You went shopping?" I ask, nodding to the bags propped by the dresser. She must have brought them back with her from the hotel because they weren't here earlier. Trust me, even with a baby on my shoulder, I scoured the apartment for signs of my wife.

She sighs. "Nothing fun. New bras. I can't fit in my old ones anymore."

"Shame." It's an invitation to look at her breasts—which, of course, I do. She's definitely gotten voluptuous. Once again, I chide myself for not having noticed, but now that I think about it, I *had* noticed. I'd just thought she'd added a few needed pounds. The woman has always been thin.

"You sound so disappointed."

"Extremely." And she's wrong—lingerie is always fun. I bend down to poke in the bags—and no, it doesn't even cross my mind to ask for permission—and pull out a white, full cup, boring granny bra. "What the fuck is this?"

Laughing, she bounds off the bed and tries to grab it out of my hand. "It's a nursing bra."

"You're three months along. Who are you planning on nursing?" I hold it out of her reach, too interested in how the thing works. I find a clasp that opens, leaving a big hole in the cup. "Though, I have to admit this is convenient."

She jumps up and swipes it from my hand. "Convenient for feeding a baby." She stuffs it back into the bag. "Audrey suggested nursing bras. She said it's a waste to buy bras that will only fit for six months and then have to buy new ones when the baby's born."

"You know you both have incredibly sufficient bank accounts."

"Lots of money doesn't mean we need to waste it." She locks eyes on me, and her smile fades as our stare grows intense. Her cheeks redden, and I wonder exactly what she's thinking about. Wonder how a woman I know so much about can still be so fucking fascinating.

"Anyway," she says, diverting her attention back to the shopping bags. She squats down to rearrange the items inside. "I got underwear too—not-sexy underwear—because everything's tight around my waist. And some loose sundresses. Audrey said they're easy to grow into."

It occurs to me that she needed her sister for this, that she wasn't just running from me. I'm starting to understand that part of what she's needed to process is the transition from who she is to who she's going to be. Until spending the morning with Dylan and his girls, I guess I'd thought that parenthood would just happen magically when it was time.

Yeah, Sabrina's always been smarter than me.

Suddenly, that constant obsession to always know everything about her flares, and I'm desperate to know all the things I've missed. "What does it feel like? Having your body change. Do you notice it?"

She glances up at me, and afraid that this isn't the time, I'm about to tell her we can talk about this later, but she beats me to talking. "Yes and no. I've been lucky, actually. According to Audrey. I've only been nauseous a couple of times, usually in the evening. My boobs feel full, but they haven't hurt. Tired. I've been tired." She puts her hands on her thighs and pushes up to a standing position. "Other than that, it's been easy to, um..."

"Ignore," I finish for her, and it hits me like a bolt of lightning that she hadn't been keeping this secret from me—she'd been keeping it from herself.

It erases the feeling of betrayal.

"Yeah."

"Yeah," I echo.

"But when I'm not ignoring it," she says more brightly, "it's actually kind of cool. I mean, this whole complicated, amazing thing is happening inside of me, and I have had nothing to do with it."

"Well, not exactly nothing."

She laughs. "No, not exactly *nothing*. But I'm not doing anything right now, and it's still happening. There's a whole other person in my stomach. I feel a little like a God."

"Always been a goddess in my book." She does look particularly sent-from-heaven at the moment. Rosy cheeks, glowing skin. A light in her eyes I haven't seen in weeks.

I take a step toward her.

Then immediately take a step away.

Then several steps. Until I'm all the way at the door. I'm addicted to her, and if I have any hope of being a better man—the kind of man who can give her space—then I need to leave before I *can't* leave.

She tilts her head, studying me. "Are you...?"

"Going? Yeah. Yes." I lean against the door, feeling the solid shape against my backside. "I came for the advice. As I've said."

"As you've said."

"Which I really do appreciate."

"I appreciate that you asked." She takes a step toward me.

I must take a step toward her too because there's air at my back now. "I'm going to bring you in more often. When I need advice."

She takes another step. "Not all the time, though. Because some of the things you're into are boring."

"Right. A lot of it's boring." If I reached out, I could touch her. "So I should probably get going..."

"You should." But she closes the gap between us. "Donovan."

I kiss her.

She kisses me back.

There's no pretending that this is just a kiss goodbye, because immediately, she's reaching for the hem of my shirt, and I'm working the button of her shorts. We're frantic and hungry, and I feel desperate with my need to touch her, love her, fuck her.

But then we break apart so she can pull my shirt over my head, and when our eyes meet again, we hesitate. Or rather, we slow. We soak each other in.

My hand cups her cheek, my thumb dusts across her bottom lip. Her hands spread across my chest, our eye contact never breaking, and this is the deepest conversation we've had in a long, long time, everything said without a single word.

I bend in to take her mouth with mine. A slow, lingering kiss this time, keeping my eyes open until she closes hers. My tongue plunges deeper, possessing her mouth, refusing to change the speed when she tries to hurry me up.

When I pull away, this time to remove her shirt, she's quick to return to our kiss. I give in to her lips momentarily, then kiss down her jaw, down her neck. Down her decolletage to her breasts spilling over her lace bra. I run my tongue along the plump flesh while she undoes the hook in the back. It falls off her, and I palm her breasts, memorizing the new weight of them. She was quick to remind me that this part of her body—a part I've worshiped for so long—has a function along with its beauty, and the strangest thing? I'm even more enamored with them now than I ever have been.

I kiss and lick then draw a nipple into my mouth, sucking it

until it's a sharp point. Then I rub my thumb across it in rever-
ence. Her breath catches, and she throws her head back,
seeming to be lost both in pleasure and agony. She wants me to
hurry. She wants me inside her. She runs her hand over the
crotch of my sweats, palming the shape of my very erect cock,
hoping to move me along.

Yes, I know what you want.

But then I keep kissing down her body. I get down on my
knees so I can do it properly, pulling her shorts down as I do,
and when I get to her bare belly, I splay my hands across the
expanse of skin. She feels different here. Her flesh tight when it
used to have give.

Right here, buried deep in her womb, this is *us*. The place
where the two of us are no longer *her* and *me* but are forever *we*.
We made this. We planted this seed. We loved this into being.

My eyes gloss over, and I look up at her. She caresses my
face with the back of her hand, and she nods, her shiny eyes
telling me she knows exactly what I'm thinking. She's feeling
it too.

And with that, my restraint meets its end.

I nudge her backward, crawling with her, until she hits the
bed. She falls back onto the mattress, and I'm momentarily torn
between the pulsing ache of my cock and the need to bury my
face in her pussy.

Just one taste...

I ignore the ache and greedily feast on her cunt. She's past
due for a waxing, staying bare not her main priority of late, and
as much as I've always appreciated her smooth, the neglect is a
major turn-on. Because it's real. Because she doesn't think she
has to work to keep me. Because she knows she's mine, whether

her body is primped or au natural, and I love her all the more for letting me have her in all of her ways of being.

I'm so into it, that I bring her to orgasm without even having to try.

I feel the need to give her another, but my cock is throbbing, and I need to be inside her more.

Standing up, I undo the drawstring of my sweats and pull them down along with my underwear. Sabrina scoots up the bed in anticipation, and so as soon as I'm naked, I stretch myself over her. She spreads her legs wide, bringing her knees up to hug my hips, and without any effort, my cock slides inside her heat.

I blink against the pleasure. It's not even the right word for what I'm feeling. It's an emotion too big to name. It's heavy and immense and pleasurable, yes, but it has depth, and for a handful of seconds I feel like I might drown.

But her eyes are locked on mine, as tightly as my cock is locked inside her, and she's a life raft, saving me once again, keeping me afloat.

"Sabrina," I whisper against her lips. Sabrina, named for the river nymph who saved the virgin from death. I was a far cry from innocent when we met, but I was as new to love—to *true* love—as she had been to sex, and she saved me. Even when I'd thought I was the one saving her.

Loving her, really loving her—the in-the-same-room love and not just the from-afar love I lived with before—has changed me into a person I sometimes don't recognize. A better person. She's taught me how to really live, how to be *in* the world and *of* the world, and not just directing it.

And I'm still changing. Still being changed by her.

I rock deeper inside her. My hand grabs her ass, bringing

her closer to me. We pitch and toss together, two souls riding an ocean. *Three* souls.

She cups my face with her hands. I kiss her, and she clenches around my cock. I slow down. I drag it out. I make it last, pushing her toward release, letting her fall, pushing her closer to the edge.

And then I can't hold on anymore.

"Come with me." I press a finger to her clit, helping her obey the command. It's me who comes first, but she quickly follows, burying her cries into my neck. So not to be heard by Audrey and Dylan, maybe. Or maybe she's worried about waking the babies.

See? Already transitioning into what's next.

We lie on the bed afterward, face-to-face, sweaty and breathless. I stroke her face and her neck and kiss her and stare and kiss her some more. She glows.

I don't want to wreck the moment, but we're on a timeline. "The blackmailer needs his response by tomorrow night." I don't need to be at home to deal with him, but there's more to the plan. "I should arrange the plane for takeoff if I want to be back by tomorrow."

She lets out a happy sigh. "Do we have time for a shower?"

I trace the crease by her mouth and shake my head. "I'm going alone."

"What? No, you're not."

She starts to sit up, but I pull her back down. "You don't need to be home for this."

"I want to be there for you."

"You were here for me. But I interrupted your time—" I place a finger on her lips when she tries to cut me off. "I want to respect that. And it can't be good for you to fly back so quickly. Jet lag on top of jet lag."

"I'm going to be jet-lagged no matter when I come home."

I ignore her. "You can spend more time with Audrey."

"I've already missed so much work."

"You've had good reason. No one will fault you for needing more. And if you really think you need to, you can go into the London office with Dylan."

She frowns, and I have the sense to change my approach. "I'm not telling you what to do."

"You're not?" She's dubious, and I deserve that.

I kiss her, then brush her cheek. "I'm telling you what I think you want to do. You came here for a reason. It was a good instinct. I think you should follow that through."

She thinks about it, and when her body relaxes, I know she sees my point. "Are you sure?"

Surprisingly, I am.

I pull her tight to me. "I want you to stay here. I want you to have your space so you can process whatever you need to. Stay through the week. But when you come home, Sabrina, you're done processing alone. From then on, we process together."

"Okay."

"Okay."

It's harder to leave her bed than it should be. We still have shit that needs to be said and our future holds a lot of unknowns.

But I've never felt more sure of us when I get in the cab and drive away.

TWENTY-FIVE

MY FATHER'S secretary sees me as I approach his office the next day. "You can go straight in," she says. "He's expecting you."

"Thank you, Erin."

"Anything for you, Mr. Kincaid." She tosses her hair and gives me a flirty smile. It's hilarious how she still tries. I've never once given her the time of day, even before Sabrina was in my life full-time. She's attractive, of course—my father wouldn't hire anyone who wasn't—but I'm pretty sure those lips have already been on his dick, and sharing with Raymond has never been my thing.

But her crush does have benefits since it means she'll always bend over backwards to work me into my father's schedule.

Without knocking, I push open the double doors and enter Raymond's office. It's twice the size of mine, and the decor is heavy and wood, partly why I was so attracted to glass and minimalism when designing Reach. How much of who I am is purposefully the opposite of him?

How much of who I am is exactly the same?

I find him, not behind his desk, but at his chess board, noodling over a move. He seems unhurried and unanxious when he glances up at me, not like a man waiting for an update on his blackmailer. I know that's because he trusts me. He knows when I say I'll take care of something, that I will.

I almost feel guilty.

"Donovan." He beckons me over with his hand. "Play this out with me, will you?"

I hesitate. I played chess competitively in high school and could wipe out most anyone, even jet-lagged and exhausted. Except for Raymond Kincaid.

Guess who taught me.

I already prepared myself for a loss before walking in today. I just didn't know it would be one that was quite so obvious.

But what Raymond Kincaid wants, Raymond Kincaid gets.

I sit across from him at the white side and study the board. It's early in the game. At quick glance, I can't see either side has the advantage. "What is this setup?"

"Something I've been playing with myself. It's hard to find a challenging partner. But I suppose you'll do." He's an asshole, but he smiles as he says it, teasing.

The truth is, as complicated as our relationship is, it's not like there isn't anything good between us.

"I'll do?" I move one of my knights. "Get ready to be pummeled, old man."

He moves a pawn in response, and quickly the game is underway. "So what do I have to do to convince you to move your money over here like we talked about? Win this game?"

I wrinkle my face in incredulity. I'm not fucking investing my money in King-Kincaid. How is that the thing he's most concerned with right now? Scamming over more potential clients. Fuck that.

"Don't you want to know how the exchange went?" I ask him instead, changing the subject.

"I figured if there was anything pertinent, you'd let me know." He moves his rook and takes my bishop. "Is there something I should know?"

In answer, I reach into my inside jacket pocket, pull out a drive and toss it on his lap.

"Is this it? You got it from him?"

I nod, but it's a lie. This is the drive from my safe. If all goes as predicted, RawData, the name the blackmailer uses in his communications, is well on his way to passing his drive on as well. Time will tell.

"How much did it cost you?"

"A pittance." The amount that I'd paid for it originally had been significant, but nothing like the millions demanded from RawData.

"You're not paying attention," he says as he takes one of my pawns.

I'm actually quite aware of what I'm doing. "Tired, I suppose. Lot going on at home."

He pauses, truly looking at me for the first time. "Everything okay with Sabrina?"

I'm almost surprised that he asked. The first time he met her, he'd tried to buy her off to leave me. Though it had been a half-hearted attempt, which with him, was as near to acceptance as one could get.

Since then, Sabrina has been instrumental in improving my

relationship with my parents. Obviously, it still needs work. One of the things she's always bugging me about is how much effort I put into it.

With that in mind, I make an effort now. "As a matter of fact, she's having a baby."

He raises a brow. "Yours, I hope?"

"Yes, mine." *Fucker.*

"Hm." He considers. "You told your mother yet?"

"Not yet. I'm sure Sabrina will want to tell her." I wouldn't say they've bonded, but Sabrina is closer to Susan Kincaid than I am.

"A baby will be good for her. Give her something to focus her time on."

My blood is boiling. "Sabrina is not a trophy wife, Dad. She has a career that she is very—"

He cuts me off. "I was talking about your mother."

"Oh." I chide myself for jumping to that conclusion as I lose another pawn.

"You and Sabrina have a different kind of marriage. I get it. I don't understand it, but I get it." With this declaration, he seems to put things in perspective. Seems to have decided my news is good news. "Congratulations are in order, then."

"Well." Okay, I'm all about effort, but I'm not giving him details on something I'm still working out with my wife.

But the conversation gets me to wondering. "Did you want children?"

It takes a lot to surprise my father, but he genuinely seems taken aback by the question. "Did we want more children? Or are you asking if we wanted you?"

"Both." I keep my eyes focused on the game so he can't see how interested I am in his answer.

"You know how your mother feels about structure. Dinner at a certain time. The house kept a certain way. She learned pretty quickly with you that kids require a bit more adaptability."

"So Mom's the reason I'm an only child."

He toggles his head back and forth, as if deciding how to answer. "I guess that would be safe to say."

"And you?" I regret asking as soon as the question is out of my mouth. This isn't helpful. I don't really want to hear this.

"I'm the reason we had any kids at all. It came to the point where I told Susan it was a baby or a divorce."

Now I'm the one surprised.

I try not to make too much of it. "Because you wanted an heir."

"Because I wanted a *kid*." He sits back, putting his hands on his thighs, and gives me his full attention. "Call it biology or what you will. I had money and success and a wife. Felt like something was missing. Turns out, I was right."

I have to take a deep breath. And I know that later I'll analyze this statement over and over, make a million excuses for it, dismiss it entirely, but for right now, I feel more in sync with him than I ever have.

"I want a kid too," I say, my throat tight.

"Yeah, well." He takes my knight. "Send him to me to learn chess, because I obviously fucked up teaching you anything."

Then, because he can't let any interaction get too warm and fuzzy, he adds, "And make sure he knows that King-Kincaid has a place for him. He doesn't need to follow his father into a pussy job."

I glare, and he laughs like it was a joke.

But it occurs to me that there had been truth in it and that my decision not to join my father in his business might have been a blow to more than his ego. If he hadn't insisted on breaking so many laws to build his financial empire, things might have turned out differently. I blame him for that, but I probably should have made an effort to explain it to him.

I can practically hear Sabrina's voice in my head. *You were the kid. He was the grown-up. Give yourself a break.*

But I'm not a kid anymore.

And it's time for what I came here to do. "So, Dad, this RawData guy..." I wait until after he makes his next move so that I'm sure he's listening. "This isn't going to be the end of it."

"What do you mean? He make a threat?"

"No. Just a feeling." More like insider information. "He says this is the only copy, but he gave it up way too easy. He's going to come back."

Dad shrugs it off. "So we refuse to pay him. Probably shouldn't have even paid him for this."

"It's good to know exactly what he has."

"You looked? Is it as bad as he says?"

I snag one of his pawns, finally. "It's bad. If it gets out, he could really cause some trouble."

"I hope you're not suggesting we take the guy out."

"No." I'm appalled. "Absolutely...no. The fact you're bringing that up as an option is literally terrifying. Have you taken someone out before?"

"I just said I hoped that wasn't what you were suggesting. Of course, I haven't taken anyone out."

I'm only mildly relieved. His phrasing could well leave room for him to have hired someone else to have someone taken out.

For once in my life, I really don't want to know. "Anyway, I think you need to take this opportunity to get ahead of it."

"Get ahead of it." Once again, he sits back, gives me his full attention, and I realize that this is what keeps me coming back to him. He trusts my advice. He thinks what I have to say is important. It's flattering, but more than that, I think it's a version of love.

It's not the worst kind of love. But I've always felt like I have to work for it, and I vow right here and now to learn how to love my kid differently.

"Come clean," I say, laying it out on the table. "Tell the world before someone else does. Admit that there was a problem, it wasn't handled well, and promise to do better. Then hire a third-party compliance officer to make sure that you actually *do* do better.

He stares at me, as if trying to decide if I'm serious or not. When he realizes I am, he laughs, but it's a mocking laugh. "You know what that would entail?"

"I do."

"We'd probably lose more money that way than if the information was just exposed." He's back to the game, already having dismissed the idea.

"Maybe. But you'd earn more consumer confidence if it's coming from you."

"We'd have to restructure almost everything. Someone would have to be fired, someone important, and do you know how much work that is to get someone new up to speed? You know how long it took us to get on our feet after we let Daniel go?"

I cringe at the mention of Daniel Clemmons. He'd taken the fall for another King-Kincaid scandal in the past, and it had landed him in jail. That was when Weston walked away from our fathers' empire.

Why I stuck around wasn't something I could have answered until recently. Until today. I think I thought I needed Raymond more than Weston needs his father. He'd never believe me if I admit that. Not that I ever will.

And maybe I thought that Raymond needed me, too. Or hoped he did.

Now I realize I need to be the right kind of man more. "You could be the one to step down," I say, sliding a pawn forward.

"Me?"

"Take all the blame. Let the board replace you." He'll still keep his stocks. He'll likely even leave with a huge severance bonus. It won't hurt him at all financially. The company will continue to thrive. It will only hurt his pride, and for Raymond Kincaid, that's big.

Too big, I suspect. But I have to try. "I'm speaking as a stockholder, Dad. Knowing the risk that the company faces from this drive out in the world, this is the route with the best potential outcome, financially. For you as well as King-Kincaid.

"But I'm also speaking as your son."

He frowns. "As my son, you want me to throw away my entire life's work—"

"As your son, I want you to care about how you play the game more than whether you win or lose. I think you'll win anyway, if you do. You have the ambition and the talent. Be better. Don't you want to be better?"

"I'll think about it," he says, after a beat. I've never been able to read my father the way I can read other people. Maybe he's really considering it. I think he's likely just humoring me.

I look at the board. I've lost more than half of my pieces, and I can see he's less than five moves away from putting me in checkmate. "Bet the game on it? If I win, you step down?"

He tries to see what I see. Several seconds pass before he shakes your head. "You're something today, Donovan." He points at the board. "You've already lost."

But he's overlooked my pawn.

Two more moves, and it will reach the other side of the board, and when it does, it can become anything I want. I'll have him in checkmate in one more move.

He deliberates, and I'm pretty sure he's a breath away from accepting the bet.

Before he does, I stand up. It won't count if he doesn't make this decision on his own, and even if he loses, there's nothing to guarantee he'll go with it. He's not the type to honor commitments.

That's the whole issue, anyway, isn't it? His honor.

"Think about it," I tell him as I button my jacket.

"You're not going to see it through?"

"No, Dad. I'm done playing this game." I don't look back as I leave, but when I'm outside his office, the doors shut behind me, I stop to undo my tie.

"Do you need a mirror?" Erin asks, eager to fawn over me.

"Nope. It's symbolic."

She gives me a strange look as I wave and stuff the tie in my pocket, finally free of my leash.

TWENTY-SIX

I STARE at the name on my caller ID, deliberating whether or not to accept. On the fourth ring, I mute the TV with the remote and answer. "There isn't a single possible good reason for you to be calling me."

"Very narrow-minded attitude, if you ask me." Holt Sebastian's arrogance is just as lethal over the phone as in person.

"I didn't ask you. That's exactly the point." But I picked up because my curiosity has no end. "So get to your agenda. I'll give you two minutes."

"I had an interesting conversation today with someone who only referred to themself as RawData. Would you know anything about that?"

Why, yes, I would.

It was my copy of the drive that I delivered to my father, but that doesn't mean I didn't also reach out to the blackmailer. Basically, I told him that he wouldn't get payment for his information from anyone named Kincaid, and then I suggested he try reaching out to a man named Holt Sebastian.

It took me out of the picture, which was exactly what I wanted.

"I'm not really into online porn sites these days," I tell him. "But if that's your thing, by all means."

Holt must be used to assholes because I don't ruffle his feathers. "He wants to sell me some data. It's a lot of money."

"Surely, your daddy has deep pockets. He doesn't want to pay for your prostitutes anymore?"

"It's not the kind of transaction that SNC would approve of. But I'm willing to pay for it personally, if it's legit."

"Hey, I'm flattered that you'd come to me to certify your pornograph—"

He cuts me off. "Is it legit, Kincaid?"

I roll my head, cracking my neck. Out of the picture was supposed to mean out of the picture. "Obviously, I can't say for certain, since I have not touched this particular piece of data that you are talking about. But I would say...buy it. If I were to advise you, as a..."

I can't think of a demeaning term fast enough, and he fills in the sentence for me. "As a friend."

"Oh no, you fucking moron, there is not a scenario imaginable where you and I are fucking friends. And considering I've done all that I can to have no contact with you, I'm about to move you to my mortal enemies list for making this fucking phone call."

"You mean a call where the CEO of a news media network reaches out to Donovan Kincaid to validate incriminating information regarding his father's company, obtained by an anonymous source? Pretty standard call. Generally, I expect to get hung up—"

It's practically an invitation so, with a smile, I click END.

My smile fades when I think about what's on the verge of happening next. King-Kincaid will be accused of book doctoring. My father will be under scrutiny. Stock prices will fall. People will lose jobs. His business will take a hit. And he'll come out of it all okay.

Strange feeling to be disappointed about a situation that I know he's going to survive, but I am. It's been three days since I went to his office and advised him to step down. I've heard nothing from him in follow-up, and I'm certain that means he's going to ignore my suggestion.

So he won't do the right thing, but I know I did, and that feels...refreshing.

With a sigh, I shake off thoughts about the impending scandal, and pick up my laptop. In the three days that I've been home without Sabrina, I've managed to catch up on all the work that I'd neglected for the last several weeks as well as some of her work. It turns out that when I don't have her as a distraction, I get a shit ton of work done.

I'm also miserable.

But not so miserable that I can't survive it. Only three more days to go before she's home. Yes, I'm counting down.

I haven't completely been without her. I've talked to her on the phone. Told her how it went down with my father and kept her up-to-speed with office news. She's made it easier by texting several times a day. Short messages telling me what she's doing.

Drinking my one cup allotment of coffee.

Braiding my hair.

Reading Breakfast at Tiffany's.

She sends pictures too, and only a couple of them have been dirty. Surprisingly, these interactions are more satisfying than logging into a security system and casually watching her go about her day or reading a detailed report from Ferris.

Not that I'm planning on ending either of those activities any time soon, but it appears that I am capable of moderation.

Tempted to reread her last several texts for the millionth time—I may have them all memorized—I turn my phone face-down and concentrate on my computer screen, trying to make sense of the conversion rates on one of our current campaigns.

I'm still not focused when my cell rings. I reach for it eagerly, hoping that it's her.

When I see that it is, I can't answer fast enough. "Hey."

"Hey."

I look at my watch. Nearly eight p.m. It's almost one in the morning there. "Can't sleep?"

"Mm. I got sucked into a show. You?"

"Just trying to wrap up the campaign report for the Brueggeman account." I close my laptop and set it aside, though, wanting to be one hundred percent present.

"While watching TV?"

I glance up at the muted television. It's odd that I have it on. I honestly can't remember the last time I watched anything before this week. "Well, Nate suggested watching sports as a substitute for..."

"Stalking me?"

"Don't knock it."

"By watching sports, I don't think he meant competitive billiards."

Actually, he'd suggested beach volleyball, but I have a

feeling he watches for the women in bikinis rather than the sport of it.

I don't say that, though, because, "How do you know I'm watching competitive billiards?" Sure I already know the answer, I tilt my head toward one of the living room security cameras.

"There you are."

"So I'm the show you're watching." I stand and walk closer to the closest camera, giving her a better look. Wishing I could see her instead.

"Apparently, I have access to the system too. Thought I'd log in and see what it's like to be Donovan Kincaid."

"Huh." I think about everything I've done since I arrived home. Kicked off my shoes. Took off my jacket. Worked on the sofa with my feet up. Did I do anything unsightly like scratch my balls? "How long have you been at this?"

"Long enough. Were you listening to music earlier or were you dancing to silence?"

Fuck. I'd had Sinatra stuck in my head. Sometimes the man makes you move, okay? "I don't think I like this."

She laughs. "Just be yourself, Donovan. Pay no attention to the woman behind the lens."

"I'm serious, Sabrina. This is not my kink."

She laughs again, but underneath the laugh I hear something else. The sound of keys jangling.

I hurry from the living room to the hallway and position myself where I can see the front door.

"Don't worry. It was fun, but I'm not into it either." The door opens, and there she is. "This was only meant to distract you so you wouldn't hear me sneak in."

I lower the phone from my ear. "You're here."

She lowers her own phone. "I can actually surprise you when you aren't watching me twenty-four seven."

"I don't like surprises." I pocket my cell and approach her, meeting her at the end of the hall after she's left her suitcase at the front door. "But this is a good one."

I cup her face with both hands. "What are you doing here? You still have three days. You need time."

She shakes her head. "I need you."

My ribs are tight, and it's hard to breathe. I kiss her, gently, before offering a smirk. "Good."

But also not good. "I was going to do a whole thing for you. Candles, roses. The whole nine yards. You really missed out." I'm not really the best at romance. It was going to be a big deal.

"You can do a whole thing another time."

"Not likely. It was a one-time-only event. Sad that you have to miss it." I take her hand as we walk toward the living room.

"You know what? It's okay. It would overshadow what I have to tell you and what I have to tell you deserves to be the main event."

"Oh." My pulse speeds up, suddenly nervous. I drop her hand so she can't feel the sweat on my palm. "I'm all ears. Should I sit down? I'll sit down."

I sit on the coffee table and invite her to sit on the couch so I can face her head-on and also be close enough to touch her. "Now, I'm ready."

She brings her purse to her lap and digs around inside. Then she pulls out a notebook and retrieves a loose paper from between the pages, the size of a standard photograph. It's creased and worn, as though she's handled it a lot. She passes it over.

I recognize it right away. It's almost an exact copy of the

ultrasound image I'd discovered in her office. She doesn't know that I have a photo on my phone and I stare at it several times a day.

But the image itself isn't the point, and I understand what she's doing. "Sabrina," I say, my tone teasing. "Are you telling me you're pregnant?"

She bites her lip and nods. "*We're* pregnant."

It's a do-over, and I try to imagine what I would have said if this was how I'd found out.

But I can't, because odds are, no matter whether she'd tried to hide it or not, I would have known before she told me. It's who I am.

She knows it too. "Don't tell me—you already know."

"I'm processing."

She swats at me, but I grab her hand and pull her to my lap. Then I bring the image in front of us so we can look at it together. "Look at that big head."

"For all her brains."

"He gets that from you."

"He?"

"I'm all man, baby. Impossible that my swimmers carry anything but pure testosterone."

She giggles.

"See there?" I point to what's obviously a limb. "Definitely a dick."

"It's her *leg*."

"The way he's pulling on it? He's trying to put it in his mouth. Trust me, every guy tries that at least once."

"Donovan! That's our baby." But she's laughing, and fuck I love the sound of her laughter. Almost as much as I love the words *our baby*.

"Oh, wait. I got something for you." I set the ultrasound on the table and her on the sofa, then run to the coat closet where I stashed the bag, then return. "I meant to wrap it. If I'd known you were coming..." I give her a stern look as I pass over the package.

"I don't need it wrapped." She peers into the bag, then pulls out the travel coffee mug. It's the same size and brand as her current favorite mug, but this one has words in fancy font.

World's Greatest Mom

Her smile quickly disappears, and I can tell she's fighting back tears. While I don't love to see her cry, it's evidence that I've hit the nerve I meant to hit.

I sit again on the coffee table, opening my legs so that my thighs frame her knees. "When you said you were worried about what kind of parents we'd be, I heard it as you were worried about what kind of parent *I'd* be."

"Donovan, that's not..."

"I know. Hold on, let me finish." I take the mug and set it next to me so I can take her hands in mine. "I heard that because I was projecting. I'm scared. I think it's natural to be scared. We have the potential to ruin a human being. Who wouldn't be scared? There's a whole bunch we can fuck up.

"But I'll tell you what I'm not scared about. I'm not scared that I'll love our kids the way I love you. Even if I loved you in a traditional way, I'd love our kids differently. I'd be a sick man if I didn't. And our son will respect women, because he'll be grounded for a year the first time he talks back to his mother. And our daughter will learn to expect princess treatment from the men she dates, because she'll see how I worship her mom.

"Not that she'll ever be allowed to date."

Tears stream down her cheeks, but she laughs.

"I know I don't have the best example from my father. And it's a travesty that your parents are gone from this earth already. But we're smart people, Sabrina. We have good role models in our friends. I mean, not Weston, but the others."

"Stop." She's still smiling.

"We'll have to learn new ways to love, but we'll figure it out together." I bring my hand to her face and lift her chin so our eyes lock. "I know you will be the world's best mom. And I'll be a decent dad."

"You'll be the best dad," she interjects.

"We'll figure out how together. Okay?"

"You won't believe me, but I was planning to say the same thing. Not so eloquently, maybe. Same gist."

"But you didn't have to say it because I know what you need, and so I said it for you."

"I would never want to be loved any other way." She reaches for me, and when she's in my arms, I move to the couch with her in my lap.

Pressing my forehead to hers, my throat feels tight. Yeah, I'm emotional too. "I love you so much, Sabrina, that it hurts to breathe because each breath I take means one less in a lifetime with you."

A sob escapes her lips.

"That wasn't supposed to make you cry harder." I palm her cheek and kiss her. Kiss her again. Kiss her once more.

The kisses do the trick and slow the tears. "I'm sorry," she says.

"Don't be."

"I mean for not telling you and for running away."

I knew that's what she meant. "Don't be."

"I love you. I don't know how I have room to love more when I already love you so much, but I already love her too."

I place my hand over hers on her belly. "So much," I agree.

"And we'll figure it out together."

"I promise."

In what feels like a blatant change of subject, she suddenly moves to straddle me. "Donovan." She grinds against my quickly thickening cock. "There's something else I need to tell you."

"I like where this is going." I move my hands under her sundress and grab her ass. The next time she bucks, my cock is exactly where she needs it. I hiss because she's exactly where I need her too.

She places her mouth near my ear. Her breath does crazy things to my nervous system. "It seems that pregnancy makes me really, really..." She punctuates each *really* with another rock of her hips.

"Horny?"

"Turned on." Because she always tiptoes around the filthy words.

"Is that so?" Fuck, I knew I wanted her pregnant. Seriously, though, as excited as I am about being a dad, I'm never not going to love what we have when it's just the two of us. "How about I take you upstairs and love you in that way that's designated only for you?"

"The dirty way?"

"The dirtiest."

EPILOGUE

TEN MONTHS *later*

"HURRY," Sabrina pleads. "Hurry."

As much as I'd like to credit my dick for her urgency, I'm pretty sure she's more concerned about not getting caught than getting fucked.

Luckily for her, I'm taking care of both.

My pants are unzipped and my cock is ready to go when I lift her onto the counter and spread her legs apart. Best thing about her nursing? She's taken to primarily wearing wrap dresses—thank you, Audrey, for the suggestion—and now it's easy access to her body anytime I want.

Well, anytime we aren't preoccupied with parenting, that is.

"What are we even doing?" she asks as I push her panties aside, too rushed to take them off all together.

"If you have to ask, I'm doing something wrong." I slide inside her, and no, I'm not doing anything wrong. This is so very, very right.

"Oh God, oh God."

I prop one of her feet on the counter, and spread her wider. My hand reaches up to cup a breast as I adopt a swift rhythm.

"Don't touch the boobs. I need to feed."

A breast milk covered dress is maybe not the best look for today's event. I rub her clit instead. Aggressively, in quickie fashion, none of that teasy shit. We don't have time for that.

She seems to think we don't have time for any of it. "Don't worry about getting me off. I'm not going to—"

"You are," I insist. My gaze moves downward, and I watch my cock as it pushes into her, wishing we really did have more time so that I could drag this out and enjoy her.

She notices I've slowed and urges me to pick up the tempo with a buck of her hips. "Quick, remember?"

"Quick is relative." I pick up my speed nonetheless.

"We should do this at home." She's distracted. "Why did we decide to do this here?"

"Because it's a church. It's hot to fuck in a church."

It's not like it's any of the holy parts of the church. Just a small private bathroom off the side of the sanctuary. It might be the minister's, actually. Still feels taboo, and if she'd just get her head into the game, she'll realize she thinks it's hot too.

"But if we get caught, they might cancel the ceremony."

"They won't cancel the ceremony. It's a very liberal church."

"I don't think 'everyone's welcome' means 'come have sex in the bathroom.'"

"Sabrina?" Frustrated with her lack of focus, I place my free hand on the side of her face so I can direct her attention. "Get here with me, baby."

In the distance, someone calls my name, but I hold her in place. "Ignore them. This is for us. Don't let them into our space. Eyes only on me."

Now she's with me.

Her breath is ragged, and she's trying hard to control her moans. Watching her fight her pleasure is a major turn-on and as soon as she starts clenching around me, I know I'm done for.

"Wait, pull out! Pull out!"

But she feels so good, and I'm already spilling into her. "Whoops." I smile because she can't resist me. "Morning after pill?"

She swats at my shoulder, pushing me away from her at the same time. "I'm not going to morning after pill a potential Kincaid child. What happens happens."

I put myself away, and she turns to the mirror and fixes herself up, not really upset with my ejaculation faux pas. It's not the first time in the four months since Sasha's birth that I've come inside her, not that I mind pulling out when I can come on her or down her throat. As long as there's no condom, I'm happy to spread my jizz around.

Frankly, I think she still hasn't resumed birth control because she already wants another baby but at the same time doesn't want to make the commitment. Typical Sabrina. Good thing for her she has me to help her with her decision making.

Seemingly unsatisfied with her appearance, she spins back toward me. "How do I look?"

Freshly fucked. "Beautiful."

Not trusting me, she turns back to her reflection and fluffs her hair with her fingers. "It will have to do."

She reaches past me to unlock the door, but I stop her. "Sabrina."

"What? We're late. We have to go."

I study her face, memorizing everything about this moment. I do that more and more lately—revel in the present. I'm realizing that it's quality that matters, not quantity. Hours of video footage and pages of reports from Ferris don't ever equate to a real-life shared smile.

She nudges me. "Donovan?"

Now I'm ready. "Let's go. Come on. They're waiting for us." I open the door and gesture for her to go ahead.

She rolls her eyes and hurries out, giving a wave to Weston as she passes him.

Weston glances over his shoulder at her then looks at me. No questions asked, he knows what we've been up to. "Seriously? We've been looking all over for you."

I shrug as we follow after her. "Like you didn't fuck your wife at your baby's christening."

"I didn't."

"You didn't? Huh. Opportunity lost."

We turn the corner and arrive at the church foyer, where several of our closest friends and family members are gathered in groups, socializing.

Sabrina's found my mother—or my mother has found Sabrina. She bounces Sasha on her shoulder. "She's been fussy."

On cue, Sasha starts to cry. "There goes my boobs." Sabrina takes the baby. "I should feed her before the ceremony."

I follow her with my eyes as she heads to the nursery to feed, half ready to follow her because they're my two favorite people in the world, and fuck everyone else.

But Weston claps a hand on my back. "Remember us? The guys are waiting."

Okay, the guys are cool too, and they're all here for me—for my offspring, but same thing—and that's a rare feat so I let Weston lead me down another hallway toward a closed door.

"Finally," Cade says when Weston and I walk in the room. It's small. Big enough to fit a cramped pair of couches and several bookshelves.

"Shut the door." Dylan rushes to do so even as he's the one barking the command. "And blow out the window."

I don't bother to tell him that I could smell the cigars in the hall. This is the thing that could get the ceremony canceled, not the sex in the bathroom.

But Sabrina's not here to fuss, and I have a high-risk tolerance. "I hope there's scotch to go with the cigars."

Before I'm done speaking, Nate has placed a tumbler in my hand with two fingers of the good stuff. "You brought real glassware?"

"The experience is half the enjoyment," he says, a quote I've heard several times from him.

I place my hand over my chest, only mocking in part. "I'm touched."

"Wait until you try this." Dylan hands me an already lit cigar.

I glance at the label before bringing it to my lips. It's an Oliva Melanio from the Serie V, one I haven't tried before. "Do I taste salted caramel?"

"Smooth, isn't it?" Dylan passes an unlit one to Weston and

then, after lighting one for himself, he heads to the window to exhale. "Discovered it when I was scouting potential new office space. The building in Fitzrovia is next to a pretty nice cigar shop."

"But it's farther from your home. You'd hate the commute." It sounds like he cares, but Cade has his own agenda. He's of the opinion that we shouldn't scale up the London office at this time and instead put all our focus on the new office in Boston.

Dylan isn't fooled. "We can't just ignore the needs—"

Nate cuts him off. "No work talk today. It's a special occasion."

"Who died and made you the boss?" Cade asks, arms crossed, a subtle reminder who the heavy is among us.

"Nobody died, and I'm the boss," I say, because I am, equal partnership or not. And technically, it's my name with the word President behind it. No one refutes it so I go on. "And I say if it's work related, you can shut the fuck up."

"Told you," Nate says.

"Asswipe," Cade replies.

"Douchecanoe," Weston says, eager as always to get in on the childish behavior.

I join Dylan at the window. "Fucking morons, each and every one of them."

"But they're *our* morons. So we'll keep them."

"If we have to." I look around the room, realizing we're at the end of an era. We've each found the woman we belong with, and all of us are fathers now, except for Nate, who will never settle down in any traditional way. Though, he and Trish did recently buy a plant together, which frankly sounds harder to take care of than a child.

Sabrina and I even bought a second home out here in Chappaqua. We're only here on the weekends, and not every weekend since both of us are happy city people. It's a relatively small house, only four thousand square feet, but there are thirteen acres of land. I'll teach Sasha how to snowshoe out here when she's old enough. Just like I'll teach her chess and debate, though with the parents she has, she's probably a natural.

The changes are even happening at the office. With the business expanding, Reach isn't just the five of us anymore. We started with a president of operations and four VP positions—Nate as head of creative; Cade, head of finance; Dylan, head of accounts; and Weston, head of marketing. Now we've added a VP of Technology, and next time we get together for business, we'll have someone else on the team as well.

"Times change," Cade says, as if reading my thoughts.

I imagine the remark is stemming from his personal life. "Tate moved out already?"

He looks wounded at the mention. To be fair, he'd missed out on most of Tate's life. After the kid graduated, all four of them—Tate, Cade, his wife Jolie, and their baby Devyn—traveled the world together, and got close. Real close.

"Yeah. Starts college summer semester," he says with a sigh.

Dylan joins the lament. "Tell me about it. Aaron starts this fall."

"We're losing our best babysitters," Cade adds.

Dylan considers. "Cheapest anyway."

"Good point." Cade's demeanor changes. "But I have other news."

Everyone looks to him as if he'll have something surprising to say, but come on. It's obvious. "When's Jolie due?"

Weston's jaw practically drops. "Another baby? Already?"

Cade's grin says everything we need to know. "September."

"Maybe it'll be a boy," Dylan says. "We need another boy in the bunch. Poor Sebastian is outnumbered with all these little girls."

"Yes, please, have a boy." As for myself, I'd be perfectly happy with a brood of girls. Though, I'll never admit it to anyone but Sabrina.

Weston and Cade start squabbling about the perks of having a son versus a daughter, and Nate pulls out his phone, probably to dirty text his girlfriend. I should probably let him know the bathroom door locks, in case they want to sneak in for a round.

I watch them and wonder how the hell we all ended up finding each other.

"You did this," Dylan says, and it's actually not the accusation I'd expect it to be considering how immature everyone is at the moment. "You saved us all. You did good."

I look at the assholes I call my friends. Feels more like they saved me.

But I'm cocky, so I'll take it.

Too soon, there's a knock on the door. Elizabeth doesn't wait for anyone to answer before she enters with a can of Lysol. "Baby is fed. Kids are sequestered in the nursery with a sitter. Minister is on the prowl. Guests are getting restless. Time for the boys' club to disperse."

She sprays the room as she walks around the room. When she gets to me, she takes the cigar out of my hand and dumps it in my tumbler. "Your wife needs you," she says and sprays my suit with Lysol.

I wave the disinfectant from my face and glare.

"I'm doing you a favor. Get your ass out there, Kincaid."

Cade taunts Weston. "Your wife is a killjoy."

"Well, your wife is pregnant and babies kill sex," Weston retorts.

"Not with my wife."

Before I get pulled into the entertainment that is watching Cade continually one-up Weston, I hand my cigar-filled tumbler to the killjoy and excuse myself from the group. "Show's about to start, boys. Let's go, let's go."

I leave, but Dylan jogs to catch up with me shortly after. "Forgot to hand this over." He holds up a bottle of wine.

Without breaking stride, I take the bottle and read the label. "Labrusco Salamino."

It's the variety of wine that Sabrina's mother used to drink. Dylan helped me round up old Lind family photographs. I scoured through them for weeks before being certain Labrusco was the right one. Sabrina and I shared our first bottle of it after Sasha was born.

See? I can know wine too.

"I ordered a whole case for you when we were in Italy last month, but it won't ship until the end of the summer so I brought this one directly. Thought Sabrina might enjoy it on this special occasion."

"Thank you." In case there's a chance one of us will get emotional, I add, "Dad."

"Fuck you."

"Watch your language," Audrey says, meeting us in the foyer. "We're in a church. And there's a baby present."

On cue, I turn to find Sabrina ready for a hand off. "She only wants me if she's hungry."

"I'll take her," my mother happily volunteers.

But Sasha has her mood face on, and both me and Sabrina know what that means. "She wants Daddy," she says.

That's me.

I hand my mother the wine so I can take the baby. "Here I am, Sashimi."

"Raw fish, Donovan?" my mother scolds. "That's not an appropriate nickname for a baby."

Eh, she's just sad that my baby likes me more than her.

She's not done lecturing. "Where have you been anyway? Aren't we supposed to start a three?"

"The photographer wanted to grab some pictures," I lie.

"But Sabrina had the baby. Why would she take pictures of just you?"

"She's a very thorough photographer." The church bells start ringing, indicating that we're right on the hour. "Listen to that. Daddy's right on time, isn't he, Sashasquatch?"

Don't ask. The nicknames that come from my mouth fly out on their own accord.

Big round saucers gaze up at me in response, and Sasha delivers one of her killer toothless smiles. She gets me with those every time. Right in the heart. Little monkey is going to be the death of me.

The bells seem to get everyone's attention, and people start filing into the nave. I balance Sasha on my shoulder and follow behind Sabrina, my mother at my side. "We're not coming to the house after," she says, apologetically.

My mother is head over heels for Sasha so I'm guessing it's not her decision. "Dad?"

"You know how preoccupied he is with everything going on right now. He wants to get back to the city since he's meeting with his lawyer early tomorrow. I'm sure you understand."

I don't understand my father's choices, but I do understand obsession. I might very well have inherited the ability to fixate from him. It's hard to be supportive about his current obsession, though. After Sebastian News Corp aired a vicious exposé about the financial improprieties administered by King-Kincaid, my father found himself embroiled in an epic scandal. In an attempt to curb company losses and regain consumer confidence —the board, including his partner Nash King—voted to oust my father from his position as company president. It was a shocking move that did not come with a severance package.

If only he'd taken my advice and stepped down on his own, he could have walked away with a big fat golden parachute.

Being the sore loser that he is, my father has decided that his best move is to sue the company that he built. The company he still owns stock in. Needless to say, he's creating a shitstorm on top of a shitstorm. I thought I'd learned my do-what's-best-for-the-stockholder attitude from him. Apparently, I did not.

I glance down the aisle and see my father is already in a pew, focused on his phone. Probably texting with his lawyers as we speak.

"No worries," I tell my mother. "We're just glad you're both here for the ceremony." Sure I'm irritated that money and ego come before my child, but I'm learning to think of my parents as close acquaintances. It has minimized injuries and made my folks much more pleasant to be around.

People are taking their seats, and when we're midway through the nave, the minister beckons me and Sabrina to come up to the front when someone calls my name from behind me.

I turn to see who it is. "Oh, hell no."

I'm about to ignore him, but he calls my name again. "Go ahead," I tell Sabrina. "I'll be up in just a second."

I walk back up the aisle to see what the fuck Holt Sebastian is doing at my baby's christening. "There's no way in hell you came out to Chappaqua for this."

"My cousin has a place in Millwood. I thought I'd stop by and deliver this." He hands me a wrapped gift. "I'm guessing this is the star of the show." He pokes a finger at Sasha who immediately reaches for his finger.

"Don't eat that, Sasha," I tell her. "No telling where it's been."

"Sasha. Cute." He extracts his finger from my daughter's hand and stuffs it in his pocket, obviously uncomfortable with babies.

Ah, I remember those days.

"Cute until she needs a nap." Awkwardly, I work on opening the gift because, whatever it is, I don't trust him. "You know, there are people here who would shoot you on sight." Not that my father's paying any attention. "How did you even know this was happening?"

I look up from my unwrapping to scan the crowd. "Oh, right. Simone." She's got her pet Sebastian with her. I'm not about to ask, but it does appear he might be a permanent fixture. Which means, like it or not, I'm stuck with the Sebastians in my world, because Simone is family.

The gift is a framed piece of art. A picture of a hand holding a match and the whole sky lit in flames. Immediately, I remember how he told me to "burn the whole thing down" when he was trying to get me to give dirt on my father. "Not really appropriate for a four-month-old."

"It's for her father. A gift of gratitude."

"Because I saved your career?"

"I wouldn't say *saved*. More like *started*."

"Semantics." I hand him the wrapping paper, which Sasha is trying to put in her mouth, and tuck the art under my arm, image facing in so I'll get fewer questions. "This doesn't make us friends."

"Never."

I don't exactly smile, but it probably reads more like that than a frown. "Okay, well, now get the fuck out of here. I have a baby to christen, and you aren't invited."

After dropping the art off at the pew where I earlier stashed Sabrina's diaper bag, I rush up to the sanctuary where my wife is reminding the minister that we want to include a moment of silence for Sasha's twin. "We're calling them Aubrey, since that name can be for a boy or a girl, and we don't know which her twin was." A tribute to Sabrina's own sister, Audrey. "We want Sasha to know she wasn't alone."

"I've got it," the minister tells her. Then she looks at me. "Now that the guest of honor is here," she says in a tone that's both friendly and admonishing, "are we ready to begin the christening for Sasha Kenzie Kincaid?"

"Yes," Sabrina says.

"Yes," I echo. But then I realize I'm not sure. "Wait."

I survey the crowd. Nate's in the back with Trish at his side. Weston and Elizabeth are next to my parents. There's Cade with Jolie across from Dylan and Audrey. My whole family is here.

I turn back to the minister. "We're ready."

Want a bonus scene featuring Donovan, Sabrina, and Sasha? Sign up for my newsletter and get it delivered to your inbox.

Ready for more Holt Sebastian? You'll find him in Brutal Billionaire.

Laurelin Paige delivers a twist on Indecent Proposal in this billionaire workplace romance featuring elements of fake relationship, marriage of convenience, enemies to lovers, and a new alphahole readers will love to hate.

And what's up with Simone and Steele Sebastian? Find out in Dirty Filthy Billionaire, a 1001 Dark Nights Novella.

I'm damn good at my job.

So if I swipe my boss's event invitations from time to time, it's kind of like a much-earned bonus. He'll never miss them, and I get a five star free meal in the company of men in well-fitted suits.

But then he shows up at an award's dinner that I'm most definitely not supposed to be at.

Lucky for me, when my boss accuses me of stealing his ticket, a hot swoony man in a tux steps in and says, "She came with me."

Now I owe the stranger one, which is totally cool.

Until I discover the hot, swoony man is none other than Steele Sebastian, a rich man with a penchant for scandal.

And the way he wants me to pay him back?

Let's just say that Steele Sebastian has a reputation as a dirty filthy billionaire, and I'm about to find out why.

Get Dirty Filthy Billionaire

ALSO BY LAURELIN PAIGE

Visit my website for a more detailed reading order.

The Dirty Universe

Dirty Filthy Rich Boys - READ FREE

Dirty Duet (Donovan Kincaid)

Dirty Filthy Rich Men | Dirty Filthy Rich Love

Kincaid

Dirty Games Duet (Weston King)

Dirty Sexy Player| Dirty Sexy Games

Dirty Sweet Duet (Dylan Locke)

Sweet Liar | Sweet Fate

(Nate Sinclair) Dirty Filthy Fix (a spinoff novella)

Dirty Wild Trilogy (Cade Warren)

Wild Rebel | Wild War | Wild Heart

Man in Charge Duet

Man in Charge

Man in Love

Man for Me (a spinoff novella)

Dating Season

Spring Fling | Summer Rebound | Fall Hard

Winter Bloom | Spring Fever | Summer Lovin

Also written with Kayti McGee under the name Laurelin McGee

Miss Match | Love Struck | MisTaken | Holiday for Hire

Written with Sierra Simone

Porn Star | Hot Cop

AUTHOR'S NOTE AND ACKNOWLEDGMENTS

Just after college, a really friend got pregnant and had a miscarriage at about three months along. A couple of weeks later, I remember her asking me, "When will my boobs go back to normal?" Since I'd had a miscarriage before she thought I'd know.

I was like, "Soon, I'm sure." Honestly, I hadn't paid attention to when my boobs went back to normal. Is that something people notice? Not me.

You've probably already guessed the next part of this story. She went to her follow up appointment with her OB/GYN and came back, surprise! Still pregnant. Baby was born healthy and is full grown now.

So for those of you who wonder if the Sabrina pregnant with twins but miscarried story might happen, it totally did to my friend!

I'm going to be honest—I don't really love pregnancy tropes, and for me, this story is not a pregnancy trope. I'm not interested in that personally. I don't need to see a breeder hero get all hot over his swollen woman. That's a me thing. Nothing wrong with the trope at all, just not my preference.

What I am interested in, though, are how the dynamics of a relationship shift when a major change happens like having a baby. I'm interested in how people deal with that. Particularly, a couple as non-traditional as Donovan and Sabrina. If you noticed, I didn't really show you what kind of father Donovan ends up being, either, because that was the point of this story. The point was not the outcome. The point is that moment where you decide you need to look at who you are and make adjustments because you want something better/different/more in your life. Truthfully, that's always been Donovan's journey— through the duet until now. He didn't have to change a lot when he accepted Sabrina into his life since she adapted to him. But confronted with a child, he's finally found a reason to change and say I love you out loud/apologize/challenge his controlling behaviors. He grew, and I did too while writing him.

I so appreciate all of you who have gone through this Dirty Universe journey with me. There have been some dang tough stories in here—some that helped me work through my own demons (Dirty Sexy Player and Games, some written with a broken arm (Dirty Filthy Rich Love and Dirty Filthy Fix), some the breath of fresh air that I needed at the time of my life (Sweet Liar and Fate). Now we close the door on this group, and I'm sad about that. Maybe we'll return sometime. But right now I'm so happy to jump into what's next. I hope you join me.

Special thanks to all the people who make a book happen in my world these days, in no particular order: Kayti McGee,

Roxie Madar, Melissa Gaston, Sarah Piechuta, Liz Berry, Amy "Vox" Libris, Ann R. Jones, Erica Russikoff, Lauren Blakely, Christine Reiss, Nina Grinstead, Kim Gilmour, Jacob Morgan, my family, my readers, and my God.

ABOUT LAURELIN PAIGE

With millions of books sold, Laurelin Paige is the NY Times, Wall Street Journal, and USA Today Bestselling Author of the Fixed Trilogy. She's a sucker for a good romance and gets giddy anytime there's kissing, much to the embarrassment of her three daughters. Her husband doesn't seem to complain, however. When she isn't reading or writing sexy stories, she's probably singing, watching shows like Billions and Peaky Blinders or dreaming of Michael Fassbender. She's also a proud member of Mensa International though she doesn't do anything with the organization except use it as material for her bio.

www.laurelinpaige.com
laurelinpaigeauthor@gmail.com

9 781957 647333